Cater To Her

A novel

By
Sean Mitchell

RJ Publications, LLC

Newark, New Jersey

The characters and events in this book are fictitious. Any resemblance to actual persons, living or dead, is purely coincidental.

RJ Publications
Cater2her69@yahoo.com
www.rjpublications.com
Copyright © 2008 by Sean Mitchell
All Rights Reserved
ISBN 0-97863735-6

Printed in Canada

March 2008

1-2-3-4-5-6-7-8-9-10-11

"CATER TO HER"

BY

Sean Mitchell

Prologue

ANGELICA
July 8, 2008

My day is finally here. The day I've dreamed about since I was a child living in a Philadelphia orphanage. Never thought it would come, but that has been the norm in my life. I've accomplished more than I ever thought I would. How many orphans do you know that have gone on to graduate top of her class at F.I.T? How many motherless little girls go on to become one of the top Fashion Buyers at Neiman Marcus? But nothing compares to today, the day of my wedding. It's the day I merge my life with the *perfect* man. Honestly, he's not the *perfect* man, but he's ready and willing to commit, treats me well and earns well into the six figures. I know I come off like some sort of self absorbed, egotistical female, but I'm not. I am just confused and if I don't think about all my groom's good points, I may as well turn around and do a Jackie Joyner Kersee down the aisle.

Everyone's jaws drop as I make my grand entrance. I'm dressed in a Vera Wang wedding gown with a beaded bodice of pearls and sequins. My chapel length train follows me as my eyes begin to water not because of the importance of this occasion, but because of the cameras flashing in my face. They are welcoming me as if they are standing before the Queen of England.

It's almost sacrilegious that I chose to wear white. A color befitting the state of this union would probably be best described as charcoal black or blood red. I'm anything but pure. Over the past month, I've done things even the most promiscuous women would frown upon. I've been in the bed of another man, showered him with my natural juices and put my mouth to every inch of his body. The same mouth I'm about to make a sacred vow with.

I look at all the faces in the crowd as I walk to the wedding march. If they could see my face underneath this veil, they would see a scared girl. This is not the first time these people have seen me with a veil, because I've been wearing the veil of deception for the better part of a month. I see Titus smiling at me, his radiant grin torturing my soul with each hesitant step. That man loves me so much I'm scared I may never measure to the woman he thinks I am.

I locate my best friend Rochelle in the crowd; see the trail of mascara going down her face. She represents the only family I ever had. I'm holding onto my groom's father's arm because there was never a parent in my life to take this walk with me. I know he can feel the vibrations coming from my body because my hands won't stop shaking. My body cannot hide my doubt.

Pastor Richards stands at the pulpit with a self-assured grin on his face. He too is fooled by the lie that my life has become. I finally make it to the altar and intertwine hands with Titus, see the tears congregating by each corner of his eyes. I know in my heart that he loves me even though I can't say the same.

Titus is a beautiful man. With skin the complexion of honey-roasted peanuts, eyes the hue of a Caribbean ocean and lips as full and luscious as a chocolate dipped strawberry. He wasn't just handsome or fine, but rather exceptionally gorgeous. Women could not resist his smile or the way his voice took on a seductive tone whenever he comforted his congregation. He was like a Snapple ice tea, made from the best stuff on earth. And he was mine for the taking, a faithful, trustworthy and hard working man I wasn't sure I really wanted.

When I met Titus at the National Baptist Singles Conference in Richmond, Virginia two years ago, I had no idea he would be the man I married. At the time, I was trying something new. In fact, I considered myself a born again virgin and had put my total trust in Christ to put an end to my insatiable urges. I had come to the conference in search of more bible-based teachings to strengthen my faith and keep me on the straight and narrow.

However, the moment I saw Titus my head filled with thoughts that were anything but holy. When he stepped off the pulpit after a riveting discourse on Singles: respected, successful and spirit filled. I wanted a closer look. He looked sharp, dressed in an immaculate beige Giorgio Armani single-breasted suit. His nails were manicured, eyebrows plucked and his mustache was shaped thin. In other words, metrosexual, just the type of man I loved. Yet, I wasn't the only woman with Reverend Rosemond on her mind as a crowd of admirers gathered around him. He was a scrap of food among ravenous lionesses. There was no ring on his finger and in his sermon; he gave examples of how he as a single man sometimes had difficulty remaining chaste.

It was the last discourse of the day and he was the only reason all the "sisters" were even awake. I couldn't even get within twenty feet as all the "born again virgins" clamored for his attention. Feeling intimidated I left, even though for a millisecond my eyes connected with his. Never to know later I'd meet my fate.

Hours later, I sat alone in the Onyx Lounge, a restaurant in the Marriot Richmond hotel where I was staying. I was dressed down, wearing an oversized Harvard sweatshirt and track pants with my hair pulled back. It's funny, because no matter how much I dressed down to avoid attention from men, they seemed even more aggressive and turned on by my laid-back style.

Men offered me drinks for most of the night and I turned down each and everyone. I didn't want to give anyone an open invitation to hit on me. It was becoming a struggle each and everyday to hold onto my private celibacy vow to God. Sometimes I craved a man's touch so badly I didn't trust myself even to harmlessly converse with the opposite sex.

I hadn't noticed Titus as he sat beside me, but the scent of Grey Flannel instantly caught my attention. My first love wore Grey Flannel, the same man who took my virginity for the first time and as I nursed my drink called, *a goodnight kiss,* I sensed from the corner of my eye someone staring at me.

"You sure know how to light up a room," a familiar voice said.

I was just about to tell him off when we made eye contact for the second time. Usually men of the cloth lack any sense when it comes to fashion. Not to sound condescending but most of them look awkward wearing anything but a suit. Titus proved me wrong; he wore black linen pants, an untucked white dress shirt that exposed his glorious pecs and a gold chain with a crucifix. And I couldn't help but look at what he was holding in those slacks.

"Sorry for being rude, but thank you," I said, placing my drink down quickly and putting my hand into my lap. I didn't want him to think I was some type of alcoholic, or worse, yet one of those women that sat in bars picking up men.

"Don't mind me. You know even the Lord had to have a drink from time to time." He laughed, raising his hand to order seltzer water.

I felt uncomfortable, not because I was sitting next to one of God's workers but because my panties were beginning to get moist. His green eyes had a mesmerizing affect on me. And the commanding tone in which he spoke had reverberated from my chest down to my toes. For the first time in four years, I had the urge to pleasure myself. He took one sip of his drink and the site of his lips becoming wet had me wanting to jump him.

"I'm Angelica Thompson. I enjoyed your discourse," I offered him my hand, but he declined.

"I don't mean to be rude sister, but little things such as a hang shake can lead to one of the devils many machinations." He nodded and gulped down the last of his drink.

"I light up a room, but you can't touch me."

"I'm aiming not to touch you physically, but spiritually. Besides I wanted to say thank you for attending my workshop."

"Why thank me?"

Looking at him, I wondered if he resembled an angel. There was not an imperfection on his body, at least not with his clothing on. His skin was clear, his teeth were as white as the wool of a newborn lamb and his hair was curly and fine.

"Unlike everyone else, you seemed to enjoy my workshop. I can tell when a person is listening with more than their ears."

"You speak beautifully. And I need all the help there is."

"And the meek will reside on the earth."

"What do you mean by that?" I asked wondering what our conversation had to do with a scripture from the bible.

"I'm humbled by you. Because I'm sure a single woman as beautiful as you can be doing something more interesting than sitting at a boring workshop. However, you feel a need to be close to God. And that in of itself makes you more attractive."

"I'm nothing to be humbled by," I admitted. If he knew all that I'd been through, if he knew the depths I had gone to get to my station in life, he would've thrown holy water on me.

"Self despair is one of the devil's most potent devices. Whatever you've done and no matter how many times you have sinned, the lord has already forgiven you."

"Tell me Reverend. Why do you even care?"

"Everyday I get on my knees and pray to my wonderful god and I ask him to find someone for me. And everyday he says

Titus just a little while longer. This has gone on for years and to be truthful, sister, I was becoming angry in the flesh. But today he answered me." He grabbed a fistful of his shirt, closed his eyes and shook his head.

"And what did he tell you."

"The first will be last and the last will be first. When you left after my workshop I knew…"

"You knew what?"

"I had found my wife…"

Silence had snapped me back from my time warp. The wedding march had ended and now was time to marry this wonderful man. Thinking back to that prophetic day I wondered what Titus had ever seen in me. Two years later and here we are about to get Married and he doesn't even have a clue as to who he's *really* marrying.

"Who gives this woman to be married?" Pastor Richard asks.

"I do," the father of the bride, answers.

In a loud voice Pastor Richard begins, "Welcome family and friends. We meet in this place to celebrate a mystery as ageless as humankind; a mystery of enduring power and inspiration…"

My hands go numb, my legs feel like jelly and I wonder if my lover cares, and if my lover's staring at me. I wonder if my man will stand when the Pastor asks if anyone has a reason why these two shouldn't be married. Will my man forever hold his peace? Will he stand and claim what is his?

Have you ever met a man that is everything you want? I mean a man that looks good, dresses well and can hold a steady J.O.B without a problem, not to mention that in bed he is the equivalent of Michael Jordan on the basketball court or Leonardo Davinci on canvas. Finally yet importantly, gives you orgasms on a mental and spiritual level. I mean when you talk to this extraordinary man the knowledge he imparts is better than the best sex. I've met that man, but it's not the man I'm about to marry…

"Underneath my Skin"

Aurelius

When I think about love, I think of an uncontrollable feeling, a force of nature, one not dictated by our own desires. Its effects are similar to a hurricane that spins us around and around, leaving our destination indiscernible. When you feel it, there's no question. Its power cannot be disputed. Even when lost, its residue reeks on our skin. That's why I fear it. In turn, I avoid it.

There's a great reason as to why I have a great condemnation of it. But I dare not think of it because I could never relive that pain. I loved once and its loss had brought out a side of me I shutter to think of seeing again. The hurt my soul mate inflicted upon me had nearly consumed me, leaving me to wonder if *love* for me even existed. Then I met Mistress Alek and my life changed.

I couldn't see through the leather blindfold, my knees hurt and my backside was in searing pain due to the force of the oak paddle my Dominatrix had pounded me with. And with a slight tug of her leash, the leather collar around my neck tightened and caused me to lose my breath. I could feel her around me, the sound of her heels clicking against the cold linoleum as the braided strands of leather from her flogger lightly touched the hairs of my chest. The scent of warm urine reeked from my skin. That's how she marked me. I was her property. I was her slave and she was my Mistress.

Taking clamps, she began to squeeze my nipples. The pain hurt so good, as I fought a losing battle with the leather of my chastity shorts. She twisted them harder. I held in my screams, bit into the ball gag and began to tear up. I hoped she didn't see the tears filtering down my cheeks. My Mistress would not like it if I appeared weak.

"Are you crying?" My Mistress asked. I shook my head no.

"You're lying to me. And I hate liars," she stated, pulling my leash tightly while digging her heels into my back. I lost my breath once more as the ball gag restricted my breathing. My coughs were hard and shallow. I was beginning to lose circulation in my neck. I gasped, felt nauseous and before I knew it, I could feel no more...

Some consider me perverted, even crazy for the lifestyle that I have chosen. But you have to understand, I get off on pain. That's why my most parts of my anatomy were pierced. And you know what? Each time a sensitive part of my body is pierced my orgasms become even more intense. Therefore, I don't need anyone's pity because the life I live is the life I choose.

If anyone wanted to know the truth about Aurelius, they wouldn't have to look too far back. I took on the name of Aurelius five years ago as an alter ego in the world of S&M. Then two years later, I became Aurelius legally. No last name and no attachments. I was someone before that, had a name and last name that I cringe even to think of. But that boy is dead now, dead with his deep and dark secrets.

Trained as a Personal chef and caterer, I've slaved at some of the finest establishments in the entire world. During my sojourn, I've apprenticed at Ristorante San Domenico in Imola Italy, Stars in Singapore and Gramercy Tavern here in New York City. But after a few too many critiques about my outward appearance, I decided to take my talents elsewhere. And two years later, Foradori catering was born. I provide personal chef services as well as fine catered food. I'm a blue-collar brotha in a white-collar world. I am not rich, at least not yet, but with a few well-placed catering events I hope to be in due time.

Unique would be the best way to describe my personal appearance. You don't see a 6'4 210lbs brotha sporting 8 facial piercings, a 70's style afro and a torso full of tattoos everyday. Even though I've been mistaken for Lenny Kravitz on more than one occasion, people are usually taken aback by my style. My black eyeliner, black finger nail polish and the black threads that I wear have turned a lot of heads, though for the wrong reasons. The only time I wear anything that's not black is when I'm at work.

My favorite pieces of art are on my body. Going up the left side of my torso is a scripture taken from the Holy Qur'an written in the Taliq script form of Arabic Calligraphy, it reads "Thee do we worship, and thine aid do we seek." Around my waist is a barbed wire design and on each of my arms are my parent's pictures along with their days of death for I wasn't scared of death, but embraced it. That's why my favorite color was black.

 Getting back to my sex life, I can say honestly that I'm attracted to beautiful women. Don't prejudge me as one of those self-absorbed brothas or one hopelessly into jungle fever. But I can appreciate an attractive white or Asian woman when I see one. Admittedly, back during my wild San Francisco culinary school days, I may have done more than fraternize with a few white girls, even fell in love with a mulatto, but that was then. Now I like my sistas and haven't had an urge to go back to the light side. At least, not since... *her.*

Sitting in the sauna of the Harlem New York sports club after an hour session of Yoga, I was exhausted. I leaned against the wooden walls with my eyes closed trying to sweat out all the negative energy that resided in my body from another busy catering affair. This was my normal Sunday routine. After a hectic week, it provided me with a sense of peace. Besides, I was alone. Since I liked to whisk in the nude, the other men in the club didn't share a sauna with me. The sight of another dude swinging from side to side put off most brothas.

It didn't take long before the mouth of my best friend Shane disturbed my peace. Shane Hildebrand is what I like to call unapologetically gay. He reveled in his gayness, the complete opposite of the down low brotha. He's the on top brotha, as in on top of a mountain screaming to the entire world that he's gay and loves it.

Shane is sort of a cross between Sisqo and Little Richard. He's beanpole skinny, all legs and arms and walks with a switch. His low-cropped hair is dyed blond and topped off with glitter because he likes his head to shimmer. His mustache, goatee and sideburns are all cut razor thin,

Shane knew me better than anyone ever knew me. Hell, he even knew my real name. I've known him since our San Francisco days when I attended The California Culinary Academy and he attended San Francisco State. Back then, we thought we were all that, having unprotected sex with as many people as the law allowed. But I never really warmed up to that life. Ignorant as I was, I actually thought there was someone out there that was especially made for me.

Speaking of Shane, there is no building, no matter the amount of floors that can hold his ego. He has his own tailored suit salon in Saks Fifth Avenue. And compared to his couture, all other high-end fashion is considered "trash" in his mind. If he as much as caught me with anything that didn't bear the Marcus Jacobs name, he would give me an hour-long lecture on the near extinction of black designers. Good thing I was naked underneath this towel, because I didn't want to hear it.

"You can start living because Mrs. Shane is in the building," Shane cooed strutting into the sauna in full America's next top model mode. Shane never ceased to amaze me as he entered without a towel, which is usually required attire when walking from the locker room into the sauna.

"It's just a matter of time before they kick your butt out into the street," I interjected.

"This pretty behind? Why would they do a thing like that? I add style to this place. And you know style isn't bought. It's born."

"Well, I know one thing; you're gonna buy yourself a one way ticket out onto the sidewalk."

"You're just being a drama queen," Shane responded, sitting down across from me with his legs crossed. "And just for that remark I'm not even gonna give you a peek of my goodies."

Shane was like a heterosexual brotha, always thinking with his smaller head and not his big head. Ever since he had a rendezvous with one of the yoga instructors in the very sauna, he's been putting his goods on display, hoping to probably score another or two.

"Getting desperate because your yoga friend ain't giving you the time of day?" I laughed, tossing him my extra towel and closing my eyes again. His hot room fling turned out to be very married and heavily in denial.

"Hell, he's still giving me a little sumtin, sumtin."

"He actually has the time, when he's not with his wife and two kids," I replied sarcastically, peeking through one eye to gauge his distaste. It wasn't like me to take pleasure in another person's pain, but I knew Shane. If he wasn't getting it from one place, he was damn sure getting it from another.

"Well, at least I have a love life. You need to dust off that python between your legs and get back into the jungle," Shane retorted.

My double life in S&M was even a secret to Shane. Not because he wouldn't take pleasure in my activities, but because some were even too hardcore for his taste. That's why I always kept two or three towels at my disposal, to cover up all the black and blues courtesy of my Mistress. I stood up and draped one towel over my waist and the other over my back to hide any evidence of last night. As I proceeded to the sauna door, I stopped in my tracks and thought about what Shane had said.

"You're right. I don't have a love life because there's no such thing as love." I laughed, but not in a funny manner. Shane shook his head, obviously annoyed by my constant negativity. "See you later biyotch."

I had just moved into *The Lenox* condominiums only a month prior, but had already had several complaints levied against me. My apartment was on the 12th floor and I had use of my very own roof top terrace. And I loved to walk around my condo in the nude, whether to enjoy the humidity outside or listen to some *Najee* while drinking a glass of red wine. However, my carefree lifestyle obviously ruffled a few feathers in the tenement building across the street because I was warned by the building superintendent to be more discreet. Still, I didn't see anything wrong in putting my chiseled frame on show in the confines of my home. I would've thought Harlem was a little more tolerant than those rich stiffs on the Eastside.

As the sun went down, a cool breeze found its way into the open terrace doors. I stood on my patio clothed in only a silk robe as I sort relaxation by way of a little hash. Below, I could hear meringue infused music coming from a fruit truck idling by. The pit of my stomach got a little queasy as I looked down. Reminded me of the times my father would throw me in the air when I was a child. The only fond memory I ever had of him.

Thinking about my parents usually caused my eyes to well. They both died in a carbon monoxide accident only two years after they banished me from their home. Regretfully, I never got the chance to apologize for something I couldn't control. Hindsight is twenty, twenty and if I knew what I know now the love of another would have never been worth the love of my parents.

I took a seat on my Teak wood chaise and took a heavy drag of my herbal ecstasy. I love the excitement that New York exudes, but when looking into the atmosphere you cannot locate one damn star. That's what I miss about Memphis. I grew up in the predominantly white suburb of Collierville, Tennessee, the token black in a sea of white faces. Underneath the southern sky, there was always time for peace. My mother and I would sit on our porch over a pitcher of homemade sun tea and talk about the future.

I was small then and she would hold me in her arms and look into my eyes with a face that reflected mine. They called her pretty Millie, because her skin was the hue of Milk and honey and her eyes were like radiant orbs of gold. Just by smiling she could light up a room and with a shake of her hip could send men to the hospital emergency room with neck injuries.

And she was a great listener, one of the many qualities that I inherited from her. No matter what I told her I wanted to be, regardless of its difficulty, she would always say, "I know you will." Sometimes I longed for her assurances, though I'm happy with how my life has evolved. I still wonder if I would've made her proud.

After finishing off my joint, I decided to go to bed and prepare for another day at the office. As much as I loved food preparation, its fast-paced nature was beginning to take its toll. With the money I made since starting my business, I could start my own restaurant and move away to somewhere hot.

"Promiscuous Girl"

Angelica

"Doesn't your job require that you try out the merchandise before you buy it?" My best friend Rochelle laughed as we enjoyed early morning gossip over caramel frappuccino and blueberry biscotti in the food court of Garden State Plaza.

"I don't even know what his tongue tastes like." I laughed while looking down at my beautiful canary yellow diamond engagement ring.

"You got to be joking?" Rochelle paused for effect and then put her face into her hand as soon as I shook my head no.

Rochelle John was what I call a brick house. I know people use the term loosely. Some people get big-boned or just plain ole fat confused with being a brick house. For example, the comedian Monique ain't a brick house, maybe after a couple of hours on the treadmill for an entire year straight she could possibly become one. Beyonce's a brick house, nice wide set hips and an ass that won't make men swear off any cow byproducts. And that was what Rochelle was, thick, not sloppy thick but firm "damn that girl is built" thick. Sporting measurements of 38d, 24, and 38 at just 5'5, she had enough ass to feed an entire Rwandan village.

I 'm not into women or anything, but I have to admit she is beautiful. Looking like Sana'a Lathan wasn't the only thing she was going for her. Unlike most of us follicle challenged sistas, she had hair going down to that big ass of hers due to her Native American heritage. Even as she adjusted her makeup in a compact mirror, I wondered how she managed to get away with wearing revealing clothes in her line of work. Post office attire doesn't exactly scream sexy.

But I got to give my girl props because she knew how to pull it off. She knew how to make postal blue look stunning. Her short sleeve shirt was unbuttoned low enough to show off the perky breast she was blessed with. And the super short navy blue skort she wore was high enough to show off the black of her ass. I hated that she had a nice body while all I had was a pretty face. They called me "olive oil" for a reason in college.

I've known Rochelle for nearly seventeen years, we shared an apartment together in Harlem when we both attended F.I.T. During that point in my life I lived, day by day. Now I've taken a different road, the road that leads to God. Moral cleanliness is the code I live by; I've given my life to the lord. I attend church with my fiancé every Sunday and feel content to wait until my marriage day when he can part my legs like Moses parted the red sea.

I'm even particular about what I put in my body. I'm a flexitarian, the fancy word to describe those few people that eat a mostly vegetarian diet, but occasionally indulge in meat eating

Truth be told, even though I've made numerous strides in my life, I'm far from perfect. I don't attend church more than once a week and there is never a passing day when I don't use some type of foul language. Not to mention that I'm a workaholic in love with the finer things my low six-figure salary provides. Titus always says that if I let go of material things god will *give* me all the necessities of life. But in all the times I've looked down at the feet of the women in his congregation, I've never noticed a pair of Christian Louboutin's. Therefore, I might as well continue to work for my necessities.

"You are definitely better than me. As gorgeous as Titus is, I would be in jail for rape already."

I had to admit being engaged to a Minister came with its disadvantages. I respected my fiancé Reverend Titus Rosemond, but we dated for over two years and he had yet to lay a solitary finger on me. I mean I am fine as hell so I know it's not from lack of visual stimulation. Yet even on those rare occasions when we're alone, things never got heated up. Hell, they didn't even get Lukewarm. For once, a man respected me and I hated it.

"Rochelle, you need to get your mind out the gutter. From what you tell me about Dexter, I know your sex life isn't all what it's cracked up to be either. You need to start going to church with me," I said.

Rochelle has been married for ten years. Yet she spent more time in my guest room than she did in her own bed. It represents all that is wrong in this world when women marry men with more inches on their penis than dollars in their pocket.

"Dexter ain't the only one man out there that's getting' this nana," she said while applying lip-gloss to her lips.

I gave her *the look*. She wasn't stupid enough to cheat on jealous ass Dexter. He worked for the N.Y.P.D as a police officer and was known to monitor her. Last year he had a detective friend of his follow her because he *thought* she was cheating. It turned out she was only planning his birthday. And that wasn't the crazy part; he damn near killed the mailman after catching him leaving the apartment after Rochelle signed for a package. I could only imagine what he'd do if she really was sleeping around.

"Rochelle, don't play with me," I warned, taking another sip of my frappuccino.

"Do I look like I'm playing?" she said taking out an opened box of condoms from her knock off Gucci purse.

During the weekdays, early in the morning, the mall served as a place to jog for some in the community. However, Rochelle didn't give two fucks that some of the men were nearly breaking their necks to stare at her once she revealed that condom box. Hating to cause a scene, I snatched them from her fingertips and put them under my left leg.

"You want to sign your death certificate? What if Dexter found these?" I reasoned.

"And if he did, forget him," she replied dismissively waving her hands. "I got more where those came from. And you do notice those are XXL condoms. Dexter ain't fitting into those."

I sucked my teeth, removed a strand of hair from my eyes and swept biscotti crumbs from off my lap. It was always some new drama in her life. We commuted together from Manhattan to Paramus, New Jersey and every morning it was the same shit. Rochelle wasn't content unless she was fighting with Dexter. Sometimes it felt as if she was addicted to makeup sex.

Dexter was jealous and broke, but he treated her like gold and took care of the child she had from a previous relationship. Not to mention he had done the unthinkable and put a ring on her finger. It took me all of thirty-four years before a man considered me marriage material. What Rochelle should do is take a look at the statistics for unmarried sistas.

However ghetto she may seem, the girl is smart as hell, but her kryptonite has always been thugs. That's why she had to drop out after sophomore year at F.I.T, because of some lame ass brotha with much game, much dick, but not enough sense. She ended up rearing his child while he sat in a cell doing twenty-five to life in Rikers.

Still, Unique, my godson, was the best thing that could've happened to her. When he was born he looked like his father and was just as bad, but he provided her with some semblance of stability. No one could ever accuse Rochelle of not being a great mother, and that's why she's so heart broken. When you can't give a child materially what they want, they sometimes feel like they have to do it on their own. Unique was gunned down last year at seventeen as he robbed a check-cashing place, leaving behind his mother's crushed heart and a son that bore his name.

That's why I look the other way as she battles an early midlife crisis. Once Unique was laid to rest, it was like her good sense was buried with him. Now, she acted as if he was never born, and buried her pain by hitting up clubs and using my guest room as her alibi. Sometimes it felt as though she had regressed to that Nineteen-year-old girl that she was when her son was born.

Once upon a time, I was no better than Rochelle. Just because I'm gonna be a minister's wife didn't mean I was an angel. My body needed the rest since I'd taken a vow of celibacy four years ago. Back in the day if a man with a great smile, a nice car and a hefty bank account even looked my way, I spread my legs. Now I respect myself, even though I still reap the regrets of my promiscuous past and I hope Rochelle would do the same.

"By the way, Angelica, you mean to tell me that you're wearing those short shorts and you're not expecting niggas to holla."

I took an inventory of my gear. My khaki short shorts did put a spotlight on my long caramel legs. But I only wore them because they went well with my brown Jimmy Choo bucket bag and the pair of sling backs on my feet.

"I don't need to impress anyone. I got a man."

"You mean, a man not giving you any of that funky stuff." She laughed as she stood, bending over the table and pulling at my brown pomegranate print camisole. "I gotta get to work, but I suggest that you cover up those tatas and put on some pants if you don't want these trifling niggas hitting on you."

Monday's are always especially busy. I worked in the Grand State Plaza Mall. As the contemporary sportswear buyer for Neiman Marcus, I barely found time for lunch. Sometimes I could just scream at all the tasks that had to be accomplished before closing. Between checking the sales reports, setting up displays, dressing mannequins, doing sample fittings and meeting with vendors, I barely had enough time for myself or my man. Not to mention that in two days my man was going away for three weeks on a missionary mission to Africa and I was going to have to plan all the tedious details of our wedding alone.

I knew the wedding plans would take all of my free time, if not more. While looking down at my desk, I remember to finalize the details with my Wedding Planner. With my final fitting schedules two weeks from now, the last thing on my mind was food. Even though I was 5'7 and a fit 126lbs I wanted to make sure, I could at least *fit* into my dress.

As I looked at the hands on my three thousand dollar Cartier San demoiselle watch, which read 4:09pm, I realized I had better call my wedding planner, Marcellus, before he was gone for the day.

"Hello, Suri wedding planning, Marcellus speaking," Marcellus said in his knockoff French accent. I wasn't hating on him, but he knew damn well he came from Harlem. Nothing against gay men, but dealing with Marcellus was like dealing with another woman. I noticed that about him as we set the menu for my wedding. Don't tell him he's wrong about something or he'll read you up and down, right to left like a real diva would. It's a damn shame that a tall, dark, chocolate brotha like him decided to switch team.

"Hi darling! This is Angelica Thompson."

"I'm glad you called mademoiselle. I just called the Reverend. I apologize for the discrepancy."

"What discrepancy?" I wanted to hide the concern in my voice but it was too late.

"You didn't get my message? The caterer double booked on the date of your wedding."

"And what does that mean?"

"They won't have the man power to cater your wedding. The other event was scheduled first."

"Because of their incompetence I have to suffer."

"Missy, they will issue a total refund of the monies paid back to you." I could sense the trepidation in his voice. I knew their game, someone with more money and importance had offered the caterer a better deal. I didn't mean to take my anger out on Marcellus, but he did recommend the caterer.

"How am I gonna find a damn caterer to cater *my* wedding a month before. I'm not serving cheese and crackers, you know." I got up and closed the door to my office, because I knew things were only going to get worse.

"I know someone that would take the account, missy."

"If you call me missy again, I'm gonna jump through this phone and choke the life out of you."

"I know you're angry, but I can recommend a great caterer for you."

"Why would I want to deal with anyone that you recommend? You did insist on the first one. And look at the situation I'm stuck in," I snapped.

"It's the least I can do due to the incompetence of the caterer's secretary," he tried cleaning up the caterer's mistake. I hated when people passed along their failures to insubordinates.

"The least they can do is send back my money for the wedding pronto or *you* both will be hearing from my lawyer."

"The Reverend was very understanding when I explained the situation. I don't understand the problem."

"You mean the groom. Did he sit down with you and go over the seating arrangements."

"No," he mumbled.

"Did he go over the menu or does he even know the type of fabric I want on the cocktail tables?"

"No," he answered in an exasperated tone.

"So why would you call him before me?" I asked

Who was he to call my fiancé? Titus had no goddamn say when it came to *my* wedding. It was going to be *my* show he was just my co-star. Marcellus knew better than asking a man to do what clearly took the precise planning and meticulous detailed touch of a woman. That's why I decided to have a small wedding party, only my maid of honor and Titus' best man would be standing front and center. It didn't make sense to have a large party of people whose sole purpose in attending would be to outshine the bride and find their next sexual conquest. No one was going to steal my shine.

Marcellus didn't have anything else to say and I didn't even care for an answer. I slammed the phone down even though I had a lot more choice words for that wannabe French asshole. A month before my wedding and things were already coming apart. Maybe it was a sign.

I fought the urge to pinch Titus butt cheeks as he prepared to roll a strike at the Chelsea Pier Lanes. For a brotha, he had a nice, cute, sumtin anotha happening in the back of his Levis. He made me want to do more than shout. But I was content to stare from a distance. I hated our dates; they were always so...casual and not romantic. Like usual, I was stuck twiddling my thumbs under the glow of the dark disco lights as a bunch of lame elderly people in the next booth did the hot potato. And the smell of the hotdogs Titus ordered had me on the verge of throwing up. I didn't eat meat, not unless you count dick.

Slowly, but surely I was beginning to lose the conviction I had when I started my vow of celibacy. In the beginning it was easy because in my last relationship I got hurt so bad I didn't want any part of a man. After putting my blood, sweat and tears into a relationship with a married man, I was left feeling lower than low. I didn't even take the time to think that since he was cheating on his wife, cheating on me wasn't out of the question. Thinking back, the realization of his deception angered me so much that I didn't want to see another naked brotha for fear that I would catch a flashback and cut off some innocent mans penis because of the unfaithfulness of another.

My naiveté got the better of me four years ago. Since then, I've learned not to take every man at his word. That's exactly why I was happy to have found someone like Titus. Sex comes a dime a dozen. But a faithful man, not to mention a man that is still a virgin is something to be treasured. Of course, my feelings for Titus weren't love at first sight, even though he's fine, but I know that *someday* I'll love him.

Titus took a bite from his hot dog as he sat across from me. He was casually dressed in a pair of black Prada slacks I bought him and a short sleeved v-neck t-shirt. His great abs and muscular arms looked great in anything. And he knew it; though he was a man of god he was still a man and felt confident about his.

I appreciated a man with great taste. I appreciated fine things in general and Titus was able to provide me with the life I deserved. Not only was he the highly esteemed leader of his own non-denominational church, but an in demand motivational speaker. Last year alone, he made well over seven figures and had also paid the mortgage on my Tribeca condominium. Though he lived in a modest one-bedroom basement apartment in Harlem, his pockets were deep.

"Angelica, what's bothering you? Is the situation with the caterer still on your mind?" he asked with sincerity in his emerald eyes. I'd long forgotten about the caterer hours ago. That wasn't my problem. I despised the fact that Titus never sat next to me or displayed any signs of affection. When I revealed my concerns once before, he told me that the devil was clouding my judgment.

"You know I love you. But sometimes I feel like you're not even into me," I whispered. Having come from where I came from, I hated wearing any emotion on my sleeves.

"I love you too and I'm here with you. But what are you exactly asking me?" He moved his food to the side, wiped his gorgeous mouth and hands with a napkin and moved his chair closer. But not close enough.

"Do you ever want me?"

"My love for you far surpasses any physical act, if that is where you're getting at."

"But how do you know I can please you?" I wondered. His jaws clenched and his eyelids narrowed. Lines began to form on his head and I knew I had frustrated him.

"I'm beginning to wonder why that's always an issue. You've supposedly waited thirty-four years and you mean to tell me you can't wait another month. Should I be worried while I'm away doing the lord's work?" His tone had sharpened, as if he was talking to a wayward member of his congregation.

Lying can be deadly. It also fills one with guilt. That night two years ago in the Onyx lounge as we talked, he asked me one question. How long have you maintained your cleanliness before god? I answered since birth. I told him that I would never give myself to a man unless he was my husband. He believed me, at that time I needed him to. Now I wished I never lied.

But I needed to impress him. Coming from a long line of Ministers and clergymen, he was shielded from the bitter world I had to face. In his closed circle of family members, I would've been considered a sinner. He said he knew I was his wife. And I needed to be viewed as someone who was worth more than lying on her back.

"I just want a kiss," I humbly confessed.

Wasn't I to be desired? I hated putting on an act for him and everyone else who expected more out of the prospective wife of a minister. Even my baggy, pink velour jumpsuit concealed everything I had to offer. If Titus had seen my outfit earlier, he'd damn near have had a heart attack. But no, I had to dress modest, wear dresses down near my ankles and always act like I was on some unreachable spiritual plain. Why, because I was a minister's fiancé?

Titus always carried a leather carrying case. It was an old beat up looking bag from when he was a child singing on the choir in his father's church. The Velcro had long ago stopped catching and when he carried it, he always had to hold it under his arm to keep it closed. As he opened his antique bag, I instantly knew what to expect. He extracted his black bound bible, turned to his appointed scripture and put on his Cartier reading glasses, in the middle of a crowded bowling alley. Like usual, he couldn't tell me from his own words why he couldn't touch me.

"Let me read you something from…"

I stood in the front pew of Mount Bethel A.M.E listening to my man give another heart wrenching Eulogy for one of his beloved Deacons, Deacon Marshall who was also City Councilman . I held hands with the widow, trying my best to provide her with much needed strength as she stared at the lifeless body of her husband in the bronze colored coffin only a few feet away. She shook her head as Titus spoke and fought back tears with a white handkerchief.

Trying her best to be the pillar of strength for her family, she would reveal a contrived smile whenever Titus made a joke to lighten the mood. At least he fortified her through candid reflections. All I could do was lean over and whisper in her ear "The lord will not fail you." Those words meant nothing to me, they just sounded like the right thing to say at this particular time.

Looking down from the altar into the eyes of Sister Marshall he said, "Your husband's in a better place. A place where his step has more spring, his legs more pep and where his love for you will never perish. Your love was a perfect love that distance, time and death could never stop. It's persevering. And the day you meet again, its radiance will not have dimmed. But it will be even more omnipotent."

Those words touched her, made her smile with fervor while crying tears of joy. Titus was always eloquent when speaking from the pulpit. Titus loved his congregation and held a self-sacrificing affection for them that he never showed me. For that reason, I was jealous of the attention he gave. If anyone were missing, he would call him or her personally. If anyone seemed down, he would impart words of encouragement, and if anyone were in need, he would provide food, both spiritual and physical.

However, he ignored who was supposed to be the most important component in his life. His congregation was his first love and I felt like a mistress.

Befitting of the mood, rain began to pelt the tinted limousine window as we drove from the burial site. We were alone, yet the silence we held had become customary in our courtship. We dated for two years without ever really talking. Our engagement was only common routine. It wasn't even spectacular, not over a candle light dinner and he didn't surprise me by getting on bended knee in front of friends and family. It was over the phone as we read the bible together.

The interior lights were on, Titus was reading from his bible, caught in the private recesses of his psyche he never let anyone near him. Everyone had another side, but his was well hidden and bolted shut with an impenetrable lock

I don't know what I was supposed to look for in a soul mate. My record of boyfriends would attest to the fact that I habitually pick no good men. It wasn't as if I had a father around to compare them to. Thus, I relied on my instincts, which were fickle to say the least. I tried the thug thing, the baller thing, even tried the white thing until I found out the myth about the size of their members was really a fair assessment. Titus on the other hand was the only honorable male to ever lay eyes on me. And I didn't want to lose a man who had saved himself all his life for me.

"Did you speak to Sister Marshall before you left?" Titus asked.

"I didn't get a chance to," I said. In reality, there was nothing for me to say, I didn't know her and better yet, I didn't know her husband. "I wasn't having one of my better nights."

"You have to make it an obligation. My congregation looks to you for inspiration. You can't have an off night. When we get to her house, make it a point to speak with her"

There were many things he said I couldn't do. I couldn't curse, couldn't hang with the wrong crowd a definition, which all of my friends fell under and I couldn't go out on the town. In all actuality, he didn't want me to be me.

I powered down the back window. Without fresh air, I was beginning to get carsick. "I need to get home. I got work in the morning and I think I'm coming down with something," I said, lying on both accounts.

"You can go to work and slave for people with low moral fiber, but you can't give support to a widow." He shook his head, took his eyes out of the bible, leaned in his seat and crossed his legs. "Until you put the work of the lord first, your job situation will never improve."

"I put the lord first," I said raising my voice.

"Then the job must go."

This man didn't realize how much I'd already sacrificed for him, for his love. Four years earlier, I sinned vehemently on a regular basis. I would stay out into the early morning, dabble in about every party drug imaginable and fornicate like it was going out of style. That life style came with a price. Forget baby momma drama, I had nigga's wife strife. Titus just didn't know that what attracted me to him more than his bank account and good looks was his baggage free life.

"Titus, you don't hear me telling you to leave the church."

"That makes no sense and you know it. This isn't a career; it's a calling and a privilege. I've worked diligently to get where I am. And until the lord tells me to stop, this is where I'll remain."

"Exactly, so why would you ask me to quit something I worked hard for?"

He hated when I went against him. I could hear his teeth grind and see his jaw lock. My defiance was killing him inside. He was old school, from a Mid-western Baptist family where women were seen, but not heard. I met his mother, Marjorie when we went to visit his family in Arkansas and could tell she had never made a worthwhile decision in all forty years of marriage. His father was unimpressive physically; barely standing an inch above his five foot four-inch wife, but was still domineering. She jumped when he spoke, making it her divine function to care for his unrealistic preferences. I detested the way he treated her and to make things worse, I had to stay in Titus' childhood bedroom as he slept in a nearby hotel. This meant I had to bear with his Father's chauvinistic ways alone.

During my stay, a snowstorm hit and dumped a foot of slush on the ground. When I awoke in the morning to the sound of a shovel scrapping against gravel, I was surprised to see Marjorie in her robe and boots waist deep in a mound of snow making sure not to scrape the shovel against her husband's Cadillac.

Titus, though, wasn't his father. He wasn't a domineering man, but didn't take after his mother either. He was sort of in the middle. I guess that's what two parents are for. Besides, he couldn't get away doing to me what his father did to his mother.

"I wished you could come with me on my missionary trip," he said, trying to turn on his natural charm.

"You can't blame my job for that," I said stretching my right hand out and showing off my ring.

"Maybe not in this instance, but there will be other times," he said.

"Hopefully those will be few and far between," I responded. The car came to a halt outside the front door of my building. I wanted to jump across the seat and put my lips against his, but it wouldn't do any good. His chastity meant too much to him, even more than my happiness.

"Well, my heart. Guess this is goodbye for the next three weeks," he said softly. He winked at me, with glazed over eyes. Obviously, our time apart weighed on his mind.

I composed myself, waited for the driver to get out and open my door. I looked in my little compact mirror, made sure my makeup looked flawless, even though it was not like I had done anything to mess it up.

"Can you join me for breakfast in the morning, I'm cooking. I'll appreciate it if you'd join me for a feast in the morning," I stated as the driver let the cool summer breeze in as he opened the door. I had never cooked in my life, didn't have a mother to teach me. My breakfast of champions consisted of a hot cup of coffee and a pastry both store bought. I tried making coffee once and ended up with something that looked like used car oil. However, I did not want him to leave like this. Besides, he never hid the fact that he wanted a domestic wife. Maybe I could cook my way into getting that elusive first kiss.

"If you're cooking, I'm there. I think that is a great idea. I'll be there with an empty stomach," he rejoiced. With a huge smile on his face, he blew me a kiss as I stepped out onto the sidewalk. I blew him one in return, praying to receive the real thing to hold me over in his absence.

As the fire detector sounded, I rushed into the living room and opened the windows, put the fan atop the gas range on high and continued to cook. I flipped the sausage over, couldn't tell whether it was done, it felt frozen to the touch but had a crispy black coat on each side. Since I prepared eggs before hand, the residue left behind had turned a licorice color, making it difficult to make the sausage look golden brown as it did on the package.

The oven timer went off. My buttermilk biscuits were done; I opened the oven door and smiled as I beheld my creation. They looked light and fluffy, the tops were brownish yellow and the sides were a light yellow. I put on the brand new pair of oven mitts I never used and took them out the oven. After placing the pan atop the plastic that covered my kitchen table, I grabbed the spatula from the frying pan where I was cooking the sausage and used it to pry the biscuits from the pan. The bottoms were baked to the pan, so I cut off the good part and soaked the pan along with the bottoms in the sink. Putting the finishing touches on breakfast, I set a place for Titus at my dining room table and lit an apple crisp candle to further entice his taste buds.

I looked at the clock, it was nearly eight and Titus told me he'd be here by that time. My suit for work was already laid out, but I decided to put on a sexy pair of pajamas I bought at La Perla instead. They weren't overtly revealing, but if he looked, close enough his eyes could behold my tantalizing curves. This would be the first time we were alone, so I wanted to make access as easy as possible without going all out and answering the door in the nude.

Taking off my robe in front of my mirror, I pinched a finger full of fat from my waist. My body wasn't in tiptop shape like I wanted it to be, thus I was going to have to cut the pastries from my diet. I didn't want Titus to be traumatized the first time he saw a naked woman. Jogging would definitely be on the menu for the weekend.

I rubbed Donna Karen's gold body lotion all over, sprayed Victoria secret vanilla lace body spray on my breasts and privates and slipped into my purple silk PJ's.

I heard a light knock at my door and couldn't restrain my smile. Titus made me feel like the luckiest woman on earth. There's nothing like the feeling that overtakes you when you make your man a home cooked meal. Wonder why I hadn't tried it earlier. Seeing the smile on his face while he dived into my food would be the ultimate compliment.

Like a real woman, I took my time to answer the door, wanted him to be good and eager when he saw me. I whistled as I sashayed down the hallway leading to my foyer and was taken aback when I peeked through the peephole and saw who was outside of my door. There was nothing wrong with Titus; he looked good dressed in one of his tailored suits bearing flowers and a smile. But it was who he brought along that concerned me and instantly killed any thoughts I had of seducing him.

"Hi. How are you doing, Sister Mathews?" I said opening the door and forcing a smile as Sister Mathews walked by me without as much as a glance.

Sister Mathews was one of the founding members of Mount Bethel A.M.E. She was in her seventies, with a polka dot face, saggy titties and a bad attitude. I sensed from our first meeting that she wished that one of her dog-faced daughters were in my shoes. Ever since my engagement, she's done everything in her power to spite me. This was the icing on the cake. I didn't understand why she hated me. Titus shared a phone line with her and sometimes when I call, she'll hang up and blame it on her sleeping pills. However, part of me felt like she had me pegged, knew my game and understood that in this day and age it was almost impossible to be a virgin. I could tell it in her deciphering stares whenever I wore something less than modest in church. A younger woman has no chance against an older woman. And surely, she had been there, seen it and probably done everything I had not so long ago. No woman married for more than forty years has a shortage of tricks up her sleeves and that's why I feared her.

"It looks great in here," Titus said shaking my hand as he stepped into my apartment for the first time. He had been in my building many times but never made the trek upstairs.

I closed the door and shook my head as Titus walked ahead. I anticipated a morning I would never forget and at that moment, I was sure of it.

Sister Mathews walked around my kitchen poking her face into every pot on top of my stove with a disgusted look.

"You've done some serious cooking in here." Titus said admiring the bowls of food on the granite countertops island.

"It also smells like she's done some serious burning as well," Sister Mathews retorted. That had Titus tickled, laughing like he needed an anti-laugh antidote.

"Well, Mama Mathews, the lord says waste not want not." Titus laughed taking her coat and placing a kiss on her cheek as she took a seat.

She held her purse in front of her; clutching it with both gloved hands like someone was gonna rob her. She wore a pink church dress that looked like it was made from cactus-like material and a huge hat adorned the matted gray naps that peeked from her black wig. The hat was pink linen as well with a lavender matte and a satin sash and bow.

"Put me down for the want not and a cup of tea," she said, staring at me as if I was her maid or something. Titus left the room and went into the living room so he could put her coat away along with his.

Like a Christian woman, I bit my tongue and asked, "I have an assortment. Do you prefer Lipton or Chai?"

"You got any Earl Grey? I got a taste for some Earl Grey," she said.

"No, only Lipton and Chai," I said with a plastic smile.

"I don't want any then. What is an assortment of tea without Earl Grey?" she said in a huffed tone.

"I can go to the store if you want."

"I'm sure you wouldn't mind if I went to the store," she said staring at me suspiciously.

"What was that?" I asked shocked by her accusation.

"No God fearing woman asks a man to come alone to her home if she has something holy in mind. You may have Titus fooled, but you're a harlot and will eventually be cast out of the lord's house," she pointed her finger rigidly in my direction making her position clearly understood.

"I don't know why you would doubt my intentions for him. I would never hurt him. But it should be of no concern to you either way, he will be my husband," I said coyly with a hint of sarcasm.

"What sinners keep in the dark, the lord brings to the light," she said as Titus walked into the kitchen, stood between us and grabbed our hands.

"Before we enjoy this meal, let's bow our heads..." Titus said with closed eyes. I didn't close mine, neither did Sister Mathews, we locked eyes and didn't budge until he said Amen.

Ignoring the battle-axe, I fixed Titus' plate, put the white roses he bought for me in a vase and sat next to him as he tried to enjoy my food. He didn't like it all that well and I knew it from the time he bit into an eggshell, but he played the role of the appreciative fiancé and didn't complain. I thanked him for that.

"This was great food," Titus said as he broke off a piece of frozen sausage with his fork.

"Tell the truth, don't spare me. It was terrible, wasn't it?" I asked.

"It was pretty bad," he admitted putting his arms around my shoulders, touching me for the first time in a romantic way.

I pursed out my lips and with puppy dog eyes playfully sobbed, "Now you see why I don't cook."

"And the world's a better place because of it," Sister Mathews stuck her two cents in. "I taught my daughters as soon as they came out the womb how to make a decent meal. It makes no sense for a married woman to not know her way around the kitchen. I say the kitchen and bedroom go hand in hand. That's why my husband, God rest his soul, had no reason to be any other place but home. In my household, I made it a priority that my daughters know how to make a man happy." She put her wrinkled hands across the table and placed them on top of Titus's. Luckily, I did not have a knife or fork at my disposal or I would have gladly crippled her.

I wanted to say something back for once, give her a taste of her own medicine, but could not since Titus thought of her as a second mother. He lived in the basement apartment of her brownstone and she always made sure to cook him three meals a day.

I could also tell she wanted a reason to berate my apartment as she looked around, but I kept my place tidy. If anything, I knew how to clean.

"I don't know what I'm gonna do when you leave," I said staring into Titus' green eyes while he sipped a glass of orange juice.

"You won't be the only one feeling lost," he said. Our faces were only inches apart, the impassioned look in his eyes told me to make my move, regardless of Sister Mathews Judgmental gaze. We moved closer, I closed my eyes. Prepared my lips to touch his, relaxed my tongue in hopes that it would intertwine with his. However, a loud gag got my attention. It sounded like someone was choking. I opened my eyes to see Titus get up from his seat and rush over to Sister Mathews.

She was keeled over looking like she was gonna spit out a lung. Titus rubbed her back and tapped it softly.

"Get me a glass of water!" he ordered me.

I went to the faucet, drew some cold tap water in a glass and handed it to him. She wasn't worth wasting Evian on. Titus held the glass to her lips as she brought her head back. She drunk from it, caught her breath and sighed intensely as if she was underwater for twenty minutes.

"Mama Mathews, are you alright," he said with concern.

"I neglected to take my medicine," she said as he hugged her.

"Okay mama, I'll get your coat," he said retreating to the living room.

"Top that, Jezebel!" she said with a wink.

They left minutes later, leaving behind not only dishes, but also the realization that maybe I was taking on more than I could bear, because when I marry Titus I marry his church as well.

"Torn"

Aurelius

I felt like I had just closed my eyes as the sun peered through the slit between the black velvet curtains hanging from my picturesque sixteen-foot windows. In my room, the sun was an uninvited guest. My walls were painted black, the mirrors were blacked out, leather bondage swings hung from the ceiling and my bed was made with built in cuffs and restraints. There was nothing bright about my dungeon.

As I stirred, I felt the icy sting of the steel manacles hidden underneath my black Egyptian sheets.

I fought to look at the time on my digital clock through hazy eyes, wishing in the back of my cluttered mind that I had a few hours left of sleep. My hopes were instantly shattered as I discovered the time. It was already 9:38am and there was nothing I could do about it. Yesterday kicked my butt and I was already more than a half hour behind today's schedule.

Today out of all days, I had to be on the ball. I sent out an e-mail reminder to all my employees. I employed mostly students that needed a supplemental income to fund their weekend drinking binges. I didn't employ any fulltime employees because I didn't need any. In my field, the size of the events I catered fluctuated. I usually gave my employees two weeks notice with a reminder the day of the event. For events the size of the one tonight, I only had one rule; if you can't show, you better let me know or risk getting on my bad side. And trust me you don't want to get on my bad side.

A client of mine was having a dinner party/fund raiser for her high society friends and she insisted that I make something spectacular. The purpose of the fundraiser was for her Reverend's humanitarian missionary trip to Africa and the cost to eat was $500 per plate. I knew how much it meant to my client to have everything run smoothly. In order for me to make her dream a reality, I had to personally check on the pounds of porterhouse steak I ordered from my favorite butcher and the fresh bass I bought from my favorite fish market before they shipped out. I could've left well enough alone and have it sent to the site, but I liked to see what I was getting. My meticulous nature made for long days and it wasn't going to be no different since one was located on the upper west side, while the other resided in Tribeca. Which meant I had to do something I detested doing; take the subway.

I could feel eyes burning holes through me. Closed-minded teenagers snickered and old women gasped as they caught sight of me, treating me with the same esteem as the mentally challenged transients that roamed the subways of New York. I stood upright, tilted my black straw fedora to the side and tugged my black disco pants below my waist, slightly covering the tongue of my black ankle boots.

My body swayed with the motion of the train as I held onto the metal bars overhead. It reminded me of the surf at Cowell's beach in Santa Cruz where the set's break two hundred yards from shore. After graduating from the California Culinary academy, I went on small journeys up the California coast to "find" myself. Those were great days: whimsical days when my only problem was deciding what patch of sand to sleep on at night.

As the train pulled into my station, I felt an equal amount of glee and trepidation. Glee, knowing I survived the unfriendly glares of an entire car of passengers, and trepidation from knowing I'd have to take the train two more times before I could exhale.

When shopping for my clients, I'm very particular. That means my steaks have to be marbled cuts. This keeps the juices from escaping the meat. I take pride in my cooking. I'm not satisfied unless my customers are. I liken cooking to sex. When making love to a woman, a man can dive in and get his. However, with that approach, there's a great chance your woman may leave unsatisfied.

Like any well-prepared meal, you must take your time, not cut corners to satisfy one's own needs. An appetizer is served before the entrée for a reason, it's the key to a person's appetite, and helps keep them anticipating of the main course. The clitoris like wise is the master key for what is hidden in the mind of a woman sexually. Brothers don't take the time to attack that part of the anatomy first; they are content showing off their virility by how hard they can sex. That's why older men tend to attract younger women. They are patient they don't go hard; they know how to stimulate with patience. I've learned to love enjoying every inch and how to satisfy a woman. Like a well-fed restaurant patron, I know she'll always come back for more.

By the time I arrived back at my apartment, I had several new messages on my voicemail. A few were from Shane, but one in particular caught my attention. It was from the Reverend of the church I rented kitchen space from. He was going to be at the Fundraiser and needed a favor. This was strange considering our relationship. Reverend Rosemond was one of those holy rollers stuck in the ways of antiquated theology. While in the beginning stages of starting Foradori, I contacted him in search of kitchen space. Our phone conversation went well, but the first time we met face to face, he looked at me like I was a relic from the days of Sodom and Gomorrah and rescinded his offer of free kitchen space. Luckily, Jada Simpson, my client and one of his most generous church members, came to bat for me. My relationship with the Reverend was strained to say the least. And for that reason, it surprised me to hear from him.

I took out my yoga mat, crossed my legs under my body and sat in the middle of the living room where the chi was most strong. Then I took a mallet and lightly taped the meditation chime placed on the floor. This gave me a moment to meditate and heighten my sensory awareness. I took a deep breath, closed my eyes and exhaled slowly as I rotated Chinese health balls in both hands. Before I could perform any daily routines, I had to find my chi. Prior to discovering Feng Shui, I lived in darkness.

My condominium was furnished minimally, though I didn't fully practice Feng Shui I believed in many of its principles. Clutter wasn't good for positive life energy. The décor of my entire home was Asian influenced minus my bedroom. My living room was painted purple so I could be guided spiritually. My loveseat and sofa bed was arranged in a circle and facing the door to let the positive energy circulate freely. The fountain by the door sat on an oriental pedestal and my most prized possession, a wooden bagua mirror, hung insignificantly on the wall. I didn't have a TV in the condo because nothing that shed a positive light on black people had been on since the Cosby Show. If I had to watch another beautiful sista shaking her ass in a song while being called a bitch at the same time, I'd go crazy.

After finishing my meditation, I got dressed in my chef's outfit and loaded up my 2006 Chrysler Minivan. It was four o' clock and I knew I'd have to rush over to Ms. Simpson's estate just to have food served on time. My order of steak and fish had arrived on site at noon. And I wanted to prep the food before my staff arrived at six.

I arrived at Ms Simpson's illustrious waterfront New Jersey estate feeling rushed. After sitting in the Lincoln tunnel's bumper-to-bumper traffic for almost an hour, I knew I was in for a long night. When I arrived, I parked my car on the side of her home, crept into the back door and into the gourmet kitchen unannounced. The driveway was filled with people who had arrived by charter bus. I didn't have time for anyone's idle chitchat that would delay my feast any further, so I avoided contact with the partygoers.

As I set up my utensils on the granite countertops, I felt someone's hand creeping into the front of my black chef pants. It's was Ms Simpson and she was up to her usual antics. Though I only came to her home once a week to prepare a week's worth of food, she always managed to sneak a quick fuck as I slaved over her commercial stove.

Jada Simpson was an entrepreneur and owner of five Lexus dealerships around the country. Her story was inspiring in that she rose from the depilated Harlem landscape to become one of the most successful and powerful women this side of Oprah. Though she was twice divorced, her confidence and beauty remained intact. And she loved nothing more than being fucked all over her modernized kitchen.

"What if someone catches you with your hand down my pants?" I smirked. There was something intoxication about an aggressive woman.

"Then I'd say I was looking for some meat." She stood on the tips of her Prada pumps and blew into my ear.

"I'm sure that would go over well with your associates from church," I moaned as I began to enjoy her touch.

Jada was a born again freak. What I mean is that after being married for so long, she had finally rediscovered variety in sex. When making love to the same individual day in and day out a person can grow bored with sexual redundancy. I believe that God created varieties of people so that we could enjoy a variety of sexual partners. The concept of marriage is medieval.

Jada shared my views. She didn't want a commitment, but wanted a great sex life. She was willing and open to new experiences. And she wasn't bad with teaching me as well. That's what we had in common, so it wasn't unusual for us to do the nasty and not communicate until the next time we met face to face. We were not bound by the imaginary handcuffs of a relationship.

Jada had the ability to stop hearts. Sometimes when making love to her, it wasn't unusual for me to stop and stare. Her D.N.A should be bottled and cloned by the millions. Her butterscotch toned skin and long black hair streaked with honey blonde highlights were only the cherries atop her 5'10 160lb frame. But it was when I looked at her lips, full, wet and perfect like her neither region, I could barely maintain a semblance of control in her grasp.

When she grabbed my hand and led me to the basement bathroom, I knew we'd give a new meaning to the word "edible."

The party planner had done a beautiful job. White tents dotted the lush green landscape. Patio lights hung from the awnings, illuminating the night. An eclectic collection of music played on the outdoor sound system, ranging from Mozart to the harmonic tunes of Duke Ellington. I didn't know if most of the revelers at this black and white affair even appreciated the harmony and scoring that Ellington brought to the table in the form of "Sophisticated Lady." And I Doubted they cared that though brilliant beyond compare, Mozart's simple and direct melodies were never appreciated in his time.

This was what I referred to as an "Ass kisser convention." Most of these types of people came to fund raisers not to give money, but to schmooze. I guess it made them feel good to give pennies away for the sole purpose of a tax write off. I watched from afar, as they sipped on medium-bodied white wine with fake smiles plastered across their condescending faces.

After putting the finishing touches on the Baked Sea Bass with potatoes and Grilled Porterhouse Steak, we began to serve the crowd. I readily helped my staff. I didn't mind helping my employees when it came to the true grind of food service. Most chefs are content to revel in praise while the rest of the team does back breaking work.

Never much for attention, I passed the plates around as quickly as possible. I hated when people took me in front of a crowd of people so they could fill my head up with insincere compliments. It didn't take us any more than thirty minutes to serve the crowd. Pleased with the success of our evening, I gave my staff an extended break before desert was to be served. As they began the festivities for the fundraiser, I retreated to the beach. Jada's house wasn't far from the shore. I disappeared behind her storage shed, ducked underneath the wooden fence that separated her house from the beach and walked onto the sand. Finally alone, I took a joint out my pocket and found a spot by one of the sand dunes nestled along the seashore. Since the hard part of the evening was over, I needed to get high.

I loved the smell of seawater. The true essence of life lived in the sea. Taking off my slip resistant shoes and socks, I began to walk barefoot along the shore. I looked into the starry heavens and thought about my parents. When I found out they had passed away, I was on one of my infamous journeys along the pacific coast highway, traveling from San Diego to Santa Clara. I remember the strong smell of the sea that night. Though I mourned my parent's death, it was that smell of "life" that kept me from becoming suicidal.

I removed my chef's toque, used my hands to comb through my hair and blew a billow of smoke into the atmosphere. I hated crowds and I needed all the help I could before facing the high society stiffs at the Fundraiser. If I had one flaw in my personality, it had to be the fact that I was ruthless when protecting my privacy. I'd rather be a loner than a friend.

I fit in with that crowd just as much as Louis Farrakhan fit in at a republican convention. Their ways of life were in direct contrast to mine. They lived the so called, "American dream," a dream that for most was minus happiness. My father lived his life in the same manner, using hard work and money as an excuse to abandon the responsibilities of a parent. I hated his life and in turn hated these people

---

The night was nearing an end when Reverend Rosemond entered the kitchen with an awkward smile on his face. The type of smile a person possesses when he needs a favor from someone he's not necessarily fond of. I was in the midst of repacking leftovers in the kitchen when he took a seat on one of the stools lined along the granite center island.

"You did a great job. I'm sure the lord was pleased with your effort," he said leaning on his elbows.

"I try my best," I said. I was uncomfortable speaking about religion, especially since I didn't believe in a supreme being.

"Are you familiar with the bible, Mr. Aurelius?"

"Yes, it's a well written book," I admitted.

"No, it's the greatest book of all time."

"It's arguably the greatest," I responded.

"You don't have any faith. Otherwise, you'd recognize the bible as God's life manual to us."

"Oh, I have faith, just not in those that represent "God," I said.

Reverend Rosemond glanced towards the marble floor, put his fingers on the bridge of his nose and squeezed. I knew I had hit a sensitive area; there was no secret that most of the religious leaders found more solace in the pockets of their "sheep" than in God's life manual. Reverend Rosemond wasn't much better. I knew his suits cost a grip, because Shane told me the Reverend habitually spent thousands of dollars shopping at Saks. As I analyzed the pricey Rolex on his wrist and the over priced Armani suit on his body, I knew he could have funded his missionary trip with his own money.

"Mr. Aurelius…"

"Reverend I mean no disrespect, but I'd appreciate it if you called me only Aurelius. Not Mr. Aurelius."

The Reverend sighed loudly and said, "I don't mean to impose, but I'm desperate."

"Exactly what are you desperate for?" I said while wiping down the kitchen countertops.

"I'm getting married in a month and I was hoping you could cater my wedding."

I started to say hell no since he had the audacity to sit there and ask me to help *him* with *his* wedding in light of his past broken promise. Besides, who did he think I was, to be planning a wedding feast without going through the proper channels.

"When is your wedding?"

"On July 8th. It's being profiled in Ebony. I'm willing to pay you very well. I think we both can benefit from this partnership," he said.

Even though I had planned a vacation for the entire month of July on the French Riviera, I was sure the press in of itself would do wonders for my planned expansion. I mean, I was successful in my business, but when it came to weddings, my business had always suffered a lull. It wasn't that I couldn't do a great job, but most of my accounts were for high society affairs, or parties. The real money was being made from catering weddings. Nowadays people are getting married left and right and I wanted a piece of the pie. And in high society where people get married four or five times in a lifetime, I would really make a large profit.

"As of right now, I can't give you a yes or no," I lied. "I'm sure I can have an answer for you tomorrow. You have my card give me a call in the evening."

"That's fine. Patience is one of the lord's many attributes," he said, standing up and fixing his silk tie. "Before I forget, Sister Simpson has told me a lot about the fine job you do for her. My fiancé is currently in the market for a personal chef. And with the wedding taking so much of her time, I wanted to hire someone to take care of her culinary duties while she goes through the tedious task of planning our wedding. Would you be interested?"

As a personal chef, I always had time on my hand. Besides, I love to cook and with my three clients on summer vacations and Jada going on the missionary trip, I was in the market for someone to help fill my schedule when I wasn't catering any events. My services didn't come cheap but for the executive types always on the run, the cost was well worth it.

"No problem, but I'll need to set up a meeting so I can establish a menu for her."

Reverend Rosemond started to walk towards the kitchen door when he suddenly stopped in his tracks, "I'll be in contact in the next day or so before I'm off to Africa. But I implore you to keep all interactions with my fiancé honorable."

"My intentions are always honorable," I said. At the time, I didn't see why not.

"Breaking Point"

Angelica

You would think a man would want to spend his last few days cuddling with his woman. But not Titus, he was attending a fundraiser without me. We had planned to go together, but that's until he brought that old witch to my apartment. I didn't want to see him. He took life too seriously; to him everything was always about church. Even the bible says there's a time and place for everything. I admired that Titus wanted to help all the underprivileged of Africa, but I needed some love too.

That's exactly why I was in one of my bitchy ass moods. Lack of sex can make a sane woman frustrated as hell. And the closer I got to my wedding day, the more I thought about sex. It's not a sin to imagine, though I'm sure Titus would have a scripture for that as well. Lately though, I've been wondering how big his package was and if he was a slow learner or a natural. I mean I got no problem teaching him how to ride, but you know how men get when a woman is too good. They start wondering whom you have been with.

I was pissed as hell as I surfed through the channels on my plasma. It was midnight and on every cable channel was someone being royally sexed. You don't know how much mental energy I had to exert in order to stop from going into my private stash of sex toys. It was damn torture so I decided to turn off the television and get something hot to drink in my kitchen.

Living in Tribeca suited me just well, but I was going to miss it here. After my wedding, I was moving into a mansion in Southampton that Titus and I had bought a month ago. It's a big departure from what I'm used to. Growing up in the Philadelphia foster home system didn't always provide me with the opportunity to smell fresh air. I spent most of my time in group homes, a place where they crowd children with severe emotional problems and no place to go or in foster homes where people treated me like dirt or a sexual object with a hollow soul.

Living was a fight, trying to survive was almost impossible. I'm a survivor and some of my emotional scars will never heal. I barely ever tell Titus about my past. I don't know if it's because it's so painful or because I'd hate to scare him off. A woman without a family or place to call her own has very few options. I'm not too proud to admit that I've slept and lived with men for a place to sleep and food to eat. Sometimes I liked it, other times I felt like dirt.

My parents are just a figment of my imagination. Yet, they are my source of inspiration. It's because they decided to leave that pushes me to succeed every single day. All the times I was mistreated as a child and wanted to lay down and die, it's their leaving that kept me alive. All the times I had to lay on my back or get on my knees, it was their memory that kept me breathing. And when I had to sell my body to pay for tuition, it was their hate that gave me a pulse.

That fire still burned, even when I graduated as valedictorian of my high school class, the flame burned brighter. When I graduated from Fashion Institute Technology, the fire grew even bigger. But it was as I received my MBA from Widener University, a small private school west of Philadelphia that I realized no matter what I did it would never bring back my innocence. Guess that is why I lied to Titus, he felt like my only savior.

I fixed myself a steaming cup of Chai tea, opened up my bible and began to read from it. Titus said that by reading from it, all my physical cravings would go away. But even that didn't help. So I found myself in my bedroom with the lights turned out and a pillow between my legs. If I didn't get to sleep, I'd just have to take some Nyquil to end my torture.

I heard my phone ring; it took me some time locating it in my dark bedroom, but I hoped it was my man.

"Hello," I said in a sleep-induced haze.

"Angie, I need a favor," Rochelle asked as I sat up in my bed prepared for the worst.

"What's going on? Do you know what time it is?" I asked playing my usual motherly role.

It sounded as if she was having fun from the giggles coming from her end of the phone.

"Can I use your spare room tonight?"

"What do you mean *use it*?" Her request was beginning to sound like it could be more trouble than it was worth.

"I'm kinda…you know messed up and you know I can't go home to Dexter like this," she said in a tipsy slur.

There was silence for a second as her phone dropped to the ground causing even more laughter. I knew she was drunk, furthermore, I knew she wasn't alone or with her husband.

"I'm sorry, Angie, but my hands were a little tied up," Rochelle said in her drunken vernacular.

"I'm sure they are. Do you know I have to be at work in the morning?"

"Sorry, but girl I *really* need to use your room."

"Who are you with?" I asked. She had fully awakened me, now I was sitting on the edge of my bed with the lights on and any thoughts of a good night's sleep long gone.

"Damn Angie, you all up in my business."

"I have the right if you bring your business all up in my house."

I was still in my funky mood. Titus had neglected to call and to make matters worse, I needed it real bad. Fuck chastity, chastity can kiss my ass and take a flying leap off the Brooklyn Bridge. At the same time, I always made it a point to be there for my girl, she had definitely been there for me. No questions asked. It wasn't like I was condoning her infidelity, she's gonna cheat whether it's under my roof or someone's else's and I wouldn't forgive myself if something were to happen to her.

"Really Angie, I need to crash at your spot."

"You got a key, so hurry up and come in quietly I'm gonna get some sleep." I hung up the phone, turned off my ringer and closed my eyes.

I woke to the sound of banging coming from the next room. The digital clock read 3:47am and my heart skipped a beat as nervousness began to set in. I lived in a building with concierge service, but it wasn't unthinkable that someone had broken in. I grabbed the miniature baseball bat that I had hidden underneath my bed, clutched it tightly and tiptoed quietly to my bedroom door, opening it slowly. I was just about to turn on the hallway lights when I heard her. I heard Rochelle's voice coming from the open guest room door and it sounded like she was in a lot of pain. I stood by the door, counted to three and stepped inside.

Rochelle didn't notice me as I entered and I couldn't blame her because she was on the bed on all fours. The brotha that was putting in work looked at me, removed the dreads from his eyes and winked. Sweat poured from every pore of his muscular body and his ass, ah his ass moved effortlessly.

The room smelled like passionate sex. The mixture of their perspiration had created an erogenous aroma. The way the room was set up made the doorway a blind side, the canopy bed was situated around the corner and unless you were sitting on the foot of the bed, you wouldn't notice if someone was standing by. But Rochelle's conquest stood by the foot of the bed and was able to see me without a problem.

I wanted to run, but his slow, precise movements had mesmerized me. As a matter of fact, he couldn't take his eyes off me. It was as if he was performing exclusively for me. His skin was dark, very dark like the shade of a freshly paved driveway. And his dreads reached down to his wide shoulders, covering his face each time he thrust.

"Mi like fi bowcat. Mi champion," he said in a sexy Caribbean accent. I didn't understand a word of what he said, but it sounded sexy.

Rochelle turned around, still unaware of my presence and spread her legs. He got on bended knee and spread her fleshy folds apart with his thumb and fore fingers, then placed her legs on each shoulder. Pulling his hair back, he dived in rabidly. Most of the men I had had the opportunity to lay with never put effort into pleasing my body the way he was doing it for Rochelle.

Rochelle pulled at his locks with one hand and ground her hips steadily against his face while lightly fondling her breast with the other. Her peeks had swollen to astronomic proportions as she grazed against them. I needed a closer look and that was when she saw me. Her eyes were slits as she gazed at me lustfully and in an intoxicated manner. She ran her tongue over her plump lips and with one finger called me over in a "come hither" gesture while at the same time offering me a sample of her mammilla.

The way she offered herself reminded me of something I encountered years earlier, a memory I prayed would never come back. But the recollection was poignant. So I ran, ran back into my room, buried myself underneath my comforter and cried to sleep.

"Was your phone off last night?" Titus asked as I leaned back in my leather swivel chair.

"Sorry, I really had a hard time getting to sleep. So I turned it off," I confessed.

I spent the better part of my morning in a fog. Visions of last night had taken over my consciousness. When I saw Rochelle in the morning, I could barely look her in the eye. As she roamed around my apartment in a bra and panties, I felt abnormally uncomfortable. Even on our ride into work, I avoided conversation by listening to my I-pod. Last night opened Pandora's Box, a box I was frightened wouldn't close.

"I've been worried that this wedding has been getting to you," Titus stated.

"Not in the least, work is what is getting to me."

"Don't be so diplomatic. Be real, be honest."

"Honestly, I just can't wait for this to be over. Sometimes I wish I could just sleep and magically wake up on our wedding day."

"Trust me, I feel guilty enough by leaving you here to deal with this by yourself. But guess what I took the liberty of doing?" he laughed. Unless it was giving a sample of his dick, I didn't see any use for it.

"What, are you canceling your trip to Africa?" I asked hopefully. Titus breathed heavily into the phone; I could imagine him being angry.

"Do you even know how important this missionary mission is? We've gone over this time and time again. Can you deal with being married to someone in my position? I do the work of God not my own."

"I'm only asking, but to be honest it irritates me that you constantly ignore me for the benefit of everyone else."

"When you marry me, you become what I am, God's servant. We are to serve and that is putting all of our personal desires secondary."

His main reason of discontent from the beginning of our courtship has always been my job. In his mind, I should stay home and be the prototypical Reverend's wife, generous and exemplary. We've avoided or mostly I avoided any conversation leading to the resignation of my current position. But I could tell it would be a thorn on the side of our doctrinaire future. It's just that I've worked so hard to get where I am. I didn't foresee giving it up for anything, God or anyone else.

I've traveled the world and always looked forward to my frequent ventures to Italy, especially when watching the catwalks of Milan. My buying trips were the only times I was able to relax and contemplate my life. I've tried so hard to be everything Titus wanted me to be, that I think I've lost a piece of myself. My job is all that is familiar to me.

I want to live the good life, complete with the white picket fence and 1.5 children. Having a family is very important to me and Titus offers the stability I need. Knowing what it feels like to be truly loved is something only a family can provide. I would do for my children what my parents could never do for me. I'll love them, cherish them and never leave them.

"So, what did you do?" I said taking a pen and started scribbling my married name in my day planner.

"I've hired a personal chef to take care of you while you deal with the wedding plans. He comes highly recommended. He catered the fundraiser and has done parties for many celebrities."

"*He*. You know I'm very particular about the food I eat," I sighed, irritated that Titus kept making decisions that I could make for myself. Besides, I didn't need another homosexual in my life. They're worse than women. And if he was a chef, he was definitely into men.

"I wanted to schedule a meeting with him for the two of us tomorrow evening. I have a full day on Thursday the day I'm flying out and he likes to make a profile of each of his clients. I thought I could at least help you with something before I leave."

"Where is this meeting taking place? Tomorrow evening is going to be bad for me because I have an important meeting with a foreign manufacturer."

"So what time is good for you?"

"Do we really have to hire a chef?"

"Darling please, let me do something for you. I feel guilty enough for leaving for three weeks."

"In that case, could I meet him in Midtown the day after tomorrow during my lunch hour?"

"I'll let you know. But I'm running behind, I have to go and meet with the church board. Before I go, let me remind you, this guy Aurelius is different. His personal appearance may shock you. And he's a serious transgressor, though I trust him to do his job, I'm not sure he's the right sort for you to hang around."

"I thought Christians are supposed to show love towards all men."

"Yes, but some people are too far along for even God to save."

After talking to Titus, my day went along as planned. I headed to Midtown Manhattan for a meeting with a vendor, requested a few samples from his showroom and traveled to back to my office for a fashion forecast meeting. I hated these meetings because they got all the buyers in a cramped windowless office and expected us to come to a coherent understanding regarding the season's fashion trends. This couldn't be further from the truth because the reality of the matter was that everyone had a healthy distain for each other and with the Merchandise Manager's job up for grabs, had every reason to self advertise.

Within Neiman's it was a known fact that the job opportunity was a two horse race, between Alexis McCrain, the biggest bitch in five-inch stilettos and me. We were polar opposites, I grew up between homes and she grew up in Malibu. To speak to her, you wouldn't even know that she was a sista. But her skin was all that was black. She had a white husband, a white best friend and even had a blonde hair weave. And you know how silly a midnight black sista looks in a blonde weave and hazel contacts.

As I sat in the meeting, all I could think about was last night. I could feel the ocean developing between my Victoria secret panties. Usually I was on point at these meetings, constantly interjecting my two cents, but not when I was feeling the way I had been feeling for the entire day.

"Why did you make that decision, Angelica?" the current merchandise manager Reba Stein asked while glaring at me through her wire-rimmed frames.

"I'm sorry Reba, but I kind of drifted off." I sat up uncomfortably in my seat as I deciphered the disapproving glares of my colleagues.

I knew my skin had turned a shade of red; it always did when I felt embarrassed. Hopefully, that's all they had attributed my flush complexion to.

"That's all right. We all are guilty of a lost of focus sometimes." Reba laughed.

Reba was an older white woman, with stained yellow teeth from her nasty smoking habit and liver spotted skin. Though she didn't give off the air of a buyer, she was well respected in our circle because of her unique fashion sense. I loved Reba, not only was she my mentor, but she had always shown me favoritism. Though I appreciated her support, I knew she had helped amplify the hatred the other buyers felt for me.

I pressed my thumb against my temple and shook my head to rid myself of my sexual frustration. "I'm ready, what was it that you wanted to know."

"I had a question about the markdowns you authorized," she asked.

"What merchandise are you referring to?"

"I noticed that despite steady sales you marked down the Roberto Cavalli Rose embroidered tee."

"Actually the sales were non-existent for the last two weeks we had it on the sales floor. If you check the sales report, you will notice that the numbers are deceiving because one customer bought about fifty tees in the same size on May 4. Since then we've sold only one."

Reba scanned the sales report and the corners of her mouth rose into a smile. "You're absolutely correct. Great instincts, Angie, you should be commended for your diligence. Guess that's why you continue to have the highest rate of turnover in the store." The hairs on my neck rose, not from her words of praise but because of the hatred, I felt in the room.

"Not to interrupt Reba, but she also has the highest rate of inventory shortages. It could be that thefts are running rampant in her department or that inventory records aren't kept correctly. In either case it hurts the bottom line for the entire store," Alexis interjected without permission.

Normally I could brush the haters off my shoulder, but her intense dislike for me had gone beyond any normal personal conflict. It was becoming clear to me that she would do anything to undermine my job performance.

"I've already planned to have a meeting with the sales personnel regarding that very problem. I'm sure it will be rectified," I said in defense of myself while locking eyes with Alexis.

When the meeting ended, Reba asked me to stay behind. I was exasperated because there was no time to talk. I needed to keep my people on their toes, especially with Alexis watching my every step. However, out of respect for Reba I put my ambition aside for the moment.

Sitting in the chair across from her, I watched as she peered at the monthly sales figures. I glanced at my watch, didn't mean to be rude but I had things to do. If I wasn't on the floor to crack the whip on the sales associates, they'd just sit around.

Reba placed her wire-rimmed glasses on her desk and smiled as she let out sigh. "I can't believe that in a little over a month from now you are going to be taking that plunge."

"You make it sound so horrible." I brightened up since I loved talking about my wedding.

"I couldn't put it into words how horrible it was for me the two times I've been married. I took the plunge and a few years later both those bastards wanted to drown my ass," she said while letting out a nostalgic giggle. "I'm sure you've picked better. You're more particular than I was."

"I hear ya. Besides, if he acts up *I'll* drown his ass."

Reba took out a cigarette from her drawer, lit it with a match and offered me one like she always did even though I never smoked tobacco. Staring at me through smoke fumes, she said, "The reason I asked you to stay is because I wanted to remind you that if you need a couple of weeks off before your wedding I'll approve it. You don't need to be over working yourself. You spread yourself too thin as it is. You've been with me for six years and you still haven't taken a vacation. I want you to have this before you dig yourself into an early grave."

"That won't be necessary. Titus has already arranged to have someone help me along," I lied, but I could rest when I was dead.

"Don't push yourself too hard, nothing's guaranteed."

"What does that mean?" I asked. She was speaking about the promotion and I didn't want her sparing my heart if there was something I needed to know.

"There have been a lot of changes in management and along with changes come new politics. This is still a man's world and good hard work isn't always rewarded."

Reba knew me well, knew my beliefs and I wanted to make sure she understood my position. "I'll leave it in the lord's hands," I said with a smile, knowing it was something Titus would have said.

"Suit yourself, you young ones don't listen nowadays. Remember, this job will not keep you warm at night. If you keep yourself too busy, you'll miss out on something you truly need."

"What is that?"

"You'll miss out on living," she said reaching into her drawer for another cigarette. That was my hint to leave.

I sat in my office and read the most recent issue of *Vogue*, trying to gauge new consumer trends as I browsed the pages. However, my mind was elsewhere. Instead, I was wondering if I was ready for the life altering step I was about to take in a little over a month. Deep in my heart, I knew I didn't love Titus. I admired him and felt strongly attracted to him, but the fact of the matter was he didn't feel like my soul mate, only an acceptable replacement.

Behind his unblemished façade of holiness, I yearned to find a man with a more complex dimension to his personality. He was perfect and I was too flawed. He was missing the main ingredient that made love worth exploring. I wanted not only his best, but his worse. The measure of real love is not only what makes a person extraordinary, but what also makes them ordinary.

Still, I wasn't getting any younger. So any thoughts of backing out of this marriage were quickly pushed aside. All my friends were married, even Rochelle and the lord knows she's no better for it, but at least she has someone who she can depend on. I need that, I need the fairytale existence we all dream about but fall short. I didn't just want to eclipse that dream but I wanted to exceed it.

I heard a light tap at the door. After inviting the culprit in, I was surprised to see that it was Alexis. I could see behind her true intentions, she wanted to know why Reba kept me behind. I wouldn't reveal anything, instead I'd let her sweat. A napkin protected her hand from the doorknob as she sashayed inside with her arms crossed under her A-cup breasts, wearing a conservative two-piece black suit. Her blonde weave bounced with each step as she entered, resembling a shorter and darker version of Ru Paul. Instead of greeting me, she inspected my office with her phony hazel eyes as if she was searching for something.

"May I help you, Alexis?" I asked. I didn't appreciate the vibe she was putting out.

She cut her eyes at me, sucked on her teeth, inspected the chairs and placed a napkin on the cushion of her chosen seat before sitting directly across from me.

"It's too cold in here. You should contact maintenance to fix that air conditioner," she said, running her hand through her hair like it was all hers.

When we spoke, our conversations were littered with long, awkward and silent pauses. When two people who can't stand each other are forced to speak, that's to be expected. Our rivalry had an extra oomph to it, considering we were the only African American buyers in our store and had once fought for the affection of a man.

It wasn't always like that. When she transferred to us from our Beverly Hills store, I took steps to befriend her. Thinking we could build a "Girlfriend" rapport and watch each other's back. However, after finding out that I came from the ghettos of South Philadelphia, she started to avoid me and eventually we stopped communicating. In her mind, I could never rise above the squalor I was born into.

"I don't want to seem rude, but I don't have much free time on my hand."

"Oh, yes you're planning your little wedding," she said looking down at her suit and picking lint from the fabric.

"Well, small or large, they all require some time and effort," I quipped sarcastically.

"The reason I came was to inform you that I heard through the grapevine that interviews for the Merchandise Manager position are going to take place next week. Are you still going for it?"

"I think we all aspire to get to that point in our career. So yes, I will be going for it."

Alexis removed wisps of polyester hair from her face, crossed her legs and leaned forward.

"Are you sure you want that job? It's very stressful. Besides, I should know, I *was* the Merchandise manager at my last location."

She loved to brag and I knew her experience proved to be a formidable obstacle in my quest for the position. Her record of accomplishment at the Beverly Hills store was impeccable and she had transferred only because her Plastic Surgeon husband relocated to an office on Madison Avenue in the heart of Manhattan. I would rather eat glass than have her ruling over me.

"Yes, but I stand an equal chance as well. My department has performed the best each quarter for the last three years." I smiled, proud of my accomplishments.

She stood and walked over to the diplomas that lined my Venetian plastered walls. "Widener University…Is that one of them online schools?" she asked.

"No, it's a small school. I got my MBA there."

"Never heard of it," she said.

"And what is that supposed to mean?"

She gave me a once over, put her hands on her hips and dismissed my question with a wave of her press on's. "Sorry, I'm only familiar with Ivy league schools. Nowadays anybody can get a degree. As a matter of fact, not only did I attend Harvard as did Reba, but we are members of the same sorority as well. "

I began to get the feeling that maybe she wanted to antagonize me. Nothing would make her feel better than if I gave her a beatdown straight from South Philly. Causing me to lose my job would definitely put her on the fast track to Merchandise Manager. I wasn't going to fall for it.

"Could you close the door behind you? I'll remember to tell my fiancé to pray for you," I said even though she didn't seem like she wanted to leave before inspecting every single framed document on my walls.

"I need no prayers. He can save that for you." She left, slamming the door behind her and leaving a dark cloud of doubt hanging over my head.

It wasn't just that she was a witch that caused our bitter competition; she had slept with my man once. And by coincidence, a little birdie told her husband.

"Golden Showers"

Aurelius

The tiled floor was cold to the touch, but I had no choice but to bear the chill as I crawled across the dungeon on my knees. My mistress stood on my back as I carried her into the bathroom. Her spiked heels pierced my skin each time I moved forward. When we entered, she slapped me with an open hand. I had moved too fast.

"Lay in the tub, toilet so I can relieve myself," she ordered. She wore a red leather corset striped with steel spikes and red leather butt-less chaps that exposed her beautiful landing strip.

I didn't say a word as I slowly lay in the large Jacuzzi tub on my naked backside. She had been my Domina for the last two years and I knew that haste infuriated her. She climbed in behind me and squatted over my face. I opened my mouth and prepared to taste the natural nectar that emanated from her temple. She proceeded to pee into my mouth and the warm putrid liquid slowly gravitated down my throat. Though I enjoyed serving her, I never got used to her taste. It was bitter and sour, an acquired taste.

"Clean me, slut," she commanded, sitting on my face as I took my tongue and cleaned her from front to back.

She started to breathe heavily as I tantalized her clit. I wanted so badly to enjoy her, but the cock ring around my dick controlled my erection. Just as I could feel her begin to quiver, she slapped me across the face once more.

"Slave, did I give you permission to do obeisance at my shrine?" she asked.

I shook my head "no" for she didn't allow me to talk unless she asked. She stepped out of the tub and ran the hot shower across my naked body. My discipline was going to be severe.

Grabbing me by my ear, she led me to her dungeon once more where I was sure discipline awaited me.

Her dungeon was huge, it dwarfed the one I had at home. It wasn't painted black like mine, but blood red. Her walls were lined with all sorts of devices specially made for a disobedient slave. When I looked at her, I could see her pupils dance in delight as she scanned her collection of paddles, wooden spoons and rods freshly taken from a birch tree.

"You dare touch me with your despicable lips, do you?" she yelled taking a pair of her panty hose and stuffing them into my mouth.

"I'll show you what I do to slaves that overstep their boundaries."

I admired her strong, muscular legs. I liked the way her thirty-eight inch ass sat when she stood in her six inch heels. I dreamed of one day dominating her, my visions were clear. I would bend her over completely, put her head by her ankles and violently thrust myself into her. Make her scream just as she had done to me on various occasions. Then I would pull out each time she tasted the cusp of orgasm. I wouldn't let her come until I felt like it. As she had denied me pleasure, I'd do the same to her.

"Whap…Whap…Whap…" I woke from my fantasy just as she pounded my naked backside with a leather strop used to sharpen straight razors.

"I've warned you many times. You stupid little cunt."

I could feel myself becoming aroused. I didn't understand why pain had always been fascinatingly enjoyable for me. It had always been that way. My first recollection of this was when I had peed on myself as a child. Mrs. James, my babysitter, had taken it upon herself to beat me because of my mistake. I still remember the strong feeling of arousal I felt as she hit me across my ass. It was indescribable and though I cried, I didn't want that sensation to stop.

After the beating at the hands of my Mistress was over, she ordered me to worship her feet. I filled a basin with water and added bath salts. No one could understand the skill required to give a woman an orgasm just by touching her feet. Mistress would never admit it, but I knew she enjoyed the pleasure I gave her by way of my fingers. Great joy always enveloped me when she came without my touch.

I scanned the *New York Times* as I sat in a booth at my favorite vegetarian bistro, *Radha*. Shane and his longhaired pink Maltese Frenchie enjoyed a plate of Barbecued Tofu and mashed sweet potatoes as they sat across from me. We were regulars in this conclave of ritualistic vegans and social pariahs. The atmosphere was calming, set among the brick paneled walls were dimly lit hanging lamps that infused the place with a romantic aura. It was late evening and the sun had set leaving behind a primrose sky.

"I saw a program on television that showed racism still ran rampant in Europe. You have these soccer players being called everything from monkeys to lord knows what else. And all they can worry about in today's paper is sex trafficking in Germany before the world cup. Shows you how much America cares about us," I said horrified by the pre-civil rights mentality in Europe.

"Honey, you know they don't give a damn about anything unless it stops their money."

"That's sad; I thought we were past the days of insensitivity," I reasoned.

"Ain't nothing changed, only now hatred is practiced behind closed doors. Besides, you got it good, you only black. I'm black *and* gay."

I looked forward to my socially enlightened conversations with Shane. Showed brothers can talk about more than big booty chicks and rims.

Shane nervously bit on his nails as he stared into oblivion. Frenchie took the opportunity to lick Shane's plate clean. Though he spoiled his dog, Shane usually scolded Frenchie something terrible if he ate off his plate, but Shane looked mentally drained. As he tucked his ascot tie meticulously underneath his white cricket sweater, I wondered what was on his mind.

"I didn't mean to bring any negative energy into your life. I just thought it was ridiculous the lack of forward movement or thought given to the race issue," I admitted while delving into my plate of Soy chicken tortillas.

"That bullshit is the least of my worries. With all the drama I got in my life, I care less if those crackers hate me," Shane vented as he typed a message into his blackberry.

"Guess whoever's on the other end of that blackberry is causing you strife."

Shane started to speak, but thought better of it. He bit his bottom lip and lines of frustration gathered across his sun beaten forehead as he typed feverishly. I'd known him for years and his actions revealed one thing. He was having man problems. It never ceased to amaze me, as a matter of fact, as I stared at the date of my paper; I realized it was about that time of the year. Summer love is the type of flu that all humans regardless of their preference seem to suffer from.

Commonsense says that when the weather is beautiful one wants to spend time with a person just as aesthetically pleasing to the senses. Though statistics show that suicides increases during the holidays, I would bet that most were due to a failed summer rendezvous.

I winced as I rubbed my chest underneath my *Bob Marley* t-shirt. My nipple ring had been ripped out at the hands of Mistress Jezebel. A patch of tapped gauze rested above my torn nipple. I couldn't even enjoy the organic tortillas for my double pierced tongue had rendered obeisance to her shrine for hours.

"That lying son of a ...," Shane blurted loudly, getting everyone's attention throughout the restaurant as Frenchie began to bark. Shane tucked his blackberry angrily into the pocket of his tight, white cargo shorts.

"Damn Shane, thanks for causing a scene." I put my hand over the side of my face blocking everyone's prying eyes.

"That heifer doesn't know who the hell she's messing with. I got a good mind to go over to her house and whoop her something terrible ."

"What heifer?"

"The heifer I'm gonna go to jail for killing. Gonna call my phone popping shit because I can satisfy her man better."

Violent outbursts were the norm when dealing with Shane. But I often wondered if there was really a thin line between his actions and his words.

"Don't tell me, Rick's wife." I rolled my eyes.

Shane turned red; I could see the boiling blood coursing through his veins like he was transparent. I always thought the best of people. Sometimes I was wrong for doing so, but I felt that Shane would respect the marriage bond, avoiding freak fests with married men altogether. I wholeheartedly disagreed with the institution of marriage, but who was he to take it upon himself to intervene in a person's relationship.

"He doesn't want to be with that prissy chick anyway. I give head better," Shane said placing Frenchie on the floor.

Shane tried in true Shane fashion to give me a condensed version of *his* story. After leaving some x-rated photos on Rick's picture phone, he received a call from Rick's wife. She not only told Shane what to do with his manhood, but also threatened to show him the Lorena Bobbitt slicing technique, and threatened to divorce Rick and take his children away from him. Sad how sloppy men get when they are messing around, because had Rick simply deleted Shane's photos, they would've avoided this mess. However, she didn't know Shane; her threats had only intensified his resolve.

"You know you wrong. That woman isn't at fault for defending her marriage." I leaned back in the booth and rubbed my throbbing chest.

"Whose side are you on anyway? You're an anti-monogamist and you gonna say some sideways ish like that," Shane said while spinning his fingers and twirling his head sista girl style.

There was no winning an argument with Shane. My way or the highway was the mantra of his life.

"Listen, if you got time to lie on a mattress of drama, you might as well make your own bed." I was way past this conversation. There was bigger fish to fry and he was caught up worrying about a nigga with a wayward penis. "Tell me, does he even take you out in public? Or is most of your time spent hidden behind a closed door."

"We would go to jail for disorderly conduct for the things we do, *you know*? Besides, there's nothing we could do outside to match the joy this mouth brings him," Shane said running his tongue over his lips.

I placed my paper down, sat upright and stared Shane in his eyes. "Would he be as mad if you had a steady man?" I asked.

"He's not as insecure."

"You mean he doesn't care as much," I stated.

"Are you my psychologist? Or do you want to mess up my flow."

"I'm just saying. That's his wife and you're nothing but an extra dick in the glass." I stood, placed my folded paper under my arm and exited. Though I loved Shane, his self-seeking ways were becoming very draining.

When I arrived home, I took a bath in my Jacuzzi tub, drank a glass of wine and prepared dinner before I called the

Reverend. I had spoken to him a couple of days prior and took his fiancé on as a client, but still hadn't given him a concrete answer regarding his wedding, because I wanted to see him sweat a little. However, I believed in Karma and didn't want to carry on my charade for too much longer.

I checked my messages and wasn't surprised to only hear the solicitous howl of a few telemarketers. No one called my house unless it was the wrong number. Not that I had a problem being unpopular, because sometimes it suited me just fine, but it would've been nice to receive a call from someone other than Shane.

As I drank from a steaming cup of chamomile and soy, I wondered if I was the only one buying into my anti-love bullshit. Being alone in the world without someone to love is a lonely existence. I didn't know if I was feeling the effects of the Reverend's impending nuptials or going through one of my depressed states. It would be nice to have someone who would call just to hear my voice.

As I began to get comfortable, my phone rang.

"Hello?"

"Aurelius, my brother, how are you doing on this blessed night?" It was the Reverend and he sounded jubilant.

"I meant to call you, but the time ran away from me," I said, walking around my condo in the nude.

"No need to apologize. From time to time it gets away from me as well." He laughed. "But do you have an answer for me. I don't mean to rush, but I'm sure you can sympathize with my situation."

"I've given it enough thought and… I accept the job. I don't usually do events on such short notice, but I think I can handle this. I do need to know how many people are coming and so forth, but I'm sure we'll work out the details in the next few days." I said instantly feeling rejuvenated from his positive energy.

"The lord is always there when you need him. He's the worker of miracles." The Reverend said in his sermon vernacular. "But I'm leaving tonight for Kenya and wanted to know if it was possible for you to meet up with my fiancé, Angelica, for lunch tomorrow. She wants to go over her daily menu"

He gave me her information and told me that she was a vegetarian, which was great because I could cook her dishes that I enjoyed. The only problem I had; was the way he spoke about her, most men would be obviously beaming over the phone. The Reverend was so reserved I wondered if he even loved her.

"My flight is boarding any minute, but don't let Angelica go crazy. I don't want anything too extravagant; my congregation could be stumbled if they thought that I was a physical man. What I'm saying is she tends to get a little materialistic. You know how women can be."

"I know how women can be. I don't mean to pry, but what gets a man to the point of trusting a woman enough to marry her?" I asked

"Well there's a reason why I decided to get married. It's for companionship, because as a man of the lord and the shepherd of my flock, it doesn't look good if I can't commit. And with all the misconceptions out there about men of the cloth, I'm getting married not out of want but necessity," he said unapologetically.

The Reverend's comments struck me as odd. He never seemed to be the type of man who had to prove anything. And what was most revealing about his comments were that he never once mentioned love as the provocation.

"Lustful Thoughts"

Angelica

"Unprofessional," I said in an angst filled tone.

I looked at my watch and wondered what had happened to this supposedly great chef Titus hired. Luckily, I had taken off the entire day, otherwise I would've been late for work. When he called last night, I thought it would be best if we meet at my place, so he could examine the size of my kitchen and see if he could even work here. Though Titus didn't want us to be alone, I was sure nothing would ever happen. Especially not now that he was two hours late.

I was on my fourth cup of vanilla roast coffee and jittery as hell. Last night was another lonely night and now that Titus was gone, I had no one to help when my mind wandered. Rochelle called a few times, but until I got over the fact that she wanted me to suck on her titties, she'll just have to wait. Our relationship would never be the same, because I didn't go *that* way and didn't want a friend who could.

When the concierge finally called with the news that an Aurelius had arrived, I was ready to cuss him out and send him packing, until I realized there were no other options this close to the wedding. Within two minutes, he was at my door and weird wasn't the word to describe him as I gazed at him. I silently began to doubt Titus' judgment; because there was no way I was going to let him alone in my house.

Though he looked to be in great shape, due to the outline of the washboard abs peeking through his black *Purple Rain* short sleeve shirt, he seemed a little too into himself. A man with piercing on his lips, eyebrow and the bridge of his nose must love to be seen for no other reason but to bring attention to his chiseled good looks.

What rock band did he belong to? Why did he dress in all black? Were the first thoughts to pop into my head and as he began to speak, he confirmed my suspicions. There was no reason for a straight man to wear a tongue piercing.

"Sorry I was late, but I had a little squabble with my building superintendent."

"Would've been nice if you called? Hope this isn't going to be a habit. Otherwise, we can stop this before it starts.

"Before this starts? You sound like *we're* going to sex each other up. No worries, I only want to cook for you," he said followed by a toothy smile. If he thought his dirty mouth was a way to break the ice, he was sadly mistaken.

"My name is Angelica Thompson and I won't tolerate such crude language in my home. I'm a Christian woman and would like to be shown the proper respect." I extended my hand.

"Ms. Thompson they are only words. I mean no harm by them, but I cater food and not to my clients personal feelings. I'm honest as unfamiliar as it may seem," he said as he lightly kissed my hand.

Prayer gave me the strength to deal with most things but I didn't see how it would prevent me from giving him a piece of my mind.

"Well try not to use those words around me. By the way, I don't think we were properly introduced."

"Aurelius is my name."

"Aurelius what?"

"I have no last name."

People without a last name clearly have something to hide. A lot of celebrities do that and go by one name. Personally, I think it's silly because no matter where you go it's always good to know where you came from. What would make a person want to disassociate themselves from their family name?

From the Foyer, I led him into the kitchen. I could tell that he found it to his liking as he peered in the sub-zero refrigerator and admired the cherry wood paneling that matched the cabinetry throughout. He ran his hand along the hood of my gas stove and smiled widely as he noticed the stainless steel appliances. Even though I didn't like to cook, I made sure that my kitchen looked good.

"It will be a pleasure working here."

"I hope so. Can we get down to business?" I asked, leading him into my living room.

"You have a nice home. What is it that you do?"

"I'm a buyer at Neiman Marcus"

"And what does that entail?" he asked, delving a little too much into my business.

"I'm sorry, but do you have something else to do today, because I do," I snapped.

After sitting on my brand new leather sectional, we went over my personal menu, wedding menu and the rules of my home. I also requested freshly made meals, which meant that he had to come and prepare them daily. I didn't do prepackaged foods. I especially wanted to stress that drugs were prohibited because he looked like he dabbled and I didn't want to come home to find anything missing. His portfolio was spectacular, but I didn't want to feed his ego by telling him so.

"Is Monday good for you?" he asked

"Yes. And please don't be late," I commanded, giving him a stern glare.

When he left, I began to clean my condo. I was one of the tidiest people I knew, but my hectic work schedule hadn't provided me the time to do a thorough cleaning in a few months. I waxed the hardwood floors, disinfected the toilets and cleaned the central air vents. Everything within my grasp was sprayed, scrubbed or dusted. When I got to my guestroom, I made sure to wash the bedding, because no telling what bodily fluids had lived in the 400 thread count sheets after Rochelle's booty call.

By time I was finished cleaning to my satisfaction, it was evening and I had missed my hair and nail appointments. My split-ends were serious and my nails looked jagged and unkempt. Not to mention that I needed my weekly dose of girl-to-girl gossip. Instead, I decided to make it a blockbuster night and ordered in. The Chinese restaurant downstairs made the best steamed fish and vegetables I'd ever tasted. And I wanted to rent Boris Kodjoe's new movie. Now, that's a gorgeous brotha.

I didn't know why but Aurelius kept popping into my thoughts. All the assholes I dated throughout my life were just like him. Just as pompous, conceited and self centered. But his mysterious aura had piqued my curiosity. There was something dark and sinister about him. Probably one of them men that got hurt real bad and no longer gave a damn. As I lay underneath my sheets with a forkful of fish in my mouth, I thanked God he was gay.

When Saturday arrived, I was ready to jump for joy. I needed the break from work and as a stress reliever; I started running two years ago. There's something about having the wind in my face that calmed me. I got up just before the sun was out, laced up my running shoes, shimmied into my spandex shorts and put on my sports bra. Then I set off across the Riverfront esplanade. As my feet pounded the pavement, I could feel my heart beating at a quickened pace. Adrenaline flowed through me and I'd never felt so alive.

I smiled at my fellow runners as I breezed by. Some I knew, others I had never laid eyes on, but there was camaraderie among us. I especially envied the couples who ran together. I asked Titus many times to come along with me, but he always had something to do. Besides, he felt a person with so much idle time on their hands should be doing the work of the lord.

That's exactly what our relationship lacked, spontaneity. The urge to go where one wants to go, not because they have to, but because the spirit moves them. Life is too short to analyze and dissect every word in god's sacred document. Sometimes it's just good to experience life and learn from our mistakes. None of us is perfect and trying to be so is nearly unattainable.

I thought about missing church the next day, but decided against it because it wouldn't look good if I didn't show up. Putting on a front for the old battleaxes in Titus' congregation was becoming a second job. They hated me without even knowing me. I saw behind their unsavory smiles and thinly veiled remarks. They would be vindicated if I so much as stepped out of line only once. Since what stood between their imagined happiness was me, I couldn't take a chance appearing as anything other than the perfect Christian woman.

One would think that New York's the last place to run alone so early in the morning, but I found it to be the only time of day that the city is somewhat asleep. Only the noise coming from the exhaust of the freight trucks that sped down each street could be heard. The engaging aroma of freshly baked goods coming from the coffee shops preparing for the early morning rush could be smelled. And the sun could be seen rising from a distance, dawning in a new day.

I ran for two miles, grabbed a cup of coffee and the day's paper and headed back to my place. As I entered the double glass doors of my condo, the doorman called me over. Clarence was an older heavyset dark skinned man with white hair on his head and face and had a cheery demeanor. He was much older, but it had never stopped him from flirting with me. As I strolled across the marble floors of the lobby over to his pear wood desk, I prepared myself for his usual fresh comments.

"Angelica, when are you gonna let me steal you away?" he flirted with his eyes examining the contents of my spandex.

"When you stop being so fresh," I said with a smile.

"If you think I'm fresh, you should see what I bees thinking." He laughed nearly causing the buttons on his uniform to burst around his beer belly.

"I could only imagine." I gave him an inquisitive stare. Really, I didn't want to imagine, Clarence had a nappy ass beard and no teeth and in my most drunken state would still be repulsive.

"You don'ts have to imagine. I cans show you."

"Come on Mr. Clarence, what do you want with me? I gotta get upstairs and change," I said hoping he would get to the point.

"Can I take a peek?" he asked but quickly stood up straight and smiled as the president of the building association came down in the elevator. He leaned across his desk. "One of them Jamaicans came looking for you. He tried going up in the elevator but I put a stop to that. He looked like one them Rastafarians."

"Did he say why he was here?"

"No he didn't, just said your apartment number and then got an attitude when I told him you weren't home. Wouldn't even give me his name, I thinks that's strange," he said with concern.

"Well next time he comes back ask him where he knows me from," I said starting to walk towards the bank of elevators.

I didn't pay Clarence no mind; he had probably seen Aurelius yesterday and just wanted a reason to talk to me today.

"One more thing."

"Yes Mr. Clarence," I said annoyed that I couldn't put down my cup of coffee as my body ached from the long run..

"You forgot to kiss my jaw."

After rescheduling my hair appointment, I made sure to take a hot shower. Funky wasn't the best way to describe the way I smelled. But keeping my body in shape made it an equal tradeoff. You can't put a price on firm thighs and tight abs. I ain't ever been scared of a little sweat. As I put on my Victoria secret push-up bra, the phone rang. I hoped it was Titus because I hadn't heard from him since he left for Kenya.

"Hello?"

"How are you, Mrs. Thompson? This is Mr. Siegel from the Alibis detective agency."

"Oh…Hello, sorry if I sound deflated but I was expecting a call from someone else," I sighed.

Last year I decided to search for my birth parents. It was around the time Titus had proposed to me and for some reason I felt an intense urge to find my real identity. After trying to locate them through online sites without any luck, I hired a professional. Since I had never been adopted, my last name was still the same, which made it a little easier, so I thought. But it had been one disappointment after the next. It was almost as if my parents didn't want to be found. And the State of Pennsylvania did very little in providing me with answers.

"Getting ready for the big day?" Mr. Siegel asked.

"Don't remind me." I laughed.

"I didn't want to excite you, because you have enough going on in your life, but I may have found your mother."

I imagined tears coming down my face after finding her when I started this journey. But instead, I was wrought with fear. My throat tightened, my heart quickened and my stomach started to churn. Fear caused me to tremble. Maybe I didn't really want to know her. Maybe I had been wrong in starting this process. But I closed my eyes, exhaled and said a silent prayer.

"Where can I find her?"

"Slow Down"

Aurelius

I winced as the needles pounded against my skin. Though I enjoyed pain, needles of any kind had always scared me. My tattoo artist Damian smiled as he noticed the look of abject horror written on my face. He took sadistic pleasure in giving pain. To see him, one wouldn't be surprised. He was a huge brotha, about six foot four and over three hundred pounds. On the right side of his face was a tattoo of a gargoyle and each of his ear lobes housed hollow bamboo ear plugs two inches in diameter. Definitely not the Wall Street type or someone you would want to see in a darkened alley.

We were finishing the spinal kanji tattoo I had commissioned for him to do and the skin on my back had already gone numb from the beating it was taking. My tattoo said live with honor in Chinese calligraphy. I wanted to get it for the last few months but was unable to do so because of prior engagements.

The Moshell tattoo parlor was like any other tattoo studio in America. Designs covered the walls, hardcore rock blared from the speakers and every word out of the mouth of the artist's consisted of four letters. I was in a spacious, luminous-room, sitting forward in a dentist chair with my eyes closed, praying for my torture to end. Normally I endured the pain, but the skin on my back was still tender due to my liaisons with the Mistress.

"Damn man, you acting like a stone cold bitch," Damian teased as he cleaned my back with alcohol swabs. "I never thought I'd ever see the day you'd cry like a pussy."

"You want to get paid, right. So hurry your fat ass up."

We hurled insults back and forth, but we did so in love. We had always bonded that way, a relationship built on truth and not sensitivity. After another unpleasant hour, we finally finished.

"Next time we'll do that face piece," he said while sanitizing his instruments.

"Unlike you, I do have my limits," I said while pulling my T-shirt over my head.

"You say so now, but give it a few months. My customers are like junkies they always come back for another hit," he said holding up his needle.

"You don't have to worry about me, because there's no way I'm going out like Mike Tyson."

"Some might say it's hideous. I say it was a vast improvement on his part." We laughed.

"I'm too pretty for that."

"For all your beauty it ain't like you have a woman," he inquired.

"What you know about women? Besides, they are more trouble than they're worth."

"A little pussy ain't hurt nobody."

"No just the entire human race."

I had come to the realization that all the problems of my life had revolved around a woman. What would make a woman leave a man that loved her without condition? Leave without any notice or provocation. I had given my all, yet it was still not enough. When I thought about her, I felt pain. In her absence, she had left a shell of a man.

"You can't compare everyone to her. Otherwise what you see in every woman will only be their flaws and not their gifts."

I was in his chair enough times to have confided in him. He knew from the look in my eye and the tone of my voice who I was really speaking about. However, his words never provided me with any consolation. No one could understand the deception I endured. My feelings are unique; in turn, my hurt is as well. How can I not judge every woman if the one that I thought was *the one* turned out to be someone other than the person I knew.

I still remember the look on her face when she brought another person into our relationship. Her secret lover, a person she had conveniently never revealed until the most meaningful day of my life. When I declined her invitation to share her with another, her eyes filled with disdain and I wondered if she had ever loved me. She held the look of a person that had never known me and a person that had never made love to me. And as her lover stood behind her, I knew I could never measure up, for her lover was a woman.

My eyes stung as the sun hit them. I stirred in my king size bed, buried my head underneath my pillow and opened my eyes. After gaining focus, I looked at my clock and knew I had slept more than twelve hours, it was six in the evening and I barely remembered leaving the club. I'd gone out the night before with Shane and was paying for it. No wonder I stayed so far away from the nightlife. It was too time consuming. I struggled to get out of bed, first I threw my sheets on the sex swing, and then I put my feet on the floor. I didn't move, still lethargic from last night I laid there for another ten minutes looking at the cracks on my ceiling and wondered if I had done more than I remembered.

On my floor were clothing that I didn't own, strewn about, a male t-shirt and boxers. I panicked jumped out of my bed quickly and headed down my hallway, hastily searching for a man with socks on and his dick exposed. I was relieved to see Shane sitting on my patio sipping from a ceramic cup dressed in my favorite Egyptian silk robe.

"You look like you done seen a ghost, chile," Shane said glancing at me for a split second as he read my Sunday paper. "Is that for me?" he asked pointing at my dick as it peeked through the slit of my boxers.

I rested my head on the doorframe as I stood between the double doors leading into my terrace and tried to catch my breath.

"I'm hungry, want anything to eat?" I asked stuffing my member back into its hiding place.

"You got nothing I want. You eat bird food and I need my meat," Shane said with a wink. "Besides, I ordered a cheese steak at noon."

"Suit yourself. Continue to poison your body with all those preservatives and byproducts."

"All I know is that when I die I want to die with a big, fat, juicy piece of …um meat in my mouth."

I ignored Shane and headed to my kitchen. He could be a little too much in the morning when he went nonstop with his sexual innuendoes. Besides, he'll be sorry when he ends up with colon cancer one day by eating all that meat. I shook my head as I walked into my kitchen, opened my fridge and took out the ingredients for my organic strawberry and banana smoothie.

After I fed myself, I hopped into the shower, smelling like sweat, alcohol and vomit. Point blank, I needed to wash my ass. I turned up the hot water as far as I could and used body wash with pumice beads to clean myself. I closed my eyes as the hot water ran down my face and let my thoughts take me back in time…

My father was sitting in his favorite rocking chair on our porch as I pulled up in his brand new candy apple red 1986 Cadillac Deville. He loaned it to me for the day as a reward for getting my license. But like any full-blooded adolescent, a fine honey stood between me and my father's strict eleven o'clock curfew.

Most Saturday's I could be found at the Crystal Palace roller rink getting my skate and dance on. But this Saturday was different, Tamara Jones was there and she was fine, at least in eleventh grade terms. I always had a thing for dark skinned women; probably because I was so light, people thought I was Spanish. But Tamara was thick, a country girl raised on collard greens, corn bread and neck bones. Unlike most of the anorexic white girls in my suburban neighborhood, she had thighs and ass for days.

I remember that day like it was yesterday…

"Yall ain't skatin, right?" Tamara laughed gliding by in tight neon green spandex giving new meaning to the term camel toe.

I was messing around with my crew of associates from Collierville high school. The DJ was playing *word up* by cameo and we thought it was the perfect time to breakout our new moves. We called ourselves the rolling zebras, looking back it was a named filled with racial overtones with me being the only black in a group of four. I was their travel guide into the hood and if not for my craving to be popular, I would have never considered hanging with any of them.

Tamara lived in south Memphis, went to East Memphis high two years before when she was head cheerleader of her cheerleading squad. Her body was ripe for the plucking, but she was out of my league. She was varsity and I was junior varsity. She was twenty years old and a stripper at Tricks, a strip club in downtown Memphis. I knew who she was, not because she told me, but because she was the topic of conversation of every teenage boy in Memphis and information got around. I smiled as I watched her through my black Ray-Ban's skating effortlessly around the rink, wearing large earrings and a baggy sweatshirt that seductively fell from one of her shoulders. Her chocolate cherry scent was hypnotizing.

Crystal palace was in the middle of the hood, yet the three white boys and I strolled in every Saturday dressed in our costumes consisting of yellow Lacoste polo shirts and khaki shorts. I wore a neatly trimmed flat top and resembled The

Fresh Prince of Bel-Air and looking nothing like the type of thugs that Tamara enjoyed socializing with.

Our parents forbade us from coming to this part of town. "It was too dangerous," they said, but I came to get a glimpse of how *my* people lived. I needed to feel like I belonged, find out where I came from, because where I lived I was nothing more than a sideshow. And the three white boys by my side were only there because they wanted to be black. On these streets, life was tragic and the people lived an impoverished life. Across the street from the rink, it wasn't out of the realm of possibility to see a drug deal going down or a prostitute doing the same. But we were guilty, guilty of having invincibility complexes.

The music was blasting as the disco ball turned, spraying a rainbow of colors across the hardwood floors. Janet Jackson's *what have you done for me lately* was now playing and I was doing 360 spins across the rink like a man possessed. I left my crew behind and decided to freestyle by myself. I barely noticed Tamara coming up on the side of me and as we crashed into each other, all I could do was brace for the fall.

I hit the floor first, knocking my sunglasses off my face and she landed beside me on her backside. I looked into her eyes expecting her to be upset, but just the opposite occurred as she smiled and extended her hand.

"Dang! My butt hurts," she said holding on to my shoulder as I stood and collected my glasses.

"I'm sorry…I didn't mean to hit you," I apologized; hoping none of the neighborhood thugs that pined for her noticed our spill.

"I'll live, besides, I gots to be gettin to work," she said looking down at her fluorescent yellow watch.

"Is there anything I can do for you?"

"You drive?" she said pulling her arm into mine.

The cat had my tongue because my mouth was open but no words were coming out, only a pool of drool. Her almond shaped eyes put me into a vegetative trance.

"What's wrong, youngin? You ain't got no car," she said, looking around possibly for another means of transportation.

I wanted to say yes, but I was new to driving and didn't know how to navigate most of the Memphis streets. The only reason I knew how to get to the rink was because it was right off of route 61. But at the same time, I felt an unfamiliar sensation in the pit of my stomach. It was nervousness, but not the scared type. It was different.

"Yes I drive," I confessed, knowing that this opportunity wouldn't come but once in a lifetime.

We returned our skates and left. I cared less how my skating crew got home. They could get chased through the ghetto for all I cared. Besides, the train station was in walking distance and Tamara looked better in the passenger seat. As we got out into the parking lot arm in arm, I noticed the looks of surprise, envy and admiration written across the faces of the brothers we passed. For the first time in my life, I felt superior.

I was feeling myself a little. Walking with my head held high and my chest poking out as I opened the door to my father's brand spanking new ride. Like a gentleman, I opened the passenger side door first, not because I was a man of chivalry but because I wanted to get a bird's eye view of her ass.

"Thank you," she said as I closed the door behind her.

Women love luxury, though most wouldn't admit it, a man with a big bank account is just as alluring as one with a twelve-inch dick. Like a kitten, Tamara cuddled against the leather seats and her eyes were wide with dollar signs. I sat in the driver's seat, put on my seatbelt like my father warned and headed out the parking lot. Before I hit South 3rd Street, my father's favorite Teddy Pendergrass tape started playing *"Come go with me,"* it was like a sign from heaven.

Teddy's hushed tone had put Tamara in a state of bliss. Her body was turned towards me, her eyes were closed and she was swaying in her seat. It didn't take me but five minutes to get her to her destination and as I looked at the clock on the dashboard, the time read 11:07. My ass started hurting as I sat knowing if I left at that moment I'll still be more than forty minutes late getting home.

The parking lot of Tricks was dark, men milled around with bottles of hard liquor disguised with brown paper bags. The club as I would find out years later had a strict no liquor policy. Thus before blowing their hard-earned money on a lap dance or a glimpse of shaven pussy, brothers would stand by their cars getting their drink on. We were parked near the side door where the dancers went between a pair of abandoned vehicles in an even more dark and secluded part of the parking lot.

"Mind if I sit here for a minute? My set don't start till twelve and those bitches in there are jealous," she said. "I don't usually go wit strangers, but I see you every now and then and you ain't never been crazy, like most of them niggas down at Crystal."

"My name's Jared McKenzie," I said holding my hand out. She looked at my hand, smiled and placed a soft kiss on my cheek.

"Where's my southern hospitality? I'm Tammy and they call me Georgia peach because I'm from Atlanta." She smiled. "You know you kinda cute."

I couldn't hold my smile or my blush. She flattered me; it wasn't like any of the girls at my school were knocking down my door. Because of my accelerated courses, I never had the time for extracurricular activities. As a matter of fact, the kiss she placed on my cheek was my very first kiss.

"Thanks Tammy," I said staring at her breasts, which were beginning to peek out her sweatshirt.

"You don't need to thank me. I should be thanking you. I don't have any gas money, but what can I do to repay you." She smiled, lifting my chin with her index finger and staring into my eyes.

"Nothing, I'm cool," I foolishly replied.

Tamara stared at the clock and started to ruffle around in the pouch bag she was carrying. "Can I change in here?" she asked. "You can watch if you wanna," she flirted.

My dick started to expand, poking against my shorts like a gremlin that ate after midnight. When she took off her shirt, I could barely contain myself, her coffee brown nipples stared me in the face and the lovely birthmark down the middle of her chest was the most beautiful imperfection I had ever seen.

"You wanna touch," she asked nonchalantly. It was no big deal to her, it was second nature.

Like an amateur, I dived in quickly squeezing her breast a little too hard. "Dang, that hurt's something terrible," she squealed. "This your first time?" she asked

I nodded yes and said, "Sorry, I didn't mean to hurt you again. How should I touch you?"

"Awww, that's so sweet. You're a virgin." She smiled, at the same time flattered that she was the first woman I'd ever touched. She took my hands tenderly and placed them flat against her hard nipples. "Let me teach you. First, rub my nipples like this," she said taking my index fingers in her hands and lightly rubbing them against her breasts in a circular motion.

I marveled at how hard her nipples were becoming, they were like smooth pebbles. And when she moaned, I never realized that the sound of pleasure from the mouth of a woman was more pleasurable than a woman's touch. She then loosened my belt, undid the zipper to my shorts and released the dragon.

Her nails were long, her palms were soft and as she began to stroke me, we kept eye contact. The glazed over look in my eye was appealing to her and every time my lip curled, it gave her justification to stroke faster. I masturbated regularly, so I thought I could hold my load and I definitely didn't want to waste it on her manicured hands.

She stopped stroking when my body looked as if it might succumb to her sweet torture. She shimmied out of her spandex, revealing the sexiest panties I ever had the pleasure of seeing up close. They were in total contrast to the grandma period panties my mother would hang from the shower rod. They were red, shiny and only covered a small portion of her privates. She lay back, spread her legs across my lap, took the index finger of my right hand and placed it inside the fabric of her crotch area.

"Pull them off," she commanded.

Pulling them off was easier said than done, because of her shapely hips and onion ass, it was more like a project. First, I had to pull the panty from around her waist and only when they were half way down could I insert my finger into the crotch area and pull them off. I enjoyed this process, it was the first time I had ever touched pussy. Sure I had seen it many times between the pages of playboy, but to touch it was another thing altogether. I looked at my finger, noticed a sticky liquid that resembled semen and marveled at it. I couldn't believe that I had actually aroused her.

I was nervous as she pulled my shorts down around my ankles and off, looking out into the parking lot, I wondered if anyone could see us. If the drunks in the parking lot had any sense, they could have witnessed a free strip show from my driver side window, but they were preoccupied with the curves of their liquor bottles.

My father's car had bench seats and an arm rest in the middle of it that went up and down, but her petite 5'3 frame had no problem lying across as the heels of her feet rested atop the metal cigarette ash tray on the door.

I took off my shirt, caressed her calves and started to climb across the seats with my pussy detector searching for treasure. Before I was halfway across her body, I could feel her hand resting atop my forehead pushing me between her thighs.

"No, if I'm gonna teach you. It got to be the right way," she said.

I promised myself I'd never eat pussy, swore I'd never even think about it. It was a thing my white friends loved to do that I deemed disgusting. However, when faced with the possibility of losing out on sex totally, my stance weakened. When I got down there, I just started to lick, not realizing that the right way was to open the fleshy folds covering the entrance to her pussy. Tamara showed me, opening them with her own fingers uncovering the pinkest of pink.

The doorway to her pussy was small, didn't look like my adolescent dick could fit in even if I wanted to and the bump over it didn't look like anything but a deformity.

"You can lick that," she said pointing towards the bump with the tip of her red nails.

I looked at the clock once more, saw that there was only fifteen minutes between my virginity and her set and knew I had to get to work. I licked it slowly, like an unsure child would lick a piece of foreign food. That's when I noticed the smell emanating from her body, though a little musty, it was very enticing. The smell alone propelled me to devour that bump, letting my tongue lap at it like an Ethiopian child lapping at newly fallen rain.

If I didn't know better, I would have thought that Tamara suffered a seizure. Her body started to convulse, her mouth released a series of inaudible moans and her thighs tightened around my neck. Then she started to aggressively push against the top of my head allowing me no room to breathe.

But as quickly as it began, it silently came to an end, and then the only sound was her labored breathing.

"I got to get ready," she said with my dick sticking at attention like a flagpole.

"Is that it?" I asked frustrated.

That taught me my first lesson, to never let a woman come until I was good and ready. I could tell that since she had gotten hers and didn't care or sympathize with the fact that I was still as hard as quantum physics she was ready to leave. I watched in horror as she put on a leaf green sequined bikini and started to exit the vehicle. She looked back at me, thought about closing the door, but for some unknown reason she succumbed to the sad look on my face.

"You gonna be quick," she said. I nodded. She straddled me, pulled her g-string to the side and inserted my stiffness into her wetness.

Like an experienced jockey, she rode my dick; I held onto her butt, ran my fingers up the crack of her ass and noticed that she found pleasure whenever I grazed against her hole. So I inserted my finger as far into her anal cavity as I could, caused her to nearly strangle me with her arm as she wrapped them around the back of my neck, burying my face into her breast. Like a leech in the Mississippi river, she latched onto my neck and gave me my first hickey.

My sensitive dick was no match for her experience and within five minutes, I came, exploding my virgin sperm into her orifice without regard of pregnancy. Tamara got frustrated, as my dick became flaccid, sucking her teeth and hissing into my ear. She got off me, took a napkin from her bag and wiped between her thighs. With a slight flick of her finger, she moved her bikini back in place and left without saying a word. I never saw her again, I searched for her at Crystal for months, but she never came back. That night my father hung me from the window; pussy would always cause me grief. I didn't know it then, but that was how sex would always be, cold, empty and followed by harsh repercussions.

"The way it is."

Angelica

Pastor Richards gave a touching sermon about love. When he mentioned that love wasn't jealous nor did it look out for its own interest, my eyes began to get misty. It made me think about my mother, because after doing research on her history I found out that not only was she addicted to heroin but had a rap sheet as long as Tupac's song list. She was currently serving time in a women's prison in downtown Philadelphia How could I take on her problems in my rather stress free existence? I always pitied those people that had drug addicts in their families, never knowing if the next binge would be the last or even how far their loved one would go for another taste.

Her name's Marjorie Thompson and she gave birth to me while she was incarcerated in Cambria county prison in Erie, Pennsylvania. When I found out I was born in prison, I could barely believe it. When I started this search, part of me hoped that my mother had died when she gave birth to me and maybe my father never knew about me. I hoped for an easy explanation of my abandonment. But to find out that I was the product of an illegal transaction, it really turned my world upside down. She was a prostitute and my father was an unknown john.

I looked at the stained glass window on the west side of Mount Bethel AME and prayed to the artist rendering of an African American Jesus. Normally I prayed for Rochelle, Titus and the power to face this world, but this time I prayed for insight. I needed him to lead me in the direction that best suited me, and that best suited my future. As I said amen, I hoped he would give me an answer soon.

Mount Bethel AME was like any black church you'll find on any corner in any black neighborhood. It was a massive brick structure, filled with many of the same people that helped build it. The older members revered their Pastors and Reverends with the same respect heaped on royalty. That's what made black churches special, a black man was actually respected within its four walls.

Within the same walls, I felt guilty. How could I come in the house of the lord with all these sexual thoughts filling my brain? I hadn't talked to Titus since he left and without his words of wisdom and strength, I didn't know how long I could last. I masturbated to Boris Kodjoe last night after finding my double penetration dildo and my born again status had become non-existent.

When the service ended, I located Pastor Richards. He was filling in for Titus and was going to be the one that married us. I trusted him and needed to talk to someone who could cast away the sexual demons invading my mind and body. When we entered his office, I took a seat, crossed my legs and folded my hands. By appearing as innocent as possible, I hoped to deflect any suspicions he might have after our talk.

Titus's office was practically a living memorial to the civil rights leaders of our day. Not only were there pictures of Martin Luther King, Jesse Jackson and Marcus Garvey but pictures of Rosa Parks and Harriet Tubman lined his walls. And there were pictures of all the members of the church, young and old, poor and rich. Even his furnishings were simple; he never wanted to draw attention from the lord so his executive size desk and the iron chairs that flanked each side were all from a consignment store.

My attention returned to the Pastor. Pastor Richards was a jolly man; if there was such a thing as a black Santa, I would imagine that it would resemble him. He was on the chubby side with a baldhead, white beard and a reddish hue to his Hershey complexion. And the aura he gave out was nothing short of comforting. Though he was 6'4 and had a commanding presence, his mellow tone could put a rattlesnake at ease.

"Angelica, whom do I owe this pleasure," he said while placing a gentle kiss on my cheek.

"I'm just in need of some spiritual guidance," I confessed.

Concern spread across his gentle face and wrinkles formed on his forehead as he placed his bible down and unzipped his pulpit robe. He took a seat at the desk, rested his chubby fingers on the bottom of his chin and stared at me almost as if he was scared to ask what was troubling me.

"Cold feet is normal when you are about to take a step such as the one you're going to take," he stated.

"Actually Pastor, I'm not here about myself, but for a friend," I lied. For all parties involved, I felt it would be clever on my part to say the problem I was having was that of a friend. I would receive the help I needed and still maintain purity in my groom's eyes.

The Pastor breathed a sigh of relief and his notorious smile once again blossomed. "A true friend doesn't look to themselves for the answer, but seeks the guidance of the lord. Your friend is blessed to have you on their side," he commended while pointing at me with the bible he now held in his hands.

"I just want to know what I can say that would make the answer to her problems clearer," I wondered.

"Sister have you recommended prayer?"

"I have, but she hasn't found it effective."

"The lord doesn't always give us an immediate or direct answer and sometimes the answer he gives us isn't what we may have wished. But prayer is *always* effective," he said.

"Like I said Pastor, I'm here for my friend." I stated in hopes that I hadn't offended him in any way.

"What exactly is the problem?" he asked.

I told him about my "friend's" issues, relaying the clean version of events to him. I expected a look of surprise to spread across his face. But he took everything in stride, listening intently and without shock or disgust. His eyes never left my face and as he held my hands for support, they never trembled.

"There's no burden that the lord cannot bear. If your friend really seeks an end to the desires of the flesh, she must fill her mind with the words of the lord." He handed me his bible, placed my hand atop the leather bound book and put his hand on mine. "The answers lie in here. We are only men, representatives on earth. If she's thirsting for the answer of life's woes, she must drink from here." He asked with a reassuring smile, "So are *you* ready for your big day?"

"My big day is slowly making me insane. When you were married I'm sure you didn't have to worry about so much," I laughed.

There was a wooden picture frame placed prominently on the desk, his fingers lovingly grazed the edges as he stared at the black and white portrait of a beautiful woman.

"Is that your wife?" I asked.

"Was, she died seven years ago. We were married for forty five years," he stated still visibly shaken by his loss. Possibly hurt that he had to use *was* for a woman he had planned to spend the rest of his earthly life with.

I don't think I ever witnessed that type love before that moment. As he stared at his former bride, I could tell in his loving expression that there was never another and if there was, he had never forgiven himself for his transgression. A tear slowly fell from the corner of his left eye, stopping mid-cheek and with a gentle swipe of his finger, it was gone.

"You must have really loved her," I consoled him.

"Still do, always will, she was a good woman. She put up with my ugly mug even when I wasn't the nicest person to be around." He held her photo in his hand, gazing at it as if he was apologizing for all the times he had made her miserable.

"How did you make it through the rough patches?"

"By making sure I didn't use excuses. When you leave a space open for divorce, you will have a divorce. We both decided that this was it for us and we would fight for our love even when we felt anything but love."

"I've never known anyone with a successful marriage. My parents weren't married. My "friend" is married, but still finds herself in other men's arms. Sometimes I wonder what makes a happy marriage."

"That's an answer you don't have to go to the bible for, during my sermon today I mentioned all that love is, well you can say that a successful marriage are all those qualities rolled into one."

Contrary to what I had led him to believe, I didn't know if I *loved* Titus. Mostly when I pictured my wedding day, most of my fantasies really had nothing to do with Titus at all. I imagined myself walking down the aisle looking stunning and becoming the envy of all the haters that wanted the man *I* was going to marry. Sometimes I wondered if my motivation was to prove that no matter what the women of his congregation thought of me they could never change the inevitable.

Thinking back on my pledge to be chaste, I concluded that it had nothing to do with spiritual or moral conviction. The truth of the matter was, in my field with all the traveling that's required I had never had the time to develop any type of attraction towards another man. One thing that separated me from other women was the need for some type of intellectual connection. That's why thugs were never really my cup of tea; I needed a man who could speak without using Ebonics, a man who could fuck me without touching me.

"Pastor, I'll do one thing for sure."

"What's that sister?"

"I'll leave it in God's hands."

"Remember, love never looks for its own interests."

His feelings epitomized what I felt about love and marriage. "Til death do us part" weren't just words, they were a commandment. Some took them lightly, accepting failure by way of divorce. The Pastor was living proof that it could be done. I hoped when I was dead and gone, Titus could look at me the same way. With love and pride, shedding tears for a woman without fault.

I left church reinvigorated about my future and with extra incentive to make sure that the next man I slept with was Titus. I wouldn't let love get in the way of my happiness.

I didn't even want to think about my plans for the coming week, not only did I have to finalize details with the florist, videographer, photographer and wedding planner, I had to attend Olympus Fashion week and with so much on my schedule an event I once looked forward to, was beginning to become a thorn on my side. Though I was sure Reba would understand if I sent my Assistant instead, it wouldn't help my chances of landing her job.

I finally buckled down and called Rochelle not because I wanted to, but because she was my maid of honor and we were scheduled for our final fittings. We had planned way in advance for this particular Monday and I didn't want this day wasted over any differences. Besides, I wanted to drive my brand new CLK-Class Mercedes for a change. Titus bought it for me on my birthday in March, two months ago and I had barely driven it.

Rochelle lived in the Manhattanville housing projects, so as I parked in the parking lot outside of her building, I drove slowly to avoid puncturing my Pirelli tires on the broken glass scattered about. Rochelle grew up in Harlem and lived in the same two-bedroom stuffy ass apartment her grandmother had raised her mother in. I didn't understand her attachment to the place outside of the dirt-cheap rent. Why would you want to come home late at night praying you won't get mugged, raped or killed as you go up in a pissy elevator?

I called her on my cell phone to let her know I was sitting downstairs in my car. There was no way in hell I was going to leave my car alone, trifling niggas can remove tires and strip a car faster than a NASCAR pit crew. I know because I lived in my share of housing projects growing up and they were all the same, dark and depressing.

I hit the power locks twice, pulled out my stun gun and positioned my car facing the exit if I had to make a fast get-away. Sometimes I felt guilty about fearing a place that wasn't much worse than where I grew up. After spending so much time in safer surroundings, I had lost the feeling of security that the streets once gave me.

When I noticed Rochelle approaching the car dressed in a skintight pair of Baby Phat jeans and red halter, I sucked my teeth. She would never change. Because she reveled in the attention the drug-dealing bums hanging by the doorway gave her as she switched by, sometimes it seemed like she had never grown up. Teasing men was her thing, while knowing damn well that the Wal-Mart diamond ring on her finger meant that she was already taken.

I started my car, enjoyed the purr of my engine, let the gold bangles around my right arm fall to my forearm and adjusted my big framed Gucci glasses in the rearview mirror. I hit the power locks again as Rochelle touched the chrome door handles and let the top down while putting the transmission in drive. I turned the volume up on my Sirius Satellite radio and drove off with my hair blowing in the wind.

"Hi, gurl. Sorry I'm running late, I had to leave Lil Unique with my next-door neighbor. I'm glad you called I wasn't trying to miss this for the world." Rochelle smiled tapping me lightly on the shoulder as she got comfortable and adjusted her seatbelt. Usually, I would return the favor and a smile, but I wasn't in a friendly mood. It wasn't that kind of day.

"So how are things going?" I responded referring to her little conquest in my guest room, hoping for an apology, but was sure she wouldn't catch my subtle hint.

"Shit's aiight, Deshawn's stupid ass is back in jail, but I'm not trying to stress over his problems. I ain't got bail money for his ass, since my mother passed the only time I hear from him is when he's locked up," she said with frustration lacing her tone.

Deshawn was her younger brother and a bonafide knucklehead. Though he was fine, with his jailhouse build, cocoa complexion and zigzag cornrows, I was glad he was in jail. Along with his looks, came a temper and violent disposition. I actually liked Deshawn, because back in the day he had the hook up on that purple haze and made me consider tossing my "No thug" rule. It was for the best that he ended up behind iron bars than where he was destined to end up, six feet below.

""Tell him I said hey," I said dryly.

"What's wrong, having problems with Titus?" Rochelle asked. If she could've seen behind my tinted frames, she would have noticed me rolling my eyes. Was she that dense or so fucked up that night that she had forgotten about what she had done?

"I'm happy as ever in *my* relationship," I snapped, still lying to myself and wondering why I hadn't heard from him in over a week. I held onto the wheel tightly as my nostrils flared and turned up the volume on Cece Winan's new song.

We barely spoke another word until I merged onto the west side highway. This wasn't leisure, it was business.

"Angie, I know that what happened that night has kind of fucked up our relationship, but I wanted to let you know I was high and not thinking clearly," she confessed over the music.

I didn't say a word, because after talking to the Pastor I wondered if Rochelle and I were ever real friends to begin with. I was clearly on the road to a lasting union when she disturbed it by bringing the foreigner with the huge tool into my home. Until then, I was leading a relatively dick free existence, now it was all I thought about. She was a bad influence from the very beginning and after my wedding, I knew I had to get rid of her.

I turned down the volume and said, "I think you really need some help, Rocky. I have always given you an open invitation to the church and I think it's about time you take me up on it. Get your marriage back to some type of normalcy."

"Church isn't going to help the problems I have."

"Have you ever considered the possibility that maybe you've brought your problems on yourself?"

I pressed the brakes as traffic came to a halt. I looked in the rearview mirror once again to fix my hair, I got blonde extensions added after church the day before and could've passed for Beyonce. Rochelle was breathing hard, whenever she didn't get her way she would usually start her tantrums that way. I ignored her and didn't care if my remark had hit too close to home.

"Not only do you go to church, you think you're God, you can't judge me," she said turning sideways, staring me eye to eye.

"That phrase is tired as hell. Why does everybody doing dirt hide behind "only god can judge me" like it's a shield. The truth is you're judging yourself."

If she wanted a fight, a fight was what she was gonna get. I've bit my tongue too long when it came to her, let her run over me and bring countless one night stands into my home like no one's business. However, this time was different, because I had never woken up before, had never seen a man fuck so well and had never wanted to be fucked so badly.

"Bitch, you have a very short memory. You forget the shit you did not too long ago. You're giving me advice is like a crack head telling a child to just say no. Now you bout to marry a *Reverend* and got the gall to turn up your nose at me!!!"

"Let me use another over used phrase for your ass. That was then, this is now. And now all I see is a college drop out turned ho."

Rochelle balled her fist, looked as if she might swing, I flinched and went for the stun gun underneath my seat. Like her brother, she had a violent disposition as well. There I was ready to put one hundred thousand volts in her ass when I watched the horror in her eyes. She brought her fists down to her side. The realization had stricken me as well. We crossed a line a friendship could not come back from.

Traffic was beginning to pick up, but the distinct click of the passenger side seat belt told me all I needed to know, she wanted to leave. As we approached 72nd street, I pulled over, watched her grab her things and opened my door. Though I had said many hurtful things, I didn't know what else to say to reverse this situation. Thus, I said nothing. She glanced at me, probably thinking the same thing as I was and stood out onto the sidewalk.

"Remember, it's me today and you tomorrow," she said slamming the door hard. I watched as she walked in the opposite direction and instantly burst into tears because I had forgotten how life was without her.

When I got home after having my wedding dress fitted *alone*, I wanted to fall on my bed and close my eyes, but the smell coming from my kitchen watered my taste buds. I almost forgot that Aurelius was beginning his first day as my personal chef. I left a spare key for him with my doorman in the morning before my disastrous day began and had totally forgotten.

The aroma of fresh thyme filled the foyer and as I entered my kitchen, the dim lighting pleasantly surprised me and candles set on my table. In the middle of the table, was a vase filled with my favorite flower, gardenias and in the middle of the kitchen stood Aurelius dressed in a tight fitting chef's uniform with a drink in his hand.

"Sit, relax and put your things down. Take a load off," he demanded. I did as he said, dropping my bag and shoes in the middle of the floor before taking a seat at my dining room table. "Here's one of my concoctions," he offered

"What is it?"

"First, take a sip." I hesitated for a moment, then after seeing the inviting smile on his face, I decided to try something new. I took a sip; let the drink settle in my mouth so I could really taste it and let it go down smoothly.

"This isn't half bad. What is it?"

"It's juice made with Ginger and lime."

"It's a little on the strong side," I said.

"That's because I didn't have a day to let it mature. Things are better matured," he flirted. I smiled, I didn't mean to but I couldn't help it.

"What did you make?" I asked

"Do you always ask these many questions? Well, it's a surprise," he said while dashing out the kitchen into the living room.

Aurelius looked pretty good in a uniform. They covered his hideous tattoos and accentuated his athletic build. I also thought he was cute with his chef's hat on; it covered that bush he called a hairstyle and showed more of his face. I could barely believe it when he put on some reggae, made me feel like I was cheating on Titus. Was he cooking or seducing?

He led me into the dining room and pulled out the seat for me at the dinner table. My place at the table was already set, complete with salad forks and so forth.

"Hope you don't mind me using your stereo. I wanted to set the mood for the Caribbean cuisine I prepared. I wanted you to feel like you were on the white sand beaches of Negril overlooking the crystal clear waters of the west end," he said, painting a perfect picture as I took another sip of his ginger and lime concoction.

"So, you've been?" I asked feeling reenergized by the refreshing drink.

"Many times, that's where I learned this recipe. My mother loved Jamaica," he smiled. "Does she go there often?" I asked. He didn't answer. He stood in place for a moment, I could tell he was thinking about her, but didn't want to speak on her.

"You cook like this for your significant other?" I asked, changing the subject and hopefully breaking the tension.

"If I had one, I probably wouldn't. I learned the hard way that it's not always good to cater for a woman," he stated matter of factly.

"You can't pass judgment on an entire gender based on your experience with one woman," I said defending my women. I hated men that looked at all women with fucked up lenses because another had fucked up their vision.

"Just a second. I'll be right back," he said before leaving.

He walked into the kitchen and brought back a stainless steel ice bucket. Placing a crystal goblet next to my plate, he then lit more red candles on my table.

"I'm sorry if I'm taking too long. I don't normally wait on anyone. I leave that to my employees," he said, draping a towel over his left arm and taking a bottle from the bucket.

"Don't feel bad about it. Actually in the house of royalty, waiting was considered a highly honorable position," I said, showing that I could also dispense a few jewels of knowledge.

"You know your history. You should've been a teacher."

"No that's not for me, I hate giving presentations at work as it is. I couldn't take doing it everyday," I confessed.

"In other words, it doesn't pay enough." He laughed, stinging me with his words then putting his hands up as I rolled my eyes. "I'm not being judgmental, hope you don't take me that way. But you just don't seem like the type of woman that could survive on a teacher's salary," he said raising the bottle and waiting to fill my glass.

"No not at all," I lied while he poured the rose-colored liquid into my glass. "This wine smells great." I put a napkin in my lap and brought the goblet close enough so that I could inhale the wines flavor.

"That's because it's from the personal vineyard of a friend of mine. It's a pinot rose and it'll bring out the flavor of your food."

"Where's your friend is vineyard located?"

"In Loire Valley, I mean in France," he corrected himself as if I didn't know the first thing about other countries.

"I've been there before and I've tasted better," I snapped.

"I'm sure you have. Hopefully your extravagant taste buds can make do with my choice," he retorted as he exited the dinning room.

Truthfully, I took offense to his examination of me. Especially since it was way off base, I bet he looked at my designer clothes and my prim and proper demeanor and pegged me as one of those self-indulged women the likes of Paris Hilton. That wasn't me at all, as a matter of fact, if it weren't for my career, I'd probably never feel the need to dress so extravagantly. Well, that was the last time I'd fraternized with the help. I wouldn't say another word to Mister Big Shit unless it was about what cycle to wash my dishes on.

He prepared me a feast fitting a queen, though I avoided over indulgence. I helped myself to seconds of the Roti, Callaloo and Coconut ice cream. He served me the ice cream while I sat on my recliner watching the newest episode of *Girlfriends*. The only thing left to do was hit a joint, but I had given that up years ago.

When I finally decided to go to bed, it was nearly ten. I was scheduled to do a dreaded presentation for all the personnel in my department, so I had to get to work extra early. I got up off the recliner, hit the power button on my remote and proceeded to the bathroom to wash my hands and brush my teeth. As I opened the door, I was shocked to see Aurelius standing over my toilet with his dick in hand.

For the second time in a matter of two weeks I stared at a dick a little too long before I made an exit. I shielded my eyes, went into my bedroom, quickly closed the door, sat on my bed and put my head in my hands. Did he notice the way I looked at his dick? I could've sworn I licked my lips.

A minute later, there was a light tap at my door and without permission, Aurelius opened it and came in.

"Did I say that you can come in here?" I asked, leery that he might have misconstrued my invasion of his privacy. Also scared that maybe he was some deranged lunatic who did that sort of thing, got off on showing unsuspecting women his penis.

"No, but…"

"But what, was that planned?"

"Did I plan what?" he asked, believingly shocked.

"Do I have to call the police?" I said, grabbing the cordless from my nightstand.

"If you think I expected you to walk in on me, the answer is no. But if you have to call the police for a simple miscommunication, do what you have to do. Obviously you're either crazy or simply delusional," he said. After giving me a disgusted look, he began to walk to the front door.

"Don't let the door hit you where the sun don't shine," I yelled cold-heartedly. Though I knew he probably didn't plan my invasion, his conceited response had set me off. And to top it off, he walked right into my bedroom as if I was some two-dollar hoe or something. Or did he think that just because other women melted when he came into a room, I'd do the same? Did he not know to respect my boundaries?

Still I had to confess, my anger was rather contrived. Honestly, I sort of enjoyed seeing a real life dick up close. Wanted to touch it, feel its heart beat and if it wasn't alive, I'd resuscitate it back to life. Within moments, my thoughts of his penis had quelled any ill feelings I held towards him. My attraction to him was instant, the moment he came into my home I didn't know how to act. And to top it off, he was romantic and a great cook. Yet I would never let him know that, men don't know how to act when you tell them you want them.

Growing up, I always had issues with men I was attracted to, started after my first crush broke my heart. His name was Curtis Phillips and he was fine, always had the latest gear and the sexiest s-curl flat top I'd ever seen. Looking back at my fifth grade year, I never would have known that one incident would forever shape my life…

Class had begun and like always, I was nibbling on an oatmeal cookie that I had stolen from the cafeteria. I hated stealing, but if I didn't, my stomach would growl and everyone in class would laugh at me. My foster mother at the time, Ms. Baxter was mean, let her kids eat whatever they wanted and only gave me the scraps. If I asked for anything she would call me ungrateful and stupid then slap me across the face like she did the last time.

Ms. Baxter was a chain-smoking, colt 45 drinking, welfare recipient that had nothing better to do but sit her lazy ass home collecting checks. She had six children of her own, by eight different men and none of them looked like her or their fathers for that matter. I'm great at math so when I said eight different fathers that's what I meant. I came to the conclusion that she probably had no idea who their fathers were. Her bedroom was like a public bathroom, pieces of shit she called men would walk in and flush their lives down the toilet once they fucked with her. Too bad two of them were giving her money for kids that weren't theirs.

We lived in a rat-infested walkup on North Fifth Street. I slept on the floor on a mattress that smelled a lot like piss, sometimes I would wake up to find rats sitting on top of my leg. I had a love hate relationship with the rats because they were the only things that scared Ms. Baxter. Whenever I screamed, "rat!" she would avoid my bedroom like the plague. At least that way she couldn't call me names.

The only upside to living with Ms. Baxter was that I liked Thurgood Marshall elementary better than the other seven schools I had attended the last five years, because the teachers actually cared. I always sat in the back of the room though; I didn't like when someone sat behind me because they could see the naps in my hair or even worse, say I stink. Everyone knows funk goes downwind. Washing up had never been a problem for me, but Ms. Baxter let her kids get their shower first and most of the time, I never got a chance before the bus came. I tried getting up early or staying up late the night before, but Ms Baxter didn't like me walking around the house when she was asleep and that day was no different.

My Teacher Ms. Dixon stood in front of the class with her usual smile. She was heavy set and on the dark side, but had the sunniest disposition of anyone I ever met. We were learning fractions this week, which meant that there would be a lot of my classmates looking for a tutor. Hopefully Curtis would need some help, but he probably wouldn't want my help anyway.

I loved to study, learning new things opened up an entire new world. History being my favorite subject was what I looked forward to. When I read history books, I liked to close my eyes and imagine myself in a different country and in a different time. If I was born in Africa in the early 1800's, I could've been a princess of the Zulu tribe. Maybe then, my parents would've stayed around.

Mrs. Dixon was going to put us in groups of two and each group had to solve a math problem within thirty minutes. There were more than thirty students in my class, which meant I'd probably end up with someone I hated. In my class, I wasn't particularly liked. They called me little orphan Angie and threw things at me when the teacher had her back turned. To my glee and surprise, she assigned me with Curtis.

Curtis was different; he never said a bad word about me or teased me. There was something soothing about him that put me at ease. All the boys followed him around, imitating everything he did. One of his friends even tried to imitate his hairstyle and ended up with nothing but a head full of scabs and blisters. Sometimes his friends would tease me along with the girls. However, Curtis defended me. He would tell them to shut up or get beat down, and everyone would listen.

They all feared Curtis, his older brothers were known drug dealers in the neighborhood and they had reputations, and spoiled Curtis something terrible. That's why he dressed so well.

When he sat next to me, I felt like putting a bag over my head. He scooted his desk next to mine; put his notebook between the two desks and turned to face me. Why would someone as cute as him want to stare in my face even for a moment?

Stylish would be the best way to describe the way he dressed, his British Walkers were always immaculate, his Cazel frames always matched his Kangol hats and his Lee's were always creased. I on the other hand, was a fashion disaster, dressed in hand me downs from Ms. Baxter's son closest in age, who happened to be over weight. I wore a gray sweatshirt and pair of his jeans with patches on the knees. My belt was at full capacity since I used the last notch to keep them from falling off my ass.

"Angie, I'm glad you're my partner. You're the smartest person in this class," he said. I wanted to smile, but was worried I might have raisins from the oatmeal cookie stuck in between my teeth.

Putting my hand over my mouth I said, "You're smart too."

"Not smarter than you, you should've been class president. Why didn't you run?" he said, staring at me. I was so used to people turning their heads when they saw me that I didn't know how to respond to actual attention. Instead, I shrugged my shoulders.

When I got nervous, I played with the back of my head, did this out of anxiety and I was doing it at that moment. It wasn't like I had any hair; the little ponytail that I sported everyday was the result of my stubborn nature. I had to struggle every morning just to make one and it had my eyes looking Chinese and my head feeling numb.

My feet tapped against the floor feverishly, the patent leather shoes hitting the linoleum sounded like a room full of girls playing double Dutch. Ms. Dixon eyed me, cleared her throat and put her thick index finger in front of her hairy lips. I stopped, slunk in my chair and pulled my book to the edge of my desk and away from Curtis.

The problem was simple. I did it within five minutes without really trying. Curtis on the other hand, looked confused and by the looks of his answer, I knew he didn't know the first thing about algebra. Like most boys, he didn't want to ask for a girl's help. And I didn't want to bruise his ego, so I asked if we could do it together, this way when I came up with the answer he would feel as if he helped.

Acting as if I was as clueless as him was a tall order. No matter how I tried to show him from the textbook how to do the problem, he just had no clue. Maybe I spoke too soon, when I said he was smart. Nevertheless, my persistence paid off and by the time Ms. Dixon's thirty minutes were over, *we* had an answer.

One by one, she called us in front of the class to give our answers and explain how we came to our conclusions. My knees were knocking as I sat behind my desk, my throat felt like I had spent a summer day in the Sahara sun without any water. There was no way I was going to speak in front of my entire class. Sometimes when I was nervous, I would stutter; putting myself at the mercy of my classmates wasn't my idea of a profitable day. I had a plan though, I would write down on paper how I came to my answer and have Curtis read it. However, just when I finished writing, it was our turn and I hadn't cleared my plan with him first.

That was my first experience with jealousy as I walked to the front of the classroom with my head hung low, my left hand holding up my pants and the paper I wrote the answer on in my right, I could hear whispering. The whispers sounded like my bedroom at night when the rats were free to roam. The girls in my class, who for some reason considered me competition for Curtis' affection, were mostly spewing the hisses of hate. They were delusional for I knew he'd never lay eyes on me in a romantic way.

"Quiet it down class, give Angelica and Curtis a chance to speak," Ms Dixon commanded, sitting behind her desk and squeezing into a chair that obviously wasn't made with a full figured woman in mind. As her flesh protruded through the sides of the chair, I silently prayed she would be able to get up as fast as I planned to get out.

Without hesitation, I handed Curtis the paper and wrote the answer on the chalkboard. He glanced at me, a look of embarrassment swept his face and he handed the paper back.

"I don't want to," I said, passing the paper back to him.

"I don't want to read either," he said, tossing the paper back to me as I let it fall to the ground. I'd made up in my mind that I wasn't going to read in front of my class no matter what. And I was sticking to my guns.

We both stood there looking down at the white piece of paper and calling each other's bluff. Curtis didn't look like he was going to bend and I for damn sure wasn't. I'd take a failing grade first. My teacher tried to stand, struggled to get out of her chair, so she held onto the arms of the chair and squeezed all her stuff out. Standing for a moment trying to catch her breath, her penetrating stare told me that she wasn't gonna play this game with either Curtis or I.

Ms Dixon walked over to us, bent over and scooped the piece of paper up. This got my class going, because Ms Dixon had ass for days and not the kind men liked to ogle. One of my smart Alec classmates insisted that he had gone blind. And the rest of the students laughed in unison only heightening the seriousness of this moment.

"I didn't require for either of you to read a paper. I only want you to explain your answer. Curtis since Angelica wrote the answer you can explain how you arrived to it." She stood with her arms folded, as I stepped off to the side and out of my classmates' field of vision, I felt guilty for abandoning my partner.

Like I expected, Curtis didn't know the first thing about Fractions, at first he tried explaining how he got his answer, but asked for the paper Ms Dixon was holding instead. He looked down at the paper, put it within centimeters of his face and tried his best to decipher the words. I had the best hand writing in my class, so I was sure he could understand what I wrote. At first, I thought he might need glasses or something, the Cazel frames on his face weren't prescription eyeglasses for damn sure. However, when he started to read, my suspicion was realized.

"Tttt…Th.Th.Th.Th… The," he read. His glasses were misty, he had broken into a sweat and he seemed inanimate as he stood in one spot.

I still remember the look of helplessness he gave me just before it was replaced by unyielding anger. Though I felt sorry for him, I still wasn't going to come to his rescue. The brother was in fifth grade and couldn't read *the*, one of the most rudimentary words in human existence. How did he even manage to fool teachers this long?

"Need any help?" Ms Dixon asked, standing by his side with her arm on his shoulder.

"He can't read!" someone yelled.

"I'll do it," I said. Ms Dixon cautiously allowed me to. I'm sure she didn't want to hurt Curtis anymore than he had already been hurt.

With my back to the class, I did the entire problem, explaining it thoroughly and without use of a paper. Afterwards, some people actually clapped for me. But the male ego is fragile, funny but with all their strength, all men are weak when it comes to dealing with emotions. I helped him, but all Curtis could see was that I had embarrassed him and worse yet, showed him up. We retreated to our seats in silence.

I got back to my seat unscathed, at least for the moment. Curtis came behind me, pulled his desk away from mine and approached me. "I hate you," he said pointing at me. "Nobody likes you because you're ugly. Your parents don't even want you. You are a throwaway and I wish I never worked with you."

My mouth fell open, I turned towards my teacher for help, yet she was oblivious to the tongue-lashing. Instead, her attention was now on another group standing in front of the class. Maintaining composure was difficult. I set my gaze away from him and tried praying the tears burning my eyes away. I could tell my reluctance to argue had only angered him more.

Curtis was light-skinned and he was so angry that he now resembled the red devil on a hot sauce bottle. Taking one of my homework assignments from my desk, he began to ball it up. Without notice, he threw the balled paper in my direction, hitting me in the face. It didn't hurt physically, but inside the affects was like he had hit me with a boulder at the speed of sound.

I cried that day, never forgave myself for that. Never forgave myself for being weak. Men only respect bitches, they may not love or care for them, but they must respect them. I've learned to mask my feelings, for better or worse. I'll never cry over a man and I'll never let them see me sweat. Instead, I would be their worse nightmare, a bitch with an attitude and her own money. Sometimes I may go too far, I could accept hate, but never disrespect. My mantra was always to show no weakness.

The door slammed, awakening me out of my daze. By the time I made it to my front door Aurelius was already entering the elevator. I ran out into the hallway, put my hand between the closing doors and crossed my arms.

"I'll see you tomorrow," I said with a smile. He gave me a confused stare, sucked his teeth, leaned against the walls and pressed for the lobby.

Admittedly, I had an elementary school crush on him and looked forward to seeing him again. I was sure I would, whether he wanted me to or not. Because he had left his utensils in my kitchen along with my spare key, I knew he'd come back to retrieve them. And though I knew in less than a month I'd be a married woman, all I could think about was his pierced dick and if I would ever see it again.

"Take Me as I am"

"I can't stand that bi-polar, pompous woman," I said to myself as I entered my living room.

I sat in a yoga position in the middle of my floor and began to breathe slowly. I needed to chill and exorcise all the negativity that Angelica had heaped on me. First, I tried closing my eyes, but all I could think about was her. My attraction to her was confusing, because if anything she had only expressed distain towards me. Nevertheless, there seemed to be a sexual tension between the two of us. Why did she stare so long when she caught me?

Earlier in the evening when I arrived at her apartment, my curiosity got the best of me. I walked around her place, wanting to get a feel for her. There were no pictures on her walls, not even a photo album lying around. In her bedroom there wasn't even a candle, it lacked any sensuality. Instead, she had made it a place only used for sleep, decorated like a man would, with too much blacks and silvers. When a person resides in a place that lacks any personality, it reflects the emptiness hidden in her soul, for what a person loves, she displays. She didn't even have a photo of her fiancé.

I discarded my clothing, stepped into the shower and relieved my stress underneath the water. I turned the faucet to the hottest that my body could bare, immersed myself in the steam and began to wash my hair. When I got down to my dick I closed my eyes took a hand full of body wash and began to massage it. While closing my eyes, I couldn't help but see Angelica's face. I imagined her the way she came home, dressed in a low cut skirt showing off those beautiful legs of hers. I bet they would taste great covered in hot caramel.

Women like her don't respect a man they could walk over; rather they need a man to dominate them. In my mind, I saw myself doing just that, imagined her walking into the bathroom unannounced once more, but instead of letting her leave, I grabbed her, ran my hands up her thighs and without hesitation stuffed them down her panties. When I was a child, my piano teacher always said that my fingers were strong, flexible yet gentle. I would play a pleasurable hard staccato on her black key. By manipulating my fingers across her body, we would recreate our own rendition of Beethoven's Tempest Sonata. However, I would remember the three rules of playing, down stroke, hold and lift.

After pleasuring myself in my bathroom, I hit up the internet and checked my e-mails. On Saturday, I was catering an event for a fashion designer in the city for fashion week. Muhammad Reith was from Saudi Arabia and had sought me out personally to cater an Arabian Night's themed party at his Hampton's retreat. It was going to be the party of the century, at least this year it would be. In his email, he gave me a head count and asked that some of my waitresses come dressed as harem women and some of my waiters come dressed as sheiks, for what? I didn't know.

Getting back from the fitness center was a chore. Every muscle in my body ached, I walked to my condo in a bow legged stance, soaked my feet in Epsom salt and started to make a few calls. In my business, I learned the best way to stay in business was to always be on the grind. The person that sleeps less makes more in the long run. That's why no matter how big I got I always knew it would be profitable to network. After sending a bevy of brochures to a few corporate event planners, I checked with my suppliers to make sure everything would be in order for Saturday's event. One mishap could ruin my entire reputation.

While checking the messages I missed during my workout, I was pleasantly surprised to hear Angelica's voice over the answering service. She wanted to talk to me and wondered if I didn't mind coming in early. Though I didn't have any objections, I hoped she would apologize when I saw her that night. I would try to act as if nothing happened when I prepared her meal, but if she had another one of those bitchy fits, I'd cancel the contract without any regrets.

"Sexual Indulgence"

Angelica
27 days till...

When I woke up this morning, I just wanted to hear his voice. Last night I couldn't help but dream about him, he had taken my thoughts for hostage. And it wasn't even like I had anything to say to him when I called him. When I got his voice mail, I made something up and told him that I needed to speak to him. In reality, I doubt I'll even be home before nine at night and if he's still at my place I'll act as if my call never happened.

Is it possible to want someone you don't know so badly? I mean I know who he is, but I don't *know* him. The few hours he was in my life made me feel wanted, beautiful even. There's just something about him, about the way he took time to cook for me and to make it special. No one had ever taken the time to prepare something so special. Most men I dated would take me to Micky D's and then want to fuck all night. And Titus, well Titus didn't want to fuck me at all.

While I slept, I dreamed about Aurelius, made love to him in my dream. It seemed so realistic, so sensual and so pleasurable. My thong was even soaked when I awakened from my fantasy. Simply put, I had a Jones for a man I never even touched, a man who quiet possibly thought I was cuckoo after the show I put on for him last night.

The Florence Nightingale effect, every woman suffers from it, the inclination to help a wounded spirit. The hope of one day rehabilitating a stray dog has found countless women flea bitten and stricken with rabies. I've seen it, hell I've done it countless times. I thought I could change a man that didn't want any changing, thought if I loved him stronger than any woman wanted to then they'd change just for me.

Aurelius though was different; he seemed to be a little deeper than most guys. I could tell his mother loved him unconditionally. Only men loved by a woman knew how to treat a woman. However, he had also been hurt and possibly shocked to find out that every woman wasn't as loving as his mother. Some can be down right mean.

My day started off rather surreal, my air ventilation was on the fritz and my condo felt like a sauna, plus Rochelle was on the same train I was on. We didn't speak, we sat across from each other and it was like we had never met. She wore dark frames and I knew she was burning a hole through me because her head was facing me and her lips were like stone, chiseled in a never-ending scowl. I felt uncomfortable, but I didn't let on that I felt so, because I wouldn't run from someone who I thought owed *me* an apology.

When I got to my office, my administrative assistant, Connie, alerted me that there were flowers from Titus along with a letter on my desk.

To: My love.

A great man said: Man does not live on bread alone, but from the utterance of my father. Down here they need both, and though it's been a trying experience, my belief in prayer has increased ten fold. These people need help, not only with sustenance but spiritually as well. They don't need a spiritual advisor who finds comfort in the luxuries of western civilization while they suffer the damndest of plights. That's why I haven't called, because while I'm here I want to live like these brothers of mine. Remember, I'm always thinking of you.

Yesterday we traveled a small dirt road into the city of Lodwar under the mask of darkness and the brothers here were playing Benga music on their guitars. The song they were playing was very soothing and though I didn't understand the words the rhythm made me think of love. Made me think of you and just as I held a picture of you in my mind, I saw a shooting star. You are my star and every time I look into the heavens over this beautiful land, I think of you. You are never far from my mind or my heart.

Let this letter find you in health and unconditional Agape love.

Love Titus

P.S —Being here got me thinking that Money and all the things that come with it doesn't bring true happiness. If I didn't have money, I know I'd be happy here, these brothers are happy with nothing at all. I wonder if I could ever live in the U.S and feel the same about life ever again. They need me here, if we sold our house, I'm sure we could build a beautiful church. I would like for both of us to live out here, permanently, but I know I have to take care of home first .And with all the atrocities that take place in our back yard, I'm ready to step to the plate and find a way to address our people's needs .

My smile faded just as quickly as it came. Living in a third world country wasn't something you can bring out at the end of a letter. Sure, I could understand that maybe he had gotten filled with joy and maybe wrote something in the mist of a fleeting moment of happiness. But if he thought I would ever consider moving anywhere without running water or air conditioning, he was losing his mind. I'm not going to give up my mansion in the Hampton's to live in a hut. Still, I wondered what else he could do for people that he wasn't doing already.

This Tuesday was going to be especially busy, with the presentation I had planned for this morning and my afternoon trip to Bryant Park for the start of Fashion week; I knew it would be late before I got home. That's why I decided to dress casual, casual for me. I went Boho chic for the day, put my hair into a ponytail, twisted it into a bun and held it in place with hair sticks made from African Picture Jasper. I wore a pink BCBG floral print dress to go with my rimless

Salvatore Ferragamo frames with the pink lenses and a comfortable pair of Prada open toe sandals. The style screamed 2005, but I found it quiet sexy.

After I called all the associates in my department to the sales floor, I tried my best to internally calm myself down for this presentation. With experience, I thought I'd eventually get over my fear, but after two years, I still got dry mouth, sweaty palms and a queasy stomach. Like usual, they took their time reaching the floor. I glanced at my watch and it was about thirty minutes to spare until the doors opened for business and I hated to see people standing around when the customers needed help.

My assistant, Lea, brought me a bottle of Evian for my dry mouth and stood by my side. She was always quiet, accommodating and classy. She stood about 5'2 and resembled Star Jones. On the chunky side, she wore her hair short and never wore a stitch of makeup. She played down her looks, but her dark skin had a radiant aura emanating from it. As my only ally in the store outside of Reba, I really appreciated her.

"Should I make another call?" Lea asked, looking up at me for guidance.

"No, if they don't get their asses here in a few seconds, there will be hell pay," I snapped automatically feeling sorry that I had directed my anger towards Lea. I looked across the sales floor, yet there was no one in sight.

This was unusual; even though I knew the sales associates didn't like me, they had never crossed me.

"You know what? I'll find them," I said, walking around the department with my arms crossed and a frustrated stare etched on my face.

I looked between each rack, behind each register and in every fitting room, but there still wasn't a soul around. As I walked by the escalator, I could hear someone voice, it was coming from Home décor, Alexis's department. I rode the escalator up one flight and found myself in the mist of a full-scale presentation being given by Alexis. By her side were the Store Manager Raymond, Reba and the other Buyers.

Not one person had informed me about the meeting, but I'm sure they all got a kick out of hearing me over the store intercom. I took my place among the group as Alexis's fake ass gave a watered down version of a motivational speech. My hard work was all for naught, because I got up at three in the morning and planned exactly what I wanted to say at my own presentation. They would never hear what I had to say.

As she finished to a thunderous applause, I couldn't help but feel an incline of jealousy run through my body. Why didn't I have that sort of affect on people? Did they really know that Alexis didn't give a damn about them, and only about the promotion? Did I come across as the cold hearted, selfish and heartless bitch that Alexis really was?

What was taking place was similar to what would be considered a pep rally. Each time we hit a new sales plateau, the Store Manager would give a speech and heap praises on all the associates. The purpose was to give the associates the motivation to make more sales. I couldn't remember anyone other than Raymond giving the speech, and now as I stood looking at the condescending smirk on Alexis's face, I knew my future prospects were looking bleak.

I love fashion week. The atmosphere's always festive. I like to call it the holiday for beautiful people. Because that's all you see walking inside the tents lining Bryant Park. Sometimes, I'm lucky enough to catch a celebrity sighting or two. Maybe even get to mingle with a few, but this year was very different; my focus was on my wedding. My phone was plastered to my ears. I wanted to keep tabs on Marcellus as he finalized the details of my special day.

There was a show I was looking forward to attending and it was taking place at the Promenade. One of my best friends from F.I.T was showcasing his spring collection. Daniel Cho was like one of my girlfriends when we attended school, though we didn't talk but once every year now, we still considered each other family. There was nothing I wanted more than to help a friend get their collection inside my store.

The weather was perfect for a showcase, the sun was out and it wasn't too humid. The white tents lining the lush greenery were flawless. And everyone in the crowd outside of the tents was dressed to impress. In my single fornicating days, my focus was usually on finding the richest, cutest and most available bachelor and showing him why the statue of liberty wasn't the only woman in New York who looked great wrapped in sheets.

However, on this day, I kept my eyes to myself and my mind on finding Daniel before the start of his show. As I entered the Promenade, I was greeted by a sexy ass brotha dressed in a UPS uniform handing out brownies on a silver platter. The myth is that men look better dressed in uniforms, but I'd be willing to bet my salary that he'd look better dressed in nothing at all. The tight brown shirt could barely hold his bulging biceps.

"Would you like to try one of these?" he asked with a smile.

"No, I'm trying to abstain from any treats," I said. He walked away and probably never considered that I really wasn't referring to the brownies.

Someone told me once that chocolate was a good substitute for sex, but there wasn't a substitute for the chocolate men that milled around this tent.

"Calm down. Remember you're engaged," I whispered to myself as I took a moment to stare at the five-carat diamond on my finger.

Trying to navigate around the paparazzi and news crews was beginning to try my patience. I didn't mind attention, but I could understand how they became victims of assault at the hands of a few disgruntled celebrities. Having someone in

your face just taking pictures of you can make you feel
violated.

I located the front desk, showed them my personal invitation
and was led to the dressing area. Models are considered
classy and lady-like, but what I was witnessing was straight
out of Girls Gone wild. They were running around, throwing
clothes back and forth, all in the nude. It wasn't like I had
never seen it before at fashion shows, but for some reason I
expected something different. What they should've had was
a buffet table for all the emaciated, pale-skinned females that
were running around.

When I located Daniel, I could only smile. Dressed in all
black, wearing a v-neck shirt and tight fitting slacks, he
looked fabulous. Since F.I.T, he had done a full 180, far from
the reserved choirboy that I remembered. His hair was spiky
and highlighted with blonde streaks. He wore eye makeup,
lip-gloss and seemed happy in his skin. I could remember
when he was still fearful that his parents would find out
about his sexual preference.

He was in the process of fitting clothes on this Amazon of a
woman as I walked up behind him. When I put my hand over
his eyes, I could feel his cheeks spreading with delight.

"This better be Angie or someone wants to get there ass
kicked," he said with sass. "You know I'm Chinese and can
do a mean roundhouse."

I uncovered his eyes and gave him a huge bear hug. I
couldn't believe how much I missed him. Seeing him
brought back so many great memories that what happened
earlier at the store barely registered a blip on my mental radar
any longer.

"You look good, Daniel."

His eyes went straight to my ring as I suspected. "You look
loved."

"I feel loved. But what have you been up to, Mr. In demand."
I laughed, playfully shoving him in his chest, taking the shine
off me and directing it towards him.

"I'm trying not to pull my hair out. These bitches can drive
somebody to Bellevue. No wonder I'm gay," he said, staring
at the Amazonian woman that he never introduced and
Daniel was never discreet.

Daniel stood about 5'6 with a petite frame and small waist,
but I was all too familiar with his tantrums when provoked.
And I could tell he was on the road to one of his famous
hissy fits, so I asked to be seated and he directed me to a seat
at the front row of the runway. The place was decorated in all
white; the seats were even covered in white sheets.
Considering Daniel's personality, I thought it was sort of
plain. But I was sure he had more in store.

His show was spectacular as I figured it would, and his
collection was hot to def. As his models switched up and
down the catwalk underneath the disco lights, they danced to
"Work It" by *Teena Marie* and other cuts from the eighties.
The music was so loud I thought I was at a concert. His
models were having fun showcasing Daniel's wearable
couture and the smiles on their faces revealed it. The crowd
was enthralled and the cameras wouldn't stop popping. Like
usual, he didn't disappoint. For the grand finale, Daniel
finished the show by doing a cartwheel down the runway.

Later after attending a few more shows, I met up with Daniel
at *Level V*, a cocktail lounge in the village. We had a lot of
catching up to do. With drinks in hand, we relaxed on one of
the black leather couches underneath the electric blue
lighting and bobbed our heads to Promiscuous girl by *Nelly
Furtado*. It was way pass my hanging out time, but since it
was job related, I said the hell with it.

"You should've called Rochelle down here. This placed is
packed with her type of men," Daniel said while gazing at all
the attractive men that came in and out. I paused, and almost

forgot to tell him about my current relationship status with Rochelle.

"We ain't talking," I confessed to Daniel's surprise.

"Not the double mint twins, you both have been practically joined at the hip for the last decade. What happened, she tried to fuck your fiancé?"

"Nothing like that at all…We just grew apart," I said taking a sip from my fig martini.

"Y'all be friends again. She probably feels like she's losing a friend because you're getting married."

"On the real, I don't think I want to be friends with her. She's out there whoring around. You know what I mean?" I said, hoping to get a response. Hoped someone shared my distaste for her lifestyle.

Daniel could've cared less about what I was saying as he made googly eyes with an effeminate, thin white guy sitting at the bar. I couldn't blame him, sometimes when you are friends with both people involved in a quarrel it's best to stay out of it. His loyalty towards Rochelle and I wouldn't allow him to belittle either one of us.

The night went smoothly. We talked about his parents and how they've finally learned to accept his lifestyle and I told him about finding my mother. He encouraged me to go meet with her, knowing how much I thought about finding my parents when we were in school.

Like always, Daniel was on the prowl. After breaking up with his partner of five years, he was intent on having all the sex he could handle.

"So you've been out here for a week and didn't even call me, shame on you," I said feeling a little tipsy due to my third martini.

"I would've called you, but the lord wouldn't have followed you into the places I go." He laughed, knowing how serious I had become about religion. His remark was humorous because I could remember when I was considered the wild one. If there was a party, I was there and if there were drugs to be found, I would partake. Thinking about my change made me feel old, like I had fallen out of the loop.

"Bet, so the next time you want to hang, I'll be game."

"And Mr. Perfect is going to be fine with that?"

"What do you mean? I'm my own woman."

"So that's why I didn't get an invitation."

"Let me explain…" I said.

Daniel put his hand on mine and looked into my eyes. "I understand. No need to explain to me, the world hasn't changed that much," he said with an impaired look on his face.

I didn't have the heart to tell him, I thought the subject wouldn't be brought up. Rochelle most likely filled him in on Titus's distain for homosexuals. Titus didn't have a biblical type of disdain but a heartfelt disdain. I once broached the subject as to why he harbored such hatred, the fire burning in his eyes told me all that I needed to know. For that reason, I never even considered inviting Daniel to my wedding. I couldn't imagine him interacting with Titus, they were from different worlds.

We drank in silence. The mood had turned sullen. Like two strangers who had never met, a sense of awkwardness resided in our rehearsed conversation.

"You remember when you got drunk and nearly gave up the ass to that ugly ass waiter at the pancake house?" he laughed trying to soften the blow.

I clutched my purse tightly, looked around and hoped no one else had heard his untactful remark. One thing I hated was bringing up my past. I was a lost girl back then, my life revolved around foolishness. A life I was now far removed from.

"I choose not to remember the past. When you think about it, we were a bunch of stupid kids who didn't know our asses from a hole in the wall."

"You've changed. You were the reason any of us really kept in touch. If it wasn't for you not letting go of our old memories, we might've disappeared into oblivion. Now you want to forget everything as if they never happened," he said shaking his head, staring into his empty glass and leaving a trail of fingerprints in the perspiration. "If you can't be you when you are in love, who is it that your man has fallen in love with?"

When we left and I finally made it to bed, I thought about his words. Was I losing myself as I felt deeper in love with Titus?

"One More Chance."

Aurelius

I stood at the granite countertop island in the middle of Angelica's kitchen, my eyes focused on the tiny sliver of light spilling into the foyer from underneath the door, hoping to see the silhouette of her feet. Part of me felt like I should've gone home, been in my bed already fast asleep, but I was here. For some unknown reason I was in the home of a woman I didn't even know, but was strangely attracted to. I bribed myself into believing that I wanted to make sure she got home safe, but there was much more to it.

Taking chances was never my forte as a young man. If anything, I avoided all things that had to do with risk. And that's why I lost my only love...

July 14ᵗʰ 2000...

When I walked in the door, she was dressed in a red corset, red leather chaps and five-inch stilettos. She smelled like vanilla scented oil and every light was turned off and replaced by one hundred burning-candles. I was barely out of my work shoes before she grabbed my hand and led me into our bedroom.

Our bed was covered in pink roses and slow jazz played as the red embers from the sandalwood incense burning on the nightstand fell to the hardwood floors. The curtains were drawn and the windows open, letting in a breeze. I could feel the cool gust of wind hitting against my chest, as I smelled the alluring aroma of the ocean. She was behind me stroking my back, kneading her knuckles into my flesh like a pastry chef would do with dough. Her name was Mystical and she was from Minnesota, the love child of a deadbeat black man and a white hippie mother.

Our place was right off the ocean in the heart of New Port Beach. From our bedroom window, we had a breathtaking view of New Port Bay. She enjoyed the ocean like me; we would walk along the sand for hours in silence, listening to waves beat against the shore. The ocean's scent was an aphrodisiac and we both yearned for its aroma. Looking into the open window of our five hundred square foot apartment, five stories above, it wasn't out of the ordinary to see us making love or to witness Mystical pleasuring herself, the ocean affected us that way.

The apartment was small and the rent cost as much as a mortgage on some three hundred thousand dollar homes, but it was ours. I was head chef for the New Port Brewing Company and could afford it. It was sure different from the patch of beach we shared the first year we met. When we met, she had nothing and because I took her home, my parents disowned me. But we worked well together and had come far.

She was mulatto, the complexion of buttermilk and her entire body was perfect to *me*. From her elongated torso, to her muscular legs, down to the inscription of my name tattooed above her pussy. But if you were to dissect her, each part of her standing on its own would be considered average to some. She wasn't classically beautiful, her hair was short and dyed bright red, and her skin was freckled from her face to the tips of her feet. Her face was pierced, twice on each lip and three times on each eyebrow. When I kissed her, I could never get quiet enough of her thin lips and when I held her ass there was barely any to grab. Her feet were too big, her teeth too gapped. But as a whole, each piece of her body in coherence created the most beautiful woman I'd ever laid eyes on, even if she was stunning only through my pupils.

While at work, I could barely fill all the orders coming through my kitchen as I waited in anticipation for my day to end. I was ready to sacrifice my individual life to become one with my soulmate and I hoped she felt the same. My parents said she was wrong for me, they said she was trash and I would never make her into an honest woman. I wanted to prove them wrong and I wouldn't show them my face unless I had.

This was meant to be a special day. It was our anniversary, our three-year anniversary and I could barely contain myself. After dinner, I wanted to surprise her with a gift, actually a proposal. Though the ring I bought for her was only one-quarter carat, she would not care for she enjoyed the simpler things in life. The meaning behind the ring would be enough for her, because the proclamation of my undying love was priceless.

"That hits the spot," I said closing my eyes as she started to massage my shoulders.

"Just relax; I ain't even getting to the good part." She laughed, sticking her tongue into my ear as she navigated her hands down to my belt. I knew it was best to stay still and enjoy it.

In sex, she was my tutor; with patience and skill, she showed me how to enjoy it. Every thing I knew about sex before I met her had turned out to be nothing but fabricated lies. Sex isn't a way to get off, because if our genitals were the only parts of our bodies that needed stimulation, why are our nipples sensitive to the touch? And why do the back of our necks tingle when they are licked? While some men celebrate when giving a woman one orgasm, I wasn't satisfied unless I gave multiple.

She introduced me to new things, helped me give up all my inhibitions and showed me how to use my body as a canvas that revealed my inner most feelings. She branded me, with a blowtorch and sheet metal she branded her initials into the fleshy part of my thighs. And for me she did the same.

Our love was fairytale, a sudden and unexplainable attraction. Before me, there was a woman in her life. A woman's touch stood side by side with that of a man's on Mystical's menu. However, she quit cold turkey, decided that her only means of salvation would be through me. Though I feared she would one day have a craving for the fish that beef could not satisfy, I hoped that love would make her allergic to seafood and its taste.

"Should I give you your anniversary gift now or later?" I asked enjoying the hand job she was giving me.

"First, let me give you mine," She said, standing up and walking into our bathroom. "And put on that blind fold."

I was still wearing part of my chef's uniform. So I removed my checks, boxers and lay across the king-size bed. While waiting for her, I massaged myself to life and thought about what I wanted to do to her step by step.

On the nightstand was a red blindfold, I hated being blind it was a fear I had, but I put it on anyway. I lay down flat in my bed and used my ears as a guide. The bathroom door opened quickly and caused a breeze to waken my other senses. The hairs on my body rose and a tingling sensation ran from my inner thighs up to my earlobes.

Her hand was around my dick and then she took my manhood to the back of her throat. I tried putting my hand on her head so she could swallow even deeper, but she grabbed my wrist.

"Lay back. Enjoy. You don't need to touch, let me take care of you. I'm in control," she whispered.

The loss of sight had only served to amplify my other senses. When she sucked my dick, I could hear her lips smack whenever she reached the head, and when she brushed her hair across my thighs, my toes began to curl. The feeling of being pleased all over was about as much as I could handle.

I reached for my mask; she knew how much I loved to watch her love every inch of me. But she grabbed my wrist again and put them down by my side. It was pleasurable torture, but I made do. I pictured her in my mind, imagined how plumb her lips became whenever she gave me head. And I imagined her moving up and down on my manhood in precise premeditated movements, as she took me all in.

I felt her tease my head with the tip of her tongue and put the steel ball on the middle of it in and out of my hole. Biting down on the bottom of my lip and clutching the sides of the mattress became my only measures of relief. My body had a mind of its own and needed to be released. Possibly feeling my forthcoming surrender, she stopped.

I heard her moan, felt the bed thrust forward and heard a hand smack across bare ass. Mystical was singing a song I hadn't heard. Then there was another thrust, the sound of wet pussy being penetrated had unnerved me. My hands were back on the mask, but this time she could not prevent the inevitable.

The scene before me was something out of a porno. Mystical was over my knee on all fours, her eyes looked heavy as if she was being fucked to sleep. Behind her was someone I knew, but vaguely remembered. She was beautiful, Spanish; thin with long black hair that fell below her elbows. And she wore a black dildo.

"What the hell is this?" I yelled. Mystical began to suck my dick as if that would shut me up. I pushed her away, jumped from the bed with my hands balled in fists, about to beat the woman with the black dick like she was a man.

The woman backed away, noticed the anger in my eye and got in the fetal position in the corner of my bedroom. Mystical jumped in front of me, her breast bouncing up and down and put her arms up.

"Please, don't," Mystical said. Sounding weak, not like the woman I had grown to love. It seemed as if she would rather sacrifice herself than see me touch a hair on the body of the unknown woman.

"Ju didn't tell im," the woman said in broken English.

"Shut up bitch," I said pointing at her, letting her know that she was lucky my hands weren't around her neck.

Most men would jump for joy at the prospect of having two women in one bed, but I didn't share Mystical, not for anything in this world. If I was a king and allowed an unlimited number of concubines, I would still only have relations with her. Her love was enough for me, one pussy to one dick, making true love.

I looked into Mystical's eyes, searching for an answer. They were cold and unyielding. All she could give me was a weak shrug of her shoulders. Was she going to actually act as if what happened was nothing? I grabbed her forcefully by the elbow, pulled her close, studied her eyes once again, but they were still unreadable.

"Who's this?" I asked with intensity. If she wasn't gonna tell me where she was coming from, I was damn sure gonna show her where I came from.

She pulled away from me as if she despised my touch. "I knew you'd make this hard," she said.

"Make what hard?"

"I thought maybe we could work through this, make it livable for the both of us," she said, sitting on the bed.

I put my hands on my head, "I don't understand."

"I've told you, but you didn't hear me. You are always working," she said

What didn't I hear? Was it possible to read the mood of a woman? When women fall out of love they can still coexist with the other party like nothing happened. I didn't even know that we had problems. I didn't even know that she felt unloved and abandoned. I was a chef and not a mind reader. There would be no convincing her otherwise, for she swore she gave me signs.

Just at that moment, I was able to put two and two together. I remembered the name of her former lover, the face from the countless pictures that Mystical could never bring herself to throw away. Sandra Vega, her Columbian obsession and my enemy. She went away, left without a reason and a trace. Now she was back to reclaim what was hers. In my heart, I knew Mystical had never gotten over her. How could she when that chapter of her life had never closed. Now I was face to face with reality, my worst nightmares now realized.

"How long has this been going on?" I asked.

"For six months," she said, walking over to Sandra. She sat beside her, caressed her face, and stared into her eyes, like she once stared into mine.

Six months before, I was promoted to head chef, though the job meant more responsibilities and later hours, it paid well. I took it so we wouldn't have to live paycheck to paycheck and nearly starve just to live next to the water. Didn't she realize I did it for us? The nights that I slid into bed in the wee hours of the morning, just to slide out a few hours later, I did it for us. Sure, we barely talked or walked the beaches anymore, but I did it for us. And this was how she repaid me.

"Why now? Why not six months ago?"

"I didn't know then, but I know now. I thought we could all have an understanding, but I know now that you want more than I can give," she said.

"What do I want?" I said picking up my boxers and putting them on.

"You want me, and I can't give all of me to you," she told me.

"But Mystical out of all days why today, why on our anniversary?"

"The day we got together was the day me and Sandra broke up. I thought that if we all came together maybe we could start anew. I wanted this to be a rebirth, something beautiful, but I knew that you wouldn't see it my way. You never do," she said, now standing side by side with her other lover.

"I don't want to share you. If you can't understand that then you might as well go," I said in unbending fashion.

"I'm not yours, I'm my own person. You don't own me, I do." She looked at me, awaiting my response, maybe hoping I'd bend, but it wasn't meant to be.

"But you own me?" I said pointing to the brand between my thighs.

The tension was so thick that it could be cut with a knife. I went into the living room and out onto the patio. Waited for both of them to get dressed and leave. Only Mystical came out and stood beside me, but kept her distance as I looked out onto the ocean. She held the same beat up travel bag she had the first time I laid eyes on her and wore the same clothes as well, leaving behind everything that reminded her of me.

"Do you still love me?" I asked with my eyes still fixed on the ocean.

"I don't know if I ever did," she confessed. "The last three years I was living a convenient existence and not the one I wanted to live."

Those words pierced my heart; I slumped down on the railing and my knees buckled. It felt like she had just ripped out my insides. I hoped it was a dream and could wake from it lying next to the Mystical that loved me. But it was real, too real.

"Jared, don't do this to me. This is hard enough. You can't deny that this has been a long time coming. You deserve someone else. You deserve better than me," she said just above a whisper.

Why do women toss aside good men? Does weakness or undying love breed repulsion? They say they want a man to treat them well, be faithful, and respect them. But in reality, they don't want those things at all. They want the chase and they want the reclamation project. It wasn't that we were having problems; it was that I loved her too much. I was too nice.

The breeze picked up a bit. On a hot July day when the California sun was at its most potent, the ocean provided a refreshing oasis. I was dressed in only my boxers and she was dressed in cut off shorts and a red bra. As I regained my composure, I wanted to set things straight.

"You knew I'd say no, right?" I asked staring at her.

"Yes. But you act as if I planned this. Everything was fine when you didn't know. It wasn't like I was fucking another man. You just couldn't leave well enough alone, could you?" She couldn't look me in the eyes, fiddled with her hands instead, trying to reason about the unreasonable.

"That speech in the room was bullshit. Really Mystical, why now?" I asked.

She looked off into the distance, walked over to the railing and turned her back to me. "When I saw the credit card statement I noticed something. There was a purchase made at Tiffany's. At first, I thought it was some mistake, because I knew for damn sure I didn't buy anything. Then I tried calling you at work, but you were in the middle of a lunch rush. So I called Tiffany's myself…" she said.

"You found out about the ring," I said, feeling a little hopeful.

"You know I don't believe in marriage. I've always told you that I didn't want to get married. Now you want to force it on me."

You can't make a person do what they don't want to do. Sure, I knew that she didn't want to get married. We discussed it on various occasions and always with the same result. She considered marriage to be some type of invisible prison. The idea of two different people coming together and forming one heart, one mind and one resolve wasn't natural to her. She said it when she met my parents, she said that they weren't happy and they were married not because of love but out of routine.

Mystical was a throwaway. Men abused and used her during her entire life. She had never met her father, only knew he was black because of her ethnic features. And her mother's boyfriends raped her repeatedly during her childhood. In her mind men were evil, made me wonder what she had ever seen in me. However, her past had only intensified my love. The prospect of being the person that made her see the light was what kept me going. I realized then that I wasn't hurt because she was leaving; I was hurt because I had failed. She was my reclamation project.

"I know that all the men you've ever known have fucked you over, but I didn't, does that mean anything?" I asked.

She stared at me for the first time. The glazed over look in her eye told me that behind her rigid stance that there was still some type of love. She couldn't dispute the love I had shown her, but she remained speechless.

"My love for you is so real that I can forgive. We can get past this, work this out. Just try on the ring, if you want to leave after trying it on then I will forever hold my silence. I will forgive you either way. My love is that real," I said, feeling my own eyes begin to water.

She put out her hand, I ran into the living room. There was an inkling of hope; her tears had finally come up. They were there at the corners of her eyes; she didn't fight them. As her chest heaved up and down in anticipation, Sandra came out the room. All three of us stood in frozen silence. My eyes were on Mystical, so was Sandra's, but Mystical seemed confused as her eyes went back and forth between her two lovers. She was going to make her decision, for one of us would mean heartbreak.

She took one step towards me, stopped then took one step toward Sandra, but she didn't stop this time and without hesitation, they intertwined hands. Her decision had been made in less than a split second, in that small amount of time she had summed up our three years together.

I got on my knees as tears ran down my cheeks, with my throat feeling like I was trying to swallow razors. Under the sofa by the door was where I hid the ring. I crawled to it, retrieved it and crawled to the door.

"Please, I promise I will never bring this up again if you marry me."

Sandra was dressed in a business suit with her hair pulled in a ponytail looking like a lawyer and not the whore that had broken up my home. She grabbed Mystical's hand tighter and stood behind her. Mystical looked at me, not with a conflicted stare, but one filled with pity.

"Do you love me?" I asked as the last resort.

"She not want ju no more," Sandra said. If I wasn't so weak, I would've gotten my Ginsu knife and sliced her into shreds.

"I didn't ask you," I responded weakly as phlegm clogged up my throat. I looked up at Mystical and that cold gaze once again resided on her face.

"I want to be with her," she said. She left leaving me a shell of a man. In my heart, I hated her. Because of her, my parents were right like usual. Because of her, I'd lost the only two people that cared for me. Not only did I alienate my parents but my family as a whole. Because of her, I could never show them my face.

Jared died that day. Sometimes I wonder if I would have been better off sharing her than not having her at all.

"Familiar Faces."

Angelica

When I walked through the door, I was shocked to see Aurelius standing over the range oven looking off into space. I didn't expect him to even be here, but I was happy that he was around. Just as I laid my keys down and picked up my mail from the floor, the pan he was slaving over caught fire. That woke his ass up right away, it was as if he had no knowledge of the damage he was about to do to my kitchen. As he fought off the flames with a pot cover, he burned the tips of his fingers.

"Are you alright?" I asked, walking up to him and grabbing his hand out of instinct.

"Oh shit. Fuck," he said, snapping back to reality.

Like a mother taking care of her child, I led him to the faucet and ran cold water over his fingers. The damage wasn't as bad as I suspected. They were only superficial.

"What the hell is going on?" I asked, taking my time as I covered his burn with a sterile pad.

I was surprised he wasn't crying bloody murder. Men act like children when they are in pain, but I didn't hear a peep from him. I felt self-conscious, because I could feel him staring at me while I took care of his burn. Damn he smelled good, I thought. Whatever he was wearing, made me want to take hours fixing his wound. But I was finished in less than a minute and standing in front of my refrigerator hoping to cool down my damn self.

"Thanks," he said, sitting down at the table and staring at his hands.

"You gotta be more careful. You got diabetes or something, because your hand was in that fire for a good while," I said, taking bottled water from the refrigerator and sitting in the chair across from his. With my air ventilation still broken, I was beginning to feel sweaty in all the wrong places.

"I'm cool. Guess my thoughts got the best of me."

"Who is he?" I asked. It was a bit intrusive to ask but I needed to know if he had someone special in his life, and if he did, who was he?

He shook his head, and then started to laugh. Did I say something funny?

"You know how to bring a brotha to his knees," he said. After thinking about the connotations of what he had said, we both broke out in laughter.

It was one of my Dr Jekyll, Mrs. Hyde type days and all I wanted to do was laugh. Aurelius also made me feel comfortable. Not to mention I hadn't touched a man's hand in a few years.

"I don't mean to jump to conclusions. But I just thought..."

"I understand, because you ain't the first person that thought I was gay. But get this, tongue rings aren't just for sucking dick. Last time I checked, women like the way it feels as well," he said, sticking out his tongue.

Normally I would've felt offended, probably would've kicked him out like I did the day before, but his raw language got me horny. It was probably the way the word dick rolled off his juicy lips. Maybe it was because when he said it he was staring into my eyes, or maybe because *his* dick had never left my mind.

"So who is she?"

"She's no one worth mentioning," he said, pulling his seat closer to mine. I started to rub my neck, crossed my legs and looked away because it was beginning to get hotter. If he made a move, there was no way I could say no. Part of me wanted him to touch me, but the reasonable, godly side of me reminded me that I was taken.

"How did you meet Titus?" I asked, trying to make friendly conversation.

Aurelius stood, walked into the kitchen and removed his chef's jacket. He was wearing a wife-beater underneath, and looked as if he hit the gym hard everyday. I nearly gagged on the last of my water as I noticed him flexing his muscles when he placed the pot he burned into the sink, ran hot water on it and began to scrub it with a Brillo pad.

"To be honest, Angelica, I'd rather get to know you better, than talk about someone we both already know. I believe in discovering new horizons and not traveling back to old ones."

"Tell me something about yourself." I asked.

"Ladies first," he said. There was that sexy mysterious part of him bubbling to the surface again.

To my surprise, there was nothing I could say, it had been so long since a man even asked me about *me*. Though I was engaged to Titus, he avoided ever asking me about my past. It seemed to me that somewhere deep inside his heart he didn't want to know. Maybe he felt the less he knew the easier it would be to trust me.

"You got time." I smiled almost sure that he didn't want to be loaded down by my issues. He smiled and after realizing that people didn't gravitate to me, I wanted to open up if only to show I am human.

"All the time in the world," he said holding up the pan and showing me the caked in grease.

"One second, let me get ready," I said, walking into my room and locking the door behind me.

My one second turned into thirty minutes. If anything, I wanted to be fresh, because you never know. By the time I was ready, he had already cleaned my kitchen and was sitting in my living room. His wife beater was still on, showing off his sexy body as the stereo played an oldie station. While he listened to Smokey Robinson, he sipped on a glass of red wine. I wore an over sized t-shirt and a pair of basketball shorts and had my hair pulled into a tight ponytail.

"You need some life in here. If I hadn't met you, I would've automatically thought you were white and old," he said looking around my plain living room. It wasn't like he was lying, but I was never the domestic type. I thought black leather and white walls gave my living room a modern type of vibe.

"Why don't you give me some tips then, Martha Stewart?" I joked as I sat on the ottoman across from the sectional he was sitting on.

"First off, you need some pictures of people. I don't mean the ones that come in the frames. I mean people you love. I'm sure your mother would have a total different vision for this room."

I put my head down; little did he know the only rooms my mother decorated since my birth came with steel bars.

"Can't have pictures of what you don't have."

"Oh, I'm sorry."

"There's no reason to apologize because nothing's your fault," I said. The room got silent; I could tell I touched a sensitive spot. Though I was never one to beg for pity, at that moment, I felt pity for myself.

He got up, sat on the arm of my chair and showed me two of his tattoos. "My parent's aren't around either. They died about five years ago. These are their pictures. Though they aren't here, it's good to keep them close."

"Your Mother's beautiful and you look exactly like your dad," I consoled as I looked into his eyes.

His eyes started to glaze over; like I had unearthed a memory, he wished to forget. I didn't know what to do, never remember knowing a man who had ever shown an ounce of emotion. Grabbing his arm was the only thing I could do to show him how sorry I felt. We both stared at each other. If we were dating, I was sure a kiss would've been a formality, but we weren't and I was promised to someone else.

"I was adopted. I lived my life in and out of foster care wishing I had met them. I learned that my father is alive, though. What I'm trying to say is, even though your parent's aren't here now, think about the memories you had and not the ones you missed."

I felt embarrassed by my actions the day before, because I didn't realize the motivation behind his actions. Here I was thinking he was a conceited ass, but in reality, he was dealing with pain he could never really get over. Same as I had throughout my life. We were kindred spirits walking the earth alone.

"Since you know your mother's alive why not find her?" he asked. Once again, he was looking deeper than any man I had ever known. And I liked that, because it felt like he wanted to know the real me.

I stood, turned down the stereo, sat on the floor and crossed my legs. I always felt that the less people there are in your life, the more uncomplicated it becomes. Last week I got some information as to where my mother is, but for some reason I don't want to go any further," I shrugged.

"You know how you said I look like my father?"

"Yeah, I remember." I wondered where he was getting at.

"Ever wonder what makes you, you? Maybe by meeting her you can discover more of yourself."

"Yeah, but she's all the way in Philly. I got a wedding to plan. And with Titus out of the country, I can't see myself going up there alone." I made excuses as to why I didn't want to go.

"Let's make a trip of it," he offered.

"And what you think Titus would have to say about that?"

"Nothing, we're here alone now, with a bed less than ninety feet away, yet were only talking, right?"

He made his point and it wasn't like Titus was checking on me anyway. In his absence, I was beginning to get used to him not being around.

"Am I that unattractive that I'm not even seduction worthy?" I flirted a little. There was nothing wrong with being a compliment seeker. All I wanted to know was if he was attracted to me. "If I said yes, would it matter?"

We talked well into the morning. And not once did the conversation veer of course into something sexual. He even looked into my eyes when we talked, not at my breasts or ass. I knew that behind his suppressed stare therein lied attraction. That was what separated him from Titus; he made me feel like a woman.

I was neck deep into work when Aurelius came into my home office. I just got the merchandising plans for the next buying season from the accounting department and was already feeling like committing suicide. A lot was riding on this particular six-month plan, because if I didn't make merchandise manager and Alexis did. I would come back to bite me in the ass. The season's projected figures had to be as close as possible to the actual figures or I would be responsible for heavy losses. Reba understood when I came up short, but Alexis would have my job because of any miscalculations.

He watched me for a moment, but his lingering stare was starting to make me self-conscious and I hated being stared at. I could sense his gaze from the corner of my eyes. It wasn't like I was looking sexy, I had tied a scarf around my head and put on a beat up pair of pajama pants to go with my oversized t-shirt.

"Can I help you?" I asked looking up from my laptop.

A film of perspiration coated his skin. He wore only a t-shirt treating, to the outline of his upper body. The aroma of sweat mixed with cologne was in the air. He rubbed his chin. I didn't notice the goatee he was now growing before as I ate dinner, but it gave him a more robust appeal. Normally I abhorred facial hair, but it made his soft features more masculine and went well with his tattoos.

I loved pretty boys but secretly fantasized about making love to a blue-collar man, a blue-collar man that didn't give a damn about a manicure or a pedicure and kept his body in shape not from working out, but because of work. Aurelius resembled that type of man, at that moment.

"I put the dishes in the dishwasher and wanted to say bye. You gonna be fine?" he asked with concern

"Bye." I said, taking my eyes off him and back to my work.

He didn't move, I could tell there was something else he had to ask and I didn't have time to waste, so I closed my laptop and sighed heavily.

"Yes?" I asked in a nasty voice.

"I was tinkering with different desserts for your wedding and I thought you might like this," he said, handing me a small bonbon cup filled with red rose blossoms and a white liquid.

"This doesn't look appetizing at all."

"Try it first before you pass judgment," he said waiting for me to partake. "You know what? I'll serve it to you so you don't look at it all day," he said, taking the cup from my hand.

He put his hand on my forehead and gently pushed my head back as he poured the liquid into my mouth. He drizzled some of the liquid down the sides of my mouth, then took his index fingers and wiped them clean. The white chocolate was delectable and the flowers were edible.

"That was better than I thought," I admitted.

"Just like you," he mentioned.

"You really think I'm a good person after all the nonsense I put you through your first day here? Everyone at my job thinks I am the biggest B.I.T.C.H to walk the earth. And

Titus's congregation treats me no better," I said, looking at the intentional puzzled look on his face.

We both laughed, it felt good to smile and it was something he constantly brought out of me. I lived life with a stern look and disposition, acting as if my façade was impenetrable. However, a lot of pain lived within me. By not allowing people in, I never had any real friends and the one friend I had, I lost.

"We all are allowed a bad day or two." He opened one of the folding chairs leaning against the wall and sat next to me.

"You're only saying that because I'm paying you." "First of all, Titus is paying me, but I'm saying it because it's true. Look at you; you're a strong sista that has accomplished great things coming from nothing. I say the people at your job fear you because of what you represent. You're getting married to the man of your dreams and got the dream job to match. And you don't think people envy that?"

"What would they envy?" I asked wanting to know why anyone would want what I have.

"Everyone in this world would like to be rich materially. Money is the root of all evil, and we live in an evil ass world, but the one thing that can't be bought no matter how much money a person has is love. Ever watch a beautiful car driving down the street and feel a part of you telling you that you have to have it?" he asked, I shook my head yes. He leaned back in the chair put his right leg over his left knee and held his chin in his hand. Continuing he said, "That's the brain talking. Compare that to watching a couple walking down the street holding hands with stars in their eyes, spewing loving rhetoric, a part of you says you've got to have it also. That's your heart speaking. You can bribe the brain all day by buying things that you think will compensate for that empty feeling. The heart, you can't bribe that no matter what you do. You can substitute the person you love with someone better both physically and spiritually, but like an incompatible body part, your body will reject it. People are puzzles and we are born with a missing piece. That's why when you find the right person it makes you better; accentuating your qualities while covering over your faults and there's no substitute for that. I am sure when people see you with the Reverend they envy you because you have found the piece that completes you. We live on food, water and love. Without those three ingredients we can't live. "

At a lost for words, all I could do was stare at him. His words were profound and resonated deep within me. For all my years in college, he made me feel ignorant, because I could have never verbalized those feelings if I rationalized the meaning of life for the rest of my years.

He slapped his hand across his shoe, sighed as if he had just released all that he held in and stood up. "Now, I'll bid you farewell," he said, walking out my office, leaving behind an impression and food for thought.

The next day when I arrived home after a long day of setting up new merchandise on the sales floor and re-checking the stock room delivery by hand, I was starved. I unlocked my front door in anticipation of Aurelius's presence. I thought on what he had to say the day before and came to the conclusion that I hadn't found my missing piece. How could I if I wasn't happy? Titus like other men before him wanted to control me. I loved god, but I was becoming something that I didn't want to be. Gone were the days when I lived for a good time. What I considered fun, Titus considered a waste of time. Daniel was right, I wasn't me.

I placed my keys and my Berkin bag on the granite countertop as Aurelius chopped onions. His sleeves were rolled up and the muscles in forearms expanded and contracted with each chop. A stained towel rested above the side of his shoulder and he smiled as I took a whiff of the sauce he was stirring.

"Smells good. Try it," he said while stirring it with a wooden spoon. He then took a spoonful and gave me a taste. I closed my eyes and savored the full-bodied flavor.

"You ain't ever lie," I said bending over and, taking off each shoe one by one. I was on my feet all day and needed to sit down

I could feel his eyes on my ass, and wondered if he could see the outline of my red thong through the white material of my mini skirt. I looked behind me, caught him staring and licking his lips. His face became flush from embarrassment, as he looked the other way. I knew I had him if I wanted, but I'd let him suffer before deciding whether or not I wanted to give him a sample of my desserts.

"Come here," he commanded.

I didn't take kind to that. Playing the little submissive Reverend's Fiancé wasn't a label I liked anymore. I sat down and rolled my eyes, sucking my teeth like he was on my last nerve.

"Excuse me?" I asked, daring him to treat me like a piece of property.

"Please, could you come here? I want to show you something."

I took my time getting up. When I finally approached him, he handed me a knife. What the hell was he up to? I couldn't cook and the only time I ever had any use for a knife was to cut off the plastic on my microwaveable dinners. He had to be insane putting a sharp object in my hand.

"I'm not in the business of taking advantage of my clients, so when I can teach them how to prepare their own meals I take the time to show them. The first time I came in your kitchen, I thought it was a waste that you owned top of the line appliances but you had never used them. If I can teach you one thing before my time is up, it can open up new possibilities for you. There's nothing sexier than a woman that can throw down. Though you have the market cornered on sexy, I'm sure the Reverend would appreciate a home cooked meal from time to time," he said while cleaning off the countertop unaware of the smile on my face.

His words were like poetry, flowing off the tips of his tongue like sugar, leaving behind a pleasant after taste. I heard every pick up line in the book, listened to every excruciatingly trite come on. However, each utterance from his juicy lips had a genuine meaning. His endearing comments were a breath of fresh air in a world of trifling ass men that thought chivalry was a disease.

He placed a wooden cutting board on the countertop, took a green pepper from a brown paper bag, inspected it for imperfections and ran it under hot water. Then he hollowed the pepper out and removed the seeds, never looking rushed, always taking his time. He was armed with patience, something few men knew anything about. Grabbing me gently by the waist, he placed the pepper in the center of the cutting board and took my hand. Holding my wrist, we sliced the pepper into quarters, sliced those quarters in half and diced them into the sauce. He replaced the knife with the wooden spoon and we stirred the sauce together.

"Wasn't that easy?" he asked as he took the spoon from the sauce and fed it to me once again.

"I need you…I mean I needed to learn that. I mean that tasted good," I couldn't believe what I had just said by mistake.

His chest rested on my back and his minty breath tickled the hairs on the back of my neck. There was nothing on the cutting board or anything else to stir but we still held hands. I could feel him getting hard making my ass the resting place for his endless longness. There was a carnal silence between us and as he took hold of my other wrist, I could feel my clit become swollen and my panties become saturated.

He used his pelvis to grind against my ass, while bending me over the countertop. The tip of his dick rubbed against the back of my pussy through the fabric of our clothing. My mouth could not trap the moan that managed to escape and my hands could not stop from intertwining with his as he thrust into me forcefully. I wanted him in me, yearned to feel that fleshy part of a man invade my walls again.

He got on his knees, feasted on my wetness through the fabric of my red thong. After getting acclimated to that part of me, he ran his tongue over my ass then used his teeth to leave bite marks up and down each of my cheeks.

"I'll... stop... if…you…want…me…to," he said between each kiss on the back of my knees.

I didn't say anything. I figured if I said yes I would really be cheating. This could easily be explained as a misunderstanding since I wasn't the one doing the actual kissing. It wasn't like I had asked him to get on his knees and explore my behind.

My mind and the fire between my legs were in a battle of wills. My mind wanted to stop and filled my head with thoughts of Titus. My pussy on the other hand didn't give a damn what my mind said.

Then the timer sounded, dinner was ready and our sexual appetites had to wait until another time when they could be satisfied.

Four weeks Tilll…

When I woke up this morning, I was feeling great. After the buyers meeting at work, it was going to be an easy day, because all I had to do was attend the rest of fashion week, which was only a hop, skip and a jump from my front door. One of the Senior VP's of Neiman Marcus was going to make a stop at the store and filling the merchandise managing position was most likely the reason for his visit.

As I arrived at my office, my administrative assistant informed me of a surprise guest. I opened my door and was surprised to see my ex-boyfriend standing over my desk with a vase filled with yellow roses.

"You look as stunning as the last time I remember," he smiled, walking to me and handing me the roses along with a kiss on the cheek.

"Brice, how has life been treating you?" I cooed in an ultra feminine voice even though he was one of the last people I wanted to ever see again.

Brice Denner was tall, light and fine, the Shemar Moore type. He was also one of the prettiest men I'd ever seen and he knew it. It had been four years since the last time we'd actually spoken and our relationship didn't end on the best of terms. After fucking him for more than a year, I finally got a conscience when his wife found out. Brice could've cared less and since I was no longer putting out he no longer felt the need to call me. It made our work relationship uncomfortable. After he was transferred from my store, we never saw each other again.

Now he was standing in my office looking stellar dressed in a Brooks Brothers black suit, with a crisp white shirt and a red tie. His hair was cut low and he wore a thinly trimmed beard. The rugged look suited him well, gave him more character, but the smile on his face was one I'd seen before; it was the same smile that once upon a time gave him access to every orifice on my body.

"What you have done with yourself is pretty impressive, Angie," he remarked, looking me up and down.

It was in his nature to woo women; he had a natural knack for flattery. It wasn't like I was wearing anything special. As a matter of fact, I was dressed casually in an ivory lace camisole with spaghetti straps and a pair of black washed Rock and Republic skinny pants. So, I wasn't paying his compliment any mind.

"So what brings you back to your old stomping grounds?" I asked

"You know nothing but business. It's seems like business is the only thing I have time for anymore. And you know it's not healthy to live without any…fun," he said in a seductive mumble as his eyes rested between my legs.

"And how's your wife?" I interjected. He cleared his throat and gave a nervous smirk.

"She's in Seattle where I left her," he snapped with an attitude. Nothing had changed about him, still the same Brice.

I took off the Gucci purse from around my shoulder and sat behind my desk. It wasn't that I didn't want to catch up, but not with a jerk with his eyes on the prize between my legs.

"You must have a reason for coming here besides telling me how good I look."

"Like I said, I'm here to take care of business." He stated, making himself at home in one of my chairs. He crossed his legs; let the sleeve of his suit jacket fall to reveal a Davis Yurman Titanium watch and began to whistle. "So Angie, is it true you're going to be taking that fall?"

"What fall?"

"That marriage bullshit. For better or worse, till death do us part. All that fantasy land jazz."

I once thought I loved this man, the person he pretended to be when I met him was unlike anyone I'd ever met. Everything he did was romantic. He prepared picnics in the park, made love to me in broad daylight on well-traveled country roads, and sent me flowers just because. Then he changed, treated me like I was good only to blow his load. Afterwards, the flowers disappeared, the picnics vanished and all he wanted to do was fuck. It was because of that lie that I chose celibacy.

"A fantasy for some is a reality for others. You should know that," I said

He laughed, didn't take my words seriously, cackled like they were down right silly to his ears, and wiped his brow with his pocket square.

"You're an optimist just like my wife. The truth is, the only thing that separates men that cheat from men who don't, is opportunity. *You* should know that."

"I'm sure you would know all about infidelity."

"I'm not here to debate. My sole purpose was to take you on a business date. And since you are one of the candidates for Reba's position, I thought it would be good if I got to know more about you."

" Haven't I already let you into my head once? Besides, I doubt you have the authority."

"As Vice President of strategic planning, I think I have a huge say into who gets that job. Is six o clock good for you tomorrow evening?" Brice smiled extracting a Cohiba cigar from his inner pocket and letting it rest on the side of his lips. "Do I have a choice?" I wondered.

He removed the cigar from his lips, held it on the tips of his fingers, "No, no you don't. Since you are going to be in the city, meet me at Nobu 57, I have reservations." He stood, arrogantly smiled and walked to my door. "And please don't be late. You know how I hate to...wait."

"Only you"

Aurelius

Mistress Alek started the evening off by letting me give oral servitude. It was out of the ordinary for her, because I usually had to put in an inordinate amount of work in order to taste the tartness of her clit. Since I started seeing her, our sessions usually began with unusual forms of capital punishment, followed by more painful forms of torture, pleasure was the least on her sadistic menu. I hoped she wasn't getting soft on me; I didn't pay her to be soft, I employed her to inflict harsh pain.

She dominated me for almost three years. Out of all the Dominatrix that I had the opportunity to serve, she was the most vicious. Some would catch feelings, others wanted to see me outside of our business arrangement, but Mistress Alek never relented nor got out of character. I loved that, in our world there was no place for the faint of heart.

The tactics I employed when serving my Mistress was much more thorough than most men had time to execute. Being a Submissive taught me how to control my lust. When your dick is incased in a ring, it becomes necessary to take your mind to a different place. And I possessed the sort of mind control most men would never understand.

Mistress Alek loved when I gave her oral servitude, if not for the strict code of ethics in the world of S&M, I was positive she'd have me do it all the time. One of my most unusual fetishes had to be the fact that I loved the smell of a woman's pussy after they have worked up a sweat. It was nature's fragrance. And Mistress unknowingly provided me with a fix.

I took three of my fingers and stuffed them in and out of her with caution. Mistress Alek hated to be rushed and as I lubricated my extremities with her juices, I could tell she was near orgasm. Her clit was the size of a child's pinky, one of the biggest I'd ever seen and when I was feasting on it the right way, she would squirt her juices like a geyser.

She leaned her head back, let her hair fall and savored my mastery. Her long nails pierced my back as she held on, she wasn't one to come easily, but I wasn't one to give up. This was when my tongue ring came in handy and with a slight flick of it I had her jerking her head back and forth like a possessed woman.

"Oh.Oh.Oh Aurelius," she moaned, sounding like a dominated woman if only for a moment. She didn't scream my name, she sung it. Letting the syllables roll off her tongue like a sweet taste.

She didn't want to come, tried to cut off my circulation with her legs. But her efforts proved fruitless and within moments she came on my face. I cleaned the sticky fluid off my cheeks with my fingers and consumed it with my tongue.

After her seeming satisfaction, I led her to the bathroom, crawled across the cold tiles as she stood on my back with her bare feet. A huge fog of steam billowed out as I opened the door. The bathroom was misty due to the steam rising from the bathtub. Mistress Alek liked her water hot and if for some reason it didn't meet her taste, she would dispense a full measure of cock and ball torture and though I looked forward to it on most nights, tonight I was eager to end our two-hour session.

Like a Great Dane, her body moved fluidly when she squeezed out of her corset and discarded her ass less leather chaps. When she winced as she stuck her long, muscular legs into the Victorian slipper tub, I knew I had met her expectations.

"Slave, wash me!" she commanded, letting her head float above the water.

I poured bath salts into the water, applied bath gel to her sponge and began the cleaning process. There was nothing sensual about the act of bathing Mistress Alek. I didn't dare touch between her thighs, across her breast or on the back of her neck unless she commanded me. As her slave, I kept silent, abstained from looking her in the eye and did as told.

For some unknown reason, Angelica invaded my thoughts. Today in particular it was happening frequently and as I bathed the Mistress, I imagined I was bathing her.

The session ended without much fanfare. For once, it didn't feel as refreshing as it usually did afterwards. As I gathered my things from the Mistress' dungeon, a light tap on my shoulder startled me.

"Aurelius, I think it would be best if we parted ways," the Mistress said, dressed in tight fitting jeans and a camisole. Her face makeup was gone, revealing a natural beauty.

I didn't know how to respond, my first reaction was to guard my face because she never conversed with me unless it was followed by a harsh reprimand.

The only word I could muster was "Why?"

"It's my policy that I terminate any agreement with any of my submissives if I can no longer reach them." She spoke in a professional tone and not the belittling growl that I was used to.

Was she blind or on drugs? Because I didn't do anything but serve her perfectly. She didn't even have to discipline me at all during our session.

"I don't understand. Every thing went smoothly," I said, bewildered.

Without her costume, she looked ordinary. If I had met her on the street, I wouldn't believe that she was the type of woman that enjoyed pain. Rather, I could see her as a career-woman, someone who was held in high regard in her other life.

"Exactly and that's the problem. Most subs are disobedient on purpose. It's not that they can't understand my orders. It's that they take pleasure in my discipline." She looked me in the eyes, treating me like an equal.

"There's no problem," I said, looking downwards.

With her hands, she lifted my chin upwards, "I see it in your eyes. Someone else has become your obsession."

"But I want to continue. I need to continue." I tried to coerce her into believing me.

"Have you been seeing someone else? You can't serve two masters and I will not share you with another Domina."

Though I hated to admit it, there was truth to her argument. Last night when I talked to Angelica, there was a connection like I had never felt before. There was something hidden beneath her egocentric demeanor that glowed. Maybe it was her past and the revelation that she wasn't this holier than thou figure that I implicated her of being. I wanted to be with her, even if my fantasies were never to be realized.

When I came to Mistress Alek, I wanted to be healed. Healed in the sense that I didn't want to hurt for a woman I could never have again. During my sessions, I learned how to hide those feelings, learned how to bury them so deep that I couldn't even tap into them. When someone treats you like dirt, over time a person will realize he's worth more. Now I had feelings of déjà vu, because Angelica wasn't available. Like Mystical, her love had already been procured. Yet I had allowed her soul to touch mine and permitted thoughts of her to enter my realm of tranquility.

"I haven't found another Domina. I just met someone special."

"Most of my clients are men or women who have lost the hope of love. They are in either unhappy marriages or looking for an escape from an unhappy life. When I look into eyes brimming with hope, then I know I've done my job. I just wish you well and hope to never see you again." She kissed me on the cheek and sent me off.

In a world filled with taboos, S&M helped me discover my inner peace. Some may wonder how a slap to the face or being used as a toilet could help an already fucked up individual find inner harmony. I would respond to those people by saying pain breeds either death or life. Mistress Alek's whips, paddles and floggers had finally resurrected the dead man within. I experienced death when Mystical left me, now I wanted to live.

It was a little over seven in the evening when I arrived at Angelica's place. I got caught in traffic on the way from my session with Mistress Alek. Though Angelica specified in her contract that I have her meals prepared in a timely manner, I was sure when she tasted my spicy vegetarian chili, tardiness would be the last thing on her mind. Besides, after our great conversation last night I liked to think that we'd developed a nice rapport.

As I chopped onions and smashed cloves of garlic, I heard the jingle of keys. The door opened and Angelica entered, looking as radiant as usual. I smiled and watched when she closed the door and sashayed across the foyer like a seasoned model. There was no smile back. It didn't seem like she was happy to see me at all.

She entered the kitchen, slammed her brief case on the dinning room table and glared at me with hands on hips.

"That's why it doesn't pay to fraternize with the help. You people like to take advantage when someone's nice enough to treat you like equals," she hissed.

"Hello to you as well," I said jokingly, but she wasn't cracking a smile. "Did I miss something?" I asked still not sure if she was serious or joking.

"I waited more than two hours for you. I called your office and your cellular, but you didn't pick up. When I come home after a long day of work, I expect to have something to eat." She rolled her eyes, tapped her heels against the floor and looked at her watch. "Weren't you supposed to be here by six?" She didn't even wait for my explanation, just walked out the kitchen and slammed her bedroom door behind her.

I was beginning to think that maybe she should've hired a shrink instead of a personal chef. Her moods fluctuated from one extreme to the other too much. It felt like she took satisfaction in giving hope and then taking it away. I excused her dramatic attitude shifts because I knew there was something hurting her.

I remembered how mad my mother would get if my father forgot their anniversary or any other event with sentimental value. She would clean the house with her lips pursed, wipe the wood furniture with excessive force and throw anything my father had lying around into the garbage. For years, I thought she was crazy, until I had a relationship of my own. I realized then that women valued time above anything else, over money and over sex. And when a man consistently slighted them, they no longer felt wanted or needed. I wanted to express to Angelica that she was wanted.

Angelica came out her bedroom, closed the bathroom door and turned the shower on as her melodious singing voice mixed with the bathroom acoustics. There was no moment better than that moment. As I walked up to the bathroom door, I started to undress. In the past, I would've left, taken her attitude as a sign to depart. But I knew women, knew how they pained when their man wasn't around and didn't care. My absence ran Mystical in the arms of another. Thus, I knew Angelica needed me now.

I took off my chef's checks and my jacket, laid them in a pile at the foot of her bathroom door. They were the only clothes I had worn since I didn't wear underwear and it was too hot for an undershirt. I touched the knob, let it turn and let myself in. There she was, naked behind a translucent shower curtain, bending over and soaping her long legs with a washcloth. She didn't hear me enter, for the shower was on full blast and my steps were light.

When I pulled the curtain back, her eyes widened with shock, her lips said no, but her eyes said yes. Taking the washcloth from her hands, I kissed her tenderly on her breast. Her breathing was labored, hard and short. It was like she had never been touched before. With my tongue, I relieved her worries, sweeping across her wet nipples until they became hard in my mouth. She stood stiffly with her hands at her side, not inviting me in yet but not fighting me off.

"Should... I... Leave?" I asked between kisses to her torso.

I stuck my tongue in her belly button and swirled it around as I held on to her hips. Soapy water trailed down my face, got into my eyes and burned. Still she was rigid, without a sound emanating from her mouth or without a movement.

I kissed from her left thigh, down her kneecap and to her feet. She held the shower rod as I took each of her toes into my mouth. Then I licked a trail from her right foot, up her kneecap and across her thigh. Her breathing was jagged and shorter, anticipating what I would do next.

"Should...I...Leave?" I asked again as my tongue made it up to her bush. I inhaled her scent and savored it for she smelled like sex. And I got on my knees, spread her lips apart, took her clit into my mouth, and tasted her bath water as it rolled down her labia. Her labia was a dark shade of black, matching her nipples and the place between her thighs where her legs spread

"Ahhhh," she moaned. The sound of her pleasure was like music to my ears. She placed her hands on my head just when my tongue penetrated her tightness. I steadied her body with my arms, wanted to protect her from falling while I fed on her ebony.

Her inner pussy was very moist, for her levees hadn't been broken in years. The water continued to pound down on top of us, beads of it residing in her pubic hair and congregating in my afro.

"I shouldn't be doing this," she lamented halfheartedly.

Her words were meaningless; she didn't want me to stop. What she meant to say was that she should have done this a long time ago. Her pussy lips had never been kissed by lips like mine. If it were a woodwind instrument, I would be playing the philharmonic, composing a song between her thighs the likes of which John Coltrane could never understand.

I penetrated her with my hooked finger and searched for that elusive g spot. When I found that spongy part of her, I applied pressure while lightly flicking my tongue across her swelled clit. Every woman's movements are different, some swirl their hips against the tongue and others grind against it. Angelica was the swirling type.

While I systematically satisfied her with my hand and tongue, her knees began to give way underneath her. I spread her legs apart, put them over my shoulders and lifted her into the air all the while never missing a beat with my tongue. Minutes later, her body started to twitch and her legs began to shake. I knew she was coming, yet I couldn't stop and as I continued, she let out a scream.

"Titus…It feels sooooo goood."

The words in itself didn't bother me. It was the fact that throughout my demonstration all she could think about was Titus. I had put in the work and he was receiving all the glory. I put her down, left her crumbled in the fetal position in the middle of her shower and collected my things.

"I wouldn't give a damn if my man said another person's name as long as I'm getting it good," Shane joked while leading me into his living room. "Why waste a good fuck over a misunderstanding?"

"That's because your man is married and in reality isn't really your man," I laughed as Shane swung his pink feather boa over his shoulder and in my face.

Shane's apartment was over the top extravagant. His living room alone was a decorator's nightmare. It was done in an African tribal motif, complete with a matching leopard skin rug and couch. Dark Brown velvet drapes hung from his windows with gold tassels, tribal masks lined his walls and Ela statues sat along the base of his coffee table. It was like being in the jungle and hideous at that. And the rest of his apartment wasn't much better.

"You are going back?" Shane asked as we both took a seat on his sofa.

"I don't think I could look her in the eye. Part of me feels like I took it too far."

Truthfully, I had never played the aggressor with a woman. Never had to, they usually sought me. I didn't know what overtook me, walking into her shower like that just wasn't my M.O. What would've happened if she resisted my advances? And to make it worse, what if I really had a chance with her? I was sure I had blown it.

"Can't look her in the eye. Hell, you went down on her and didn't ask for payback and you think she got a reason to complain."

Shane didn't understand. Angelica placed a very high standard on her morals. To her, sex wasn't something to be done leisurely. The act was supposed to be shared between two married individuals. And though I didn't believe in the covenant of marriage, I didn't feel it was right to pressure her with my own lustful ambitions.

"Fuck, I knew I should have done my job and not get involved the way I usually do."

"I don't know why you're killing yourself with all that self doubt, because if she didn't want it, she would have never taken that shower. What woman discards their clothes around a man they don't want? She could have waited till your ass left before she got into that shower."

"It doesn't make it right."

I leaned back on his couch, watched the ceiling and inwardly debated if I should go back and apologize

"Sweetest Kiss"

Angelica

While biting on the bottom of my lip, I tried to head off another rippling orgasm. Sitting in my tub with my hands in between my thighs, I could barely move. Aurelius had broken me down, turned me into an invalid with the touch of his unbelievingly long tongue. Now I felt silly for ever questioning the legitimacy of his tongue ring.

I heard the phone; it had been ringing for the last two minutes. Someone really wanted to get in touch with me and here I was in the middle of my tub hoping that another wave of pleasure would ripple forth. Knowing I couldn't stay in the tub forever, I finally decided to get up, rush into my room and pick up the blaring receiver. On weary legs, I sprinted into my bedroom, crawled onto my bed and grabbed the phone.

"Hello," I said, unsuccessfully trying to catch my breath.

"My Malaika mzuri. I've missed you," Titus said. I would know his voice in a crowd.

"What did you call me?"

"I called you beautiful angel in Swahili."

"I didn't know Swahili could sound so sexy."

"Not everyone in Africa speaks in clicks." He laughed. "God created all languages to be beautiful."

Didn't know how much comfort I took in speaking to him. His powerful voice put me at ease, but an unmitigated feeling of guilt possessed me. I hoped it wasn't discernable to the ear. Titus proved to be a man capable of exposing a person's true feelings and at the moment, my thoughts were as uncertain as ever.

"You don't know how much I missed you," I admitted, beaming as I got underneath the thousand thread sheets.

"I've missed you too. What have I missed? Fill me on everything that has transpired the last two weeks."

I instantly thought of Aurelius. But I cleared any thoughts of him out of my mind for the moment. "I've found my mother."

"That's nice. Did you like the flowers I sent?" He changed the subject.

Did he just say that's nice? Obviously, he didn't care.

"Did you hear me? I said I found my mother."

"I heard you, but what do you expect me to say? I don't know the woman and what do you even know about her for that matter?"

"She's my mother. Besides, don't you have a bible nearby since you can never speak to me from your own heart?"

"I speak the word of truth regardless of where it comes from. And there is no better truth than God's word. The truth is you've been better off without her. So let lying dogs be," he retorted callously.

"She's currently incarcerated and I was hoping we could visit her when you got back."

"Why do you have to know this woman? She didn't want to know you."

The line got quiet, and he hit a nerve. He said something I avoided saying to myself throughout my life. Without trying, I thought of Aurelius, wondered how he would've handled this situation. I'm sure he would have had something uplifting to say, made me feel optimistic instead of the way Titus was making me feel.

"I guess you're right," I said submissively like the Christian woman I was.

"Be patient, two weeks will go by quickly. Before you know it we'll be together again," Titus said, trying his best to lessen the blow.

"Two Weeks?"

There was a commotion on his end, I could hear him place his hand over the phone, heard the noise in the background grow weaker.

"That's why I called. The territory is vast and I think it's gonna take at least another week before I'm able to reach everyone," he said slightly above a whisper.

Fighting with him was out of the question. He always managed to make me feel selfish whenever I wanted more of his time.

"Can you talk? Why are you whispering? You aren't coming back until a few days before our wedding?" The questions came from my mouth in frenzy.

"I don't know what to say. You're more important to me than anything, but God's work has to be done. Besides, Sister Simpson has even pushed back her own commitments to stay longer."

"Sister Simpson has done what, is she with you?"

"Yes she is, only to help spread God's word. I called you to say hi, but if you want to fight then I think it's about time that we end this conversation," he chastised. The only thing Sister Simpson was thinking about spreading was her legs.

Jada Simpson was the harlot of our church. If pussy were a commodity, the market would have crashed because of her ass. She was one of those types that thought every time she sinned she could wash it away by giving the church a blank check. What really had me concerned was that Titus had once dated her; sometimes I wondered why they'd ever parted ways. One rumor that swirled around the congregation had them two going too far for Titus's taste. How far, I wasn't sure?

If Titus weren't such a naïve man, he would've considered the possibility that just maybe Jada wanted more than his time. With her there by his side playing the role of self-sacrificing sister of the year, maybe doing my thing with

Aurelius wasn't as bad as I thought. Payback's a bitch in Chanel pumps.

Nobu 57 was packed when I walked in. On a Friday night, it was the hottest ticket in New York City. The restaurant was gorgeously decorated. Seashells hung from the chandeliers, sake barrels stood high above the first floor bar, and terrazzo tiles served as the flooring of choice. The eclectic crowd of professionals, A- list celebrities and the social elite made it the place to be. Didn't know Brice had so much influence in this city. Usually in order to get a reservation you had to call a month in advance.

Only the hip and wealthy were allowed to show their faces in the spectacular confines of its four walls. Yet, I appeared as anything but hip and wealthy. For a job interview, the best course of action was to dress modestly. Since it was a chilly June night, I wore a floral chiffon blouse and black velvet trousers. Didn't want to come off as the type of woman who used her assets to get what she wanted

The waiter led me to a private dining room on the second floor. As I entered the room, Brice stood with an ear-to-ear grin on his face. He could always fit a suit and as I took an inventory of his navy blue Brooks Brothers' single breasted, I was reminded of old times. Times in the past when he was all I ever thought about, hours that were wasted envisioning him in the buff holding a rock hard stiff one.

The soft lighting produced an alluring ambiance. R Kelly played in the background, singing songs of a sexual nature. Songs, which were candidly salacious. The message coming through the speakers fit Brice's libido to a tee. He was an upfront man; bashfulness was never his forte. A man who preferred fucking to making love.

The waiter led me to my seat, pulled it out and waited until I was comfortable. "May I get you both something to drink?"

He asked. Brice took his seat, took a long velvet box from his inner pocket and placed it on the table.

Taking the menu from off the table and scanning the cocktail selection with my newly manicure fingers, I settled on a Matsuhisa Martini and he choose a Lychee Martini.

"I'm glad you were able to make it. And right on time like usual. You always *come* right on time," he said looking into my eyes with a galvanizing leer.

"What is that?" I said ignoring his honeyed words and directing my attention to the box.

"It's an early wedding present. I didn't get an invitation, so I thought I'd give it to you now," he said sliding the box across the table.

I wondered what was inside, picking up the box I noticed that it had a little weight to it. Without seeming too eager, I opened it. As I beheld the exquisite, flawless, diamond necklace, I could barely hide the stars in my eyes. I held it above my head, let the lighting hit the diamonds and watch them sparkle. Brice had exorbitant taste so I knew it wasn't cheap. Probably something I could barely afford on my six-figure salary.

"What is it for?" I wondered, placing the necklace back in its case. As the old saying goes, you don't get something for nothing.

The waiter came back with our drinks, placed them in front of us and stood to the side, "Have you decided what you want to order?"

Without hesitation or confirmation from me, Brice ordered for the both of us. "I'll have the rib eye beef dinner and the lady will have the lobster dinner."

"As I was saying, what is it for? You don't owe me anything."

"According to who? I don't think I ever got a chance to apologize for what I did to you."

"You mean, what you did to your wife," I said stating the plain facts.

Being a home wrecker was one of the most callous things I had ever done in my life. Never did I imagine myself addicted to the high that adultery had brought me. It was fun to me, calling his home and hanging up when his wife answered, fucking him in his marriage bed just minutes before she got home and to make it worse, I was willing to do anything to make him mine. It was our little secret and I cringed to think about what I would've done had our affair continued any longer.

"What I did to her is beside the point. She knew what I was before we got married. A leopard doesn't change its spots just because you have it trapped. But you, I lied to you. I should have never fucked with that other girl. "

"You don't even remember her name," I said.

"I only remember what's important. And she wasn't worth the lent on my dick. I've changed," he said in an unpleasant tone. "Oh, that's why you took me out instead of her," I said. Then we locked stares and I knew what he really was speaking about.

During our tumultuous two-year relationship, he treated me like his property. It was all right for him to go home to his wife, but if I'd even thought about having a man of my own, he would flip. Nothing steamed him more than the thought of losing control and whenever I stepped out of line, he would check me. First, it started off as heated words, then the hitting began and after he nearly choked me to death for going on a date with another man, I started to fear him. As I watched his demeanor, I could tell he was becoming frustrated. And he had the nerve to say he changed.

Why did people claim to change but still exhibited the same types of behavior? There was nothing different about him. There wasn't even remorse for his long-suffering wife. If he had *changed,* I would've suspected a little bit more devotion towards his better half. As it was, he hadn't changed at all.

The waiter came back, placed the food in front of us and we began to eat. I wasn't particularly thrilled by my entree. Aurelius could cook circles around the chef that cooked my lobster any day. That's why I didn't mind when Brice started to eat off my plate. He thought I was being nice or had forgiven him for what he did years ago. But no, Aurelius was on my mind.

We discussed the job requirements, but it was only procedure. Brice had other aspirations. After a few drinks, his intentions became clear. I knew him, could see it in his eyes as he looked at me. A blank look resided on his face whenever I opened my mouth and tried to sell him on my ability to perform the job. He could've cared less whether or not I was qualified as long as we ended the night together.

We passed the rest of the time talking about my impending wedding. To his dismay, I discussed my newfound faith. I didn't want to lead him on or give him the impression that I was the same person he once knew. When I divulged to him my decision to be celibate until marriage, it took the wind out of his sails. To seal the deal, I even invited him to church the next time he was in the city.

After dinner ended, I was ready to get back to my life. Eating with him felt so awkward and I didn't like the tension building between us. "I gotta get back to the office to go over the weekly sales and stock reports," I said with a slight yawn.

"Well I'm going that way as well, I'll drop you off. You look ready to pass out"

"That's okay, Brice. I don't want to take you out of your way."

"No, it'll be my pleasure; my rental is parked around the corner. I'll drop you off and have a car take you back."

I had to admit the meal had made me tired. There was nothing wrong in accepting a ride from Brice. I doubted if he'd try anything before he dropped me off, at least not while I slept.

It was brisk as we walked along Hudson Street. Brice took off his jacket, draped it over my shoulder and rubbed my arms to warm me up. As I took in a whiff of his Grey Flannel, I couldn't help but be reminded about the past. I placed my head on his shoulder, feeling at home and secure in his embrace. It was the first time in a long time a man held me.

Maybe Brice was beginning to change. In public, he had always been so distant. Now he was showing affection without being overtly sexual. That was a step in the right direction. Hopefully he could continue his transformation when he got home to his wife.

Like he said, his car was parked around the corner. Once inside the vehicle, I reclined the seat shut my eyes and dozed off.

The mall was near closing when we got back. Brice insisted on walking me into the store, so as I opened my office door I was expecting to see him off. However, he had others ideas on his mind and I took notice as his hands grazed up my thigh.

"What in the hell are you doing?" I said as he began kissing me on the back of my neck.

"I am doing what we usually do," he said, while unbuttoning my pants.

I pulled away from him and ran around the other side of my desk to put distance between us.

"I knew this didn't come without strings attached." I took off the necklace he had given me and tossed it to him "You can have it if sex is what you had in mind when you gave it to me."

Brice loosened the Windsor knot on his tie, unbuttoned his French cuff shirt and unzipped his pants. "Like I said before,

I owe you that. But if you want this position, you're gonna owe me. Just like old times"

When he said that it was like old times, he wasn't lying. Five years ago when he was store manager, I used sex to go from the laborious job of Assistant Buyer to my current cushy position. That was how we started our affair and in the mist of my ambition, I fell in love. Back then, I had no qualms about using my pussy to jump ahead of the pack.

"Then you can take that job and stick it up your ass," I said as he came around the table and grabbed me by the waist.

"You don't mean that. I know you want this job, and I want you to have this job. You can walk out if you want. It's your choice." He waited for my answer, but knew me too well. I needed this job, it was my life.

He forced his tongue in my mouth, grabbed my arms forcefully and pushed his pelvis into mine. I wanted to fight him, but I couldn't, he was too strong. I froze up out of fear, knowing how violent he could get if he didn't get his way. He never had a problem hitting me across the face if I exhibited any independence.

He shook me with wide eyes. His face was stoic, angry and I knew there would be no dispute for he was going to get what he came for.

"Okay." I said timidly. I Stepped away from him and began to undress, first I pulled my camisole over my head. Then I pulled down my pants. I undressed slowly, taking each piece of clothing off one at a time. In the back of my mind I hoped he would find it in his heart to leave well enough alone, because if we started up, I didn't know if I could stop. He would open a door of desire I had concealed for far too long. He knew how I was, knew how nasty I could be. He didn't care sitting on my desk with his penis in his hand, massaging it back to life with a victorious grin on his face.

"Damn, you looking good, girl. Don't worry this will be as pleasurable for you as it will be for me."

I walked over to him once I was out of my La Perla. "Is this the only way?" I asked. In response he pointed towards the door. There was no other way.

He stood, dropped his pants around his ankles and took the position. I got on my knees and put my hands around his dick.

"Speak into the mike and tell me something good," he said, grabbing the back of my neck and thrusting himself into my mouth like a beast; his moans were barbaric as he pulled at my weave with his hand. I could've left, went out the door and never looked back. Titus provided well for himself, but it was something about Brice that had me wanting to taste him. Once I tasted him, I knew my hedonistic appetite was once again resurrected.

"Whispers."

Aurelius

My morning was spent taking care of the preparations for my Saturday event. This meant I had to promise to make life a living hell for those purveyors that dared to deliver any of my needed ingredients late. To make matters worse, the mansion where the party was taking place didn't have a licensed commercial kitchen. So I was forced to use the tight confines of the church. I shouldn't have been complaining, because I paid a relatively low rent for the place, but with parties the size of which I was undertaking, it was beginning to be a nuisance.

Standing alone in the basement of Mount Bethel A.M.E was something out of a horror film. The church was old and complete with unusual sounds that also shared a basement with a funeral home. On those rare occasions when a funeral was taking place and there was actually a body down there with me, I could barely contain myself. Death scared me; it was something about looking upon a dead body that brought things into perspective.

There are people out there who will live and die without finding true love and that sobering reality is what fucks with me. I do believe that in this large world there is someone that is my soul-mate but who's to say they live in the same state as me, same country or are even available. That's why I pity people who seek mates just because of physical beauty and end up spending years married to a person only based on superficial qualities.

Most men and women see Halle Berry and Denzel Washington and say to themselves, that's the person who I want my soul-mate to look like. What if our soul-mate isn't really much to look at all? Would we choose to spend your life unhappily with a trophy on our arm, or would we rather have a connection that transcends the naked eye? Have you ever talked to a person and felt like you knew them forever? That's a connection. Beauty fades, but a real connection only deepens.

Without the hope of true love, I would rather be dead.

The timer awakened me from my daze. I opened the oven, letting a poof of steam hit me in the face. I placed the pot on the wooden cutting board and opened the top to let the food breathe. Taking my thermometer, I stuck it into the meat to make sure the lamb was at its desired temperature and sliced into it to check its coloration and texture.

The aroma filled the kitchen, smelling good enough to make me consider eating meat. Shane always thought that it was weird that I cooked meat even though I was a vegetarian. Most people wondered how I knew it was even ready if I didn't eat it. The truth is, I've cooked for so long I can tell it's ready just by smelling it or slicing a piece off.

My phone started to vibrate and I braced myself for bad news because no one called this late unless it was an emergency. As I looked at the number, I wondered if I should even pick it up. It was Angelica's cellular and she was probably mad that I didn't show up at her apartment, but to be honest I didn't know where we stood after last night.

"What's up?" I asked waiting for her to start screaming, but that wasn't what I heard. She was sobbing. "Are you alright? Is there something wrong?" I said anxiously.

"Can we talk? I know it's late but I really need someone I can talk to," she said clearing her nose and steadying her voice.

"Sure, I'll be right over."

"No. I was wondering if I could come to you. I'm in a cab and the last place I want to be is home. Mind if I stay at your place for the night?" she said, sounding needy. "Where do you live?"

"You sure it's right that you come to my place."

I didn't mean to make it seem like I didn't want her to come to my place. Having her in my home and preferably in my bed was one of my ongoing fantasies. But she had real feelings for her fiancé, which she had made clear to me the night before. It would only confuse the feelings, which I was beginning to develop if she came.

"We've already gone beyond right. Don't you think?"

"Meet me on the corner of 123rd and Lenox."

"I'll be there in five," she said. Then the phone went silent.

A summer thunderstorm was dumping buckets of water on the streets of uptown. Films of water blurred my vision and soaked my pants. I stood on the corner of Lenox and 123rd with an overmatched umbrella in one hand and my eyes focused on every yellow cab that passed my way. With the weather conditions the way they were, I hoped she hadn't passed me by or decided to go home altogether. She was already thirty minutes late and I thought about leaving the scene numerous times. Yet every time I gave myself a two-minute waiting limit, I found myself giving her another two-minute grace period.

On the streets of Harlem at nearly midnight there were only two types of people I could be confused with, either a dealer, or user. The trouble seeking N.Y.P.D made it clear every time they drove past barely in excess of five miles per hour. They would look my way and I would glare back or give them the one finger salute. I resented the assumption that all black men standing on street corners at the break of dawn were only up to something sinister.

I tried calling Angelica, but the call went straight to voicemail like it had the other six times I had called previously. Either, she didn't want to speak or had found a better alternative. With that in mind, I started making my trek back to my building. Her grace period had finally run out. Besides, I didn't like playing the role of desperado.

The sidewalks were littered with dog shit, used baby diapers, broken bottles and Chinese food containers. I was only a block away from my luxury condominium, yet it was a different world on this side of the street. Harlem regrentrification Atlantic City style, prosperity surrounded by squalor. When I bought my place, they omitted this side of the street from the brochure. It was only a footnote in what was advertised as the new Harlem renaissance.

I heard a honk, and then watched a black Lincoln Continental slow up next to me, and the power windows went down. I walked up to the backseat window, bent down and peaked in. Angelica was leaning back on the leather seats with her hair looking like a bird's nest and eyes resembling those of a rabid raccoon. Her arms were crossed as she gave off much attitude even though it was I, who had waited. I leaned into the window and said, "Rough time getting here? Didn't think you would come. How'd you notice me all the way down the street?"

"Because of your bony ass. You need a belt."

"You stand me up then you insult me. You're cold blooded," I laughed.

"I know it's really late, but do you have time to talk. You're such a great listener and I really need one."

"It's that heavy."

"Worse."

"Try me," I said, placing my hand through the open window, intertwining with hers.

During our ride in the elevator, she failed to mention anything about what happened last night. There was something more pressing on her mind; her silence was conspicuous. Like I promised, I would provide a listening ear. Ruining our conversation with selfish dialogue wasn't my intention.

As soon as we entered my door, I hit my bedroom to take a quick shower and freshen up in my robe. Angelica on the other hand walked around my condo inspecting everything within arm's reach. I was a stickler for order, but for some reason I didn't mind her curious hands. I wanted to make her brief stay as comfortable as possible. Underneath my arms, I held a comforter and a few sheets for the sofa bed, she was a lady and I didn't want to treat her as anything else.

"What is this used for?" she asked pointing to my Tibetan Pomander.

"Traditionally pomanders are used to hold aromatic substances. Such as oils, in the past they helped ward off infections. Let me show you," I said.

While handing me the pomander we touched hands. I didn't mind, but she seemed uncomfortable and I wondered if it was because of the night before. We maintained eye contact as I poured a drop of oil from the pomander and placed it on her wrist.

"This smells weird," she said with her lips twisted upwards as she smelled her wrist up close. "It's unique. I've never smelled this before. What's it called?"

"It's Jojoba oil and it's for the skin and hair. You can find it in most hair products. It's not the most aromatic fragrance, but it's the best skin moisturizer on the market. Most of the spas should use this type of oil for their massages. There's nothing like it."

"Like you know about massages," she teased.

"I could give you one better than you've ever had," I said with confidence.

She walked over to me, getting so close that I could smell her deodorant.

She grabbed me by the collar, brought me eye to eye and whispered into my ear softly, "Is that right?"

I set up her bed, lit some candles, and brought two glasses and a new bottle of chardonnay to her bedside. She was lying down, dressed in my favorite t-shirt with her hair down to her shoulders, looking like she was attending a sleepover. I opened the terrace doors and let in a cool breeze, and put an R&B mix CD on my Bose entertainment stereo. I handed her a glass, filled it until she was content then took a seat on the edge of the bed.

"That's some of the wack ass wine I served you a while back," I said.

She smiled took a sip and looked around my living room. "Sorry about that, I was in one of my moods. I forgot to mention that even though I may act like a bitch sometimes I appreciate your food and your conversation."

"Bitch is a rather strong word for a Christian woman to use." I took a long sip from my glass, sighed and looked at her lovely legs. My t-shirt barely covered her thighs and only accentuated her nicely proportioned lower body.

"Even I don't feel like being Christian from time to time. No one's perfect, definitely not me." She didn't reveal this to be introspective, the twinkle in her eye suggested that it was her way of excusing her actions the last two nights.

"I think I've become an expert on your mood swings the last few weeks," I smiled back, letting her know I didn't mind her occasional tantrums.

"The sky is clearing up," she commented, staring out the terrace doors and into the midnight sky.

"Want to take a look at my view?" I asked standing and holding out my hand. She obliged, taking hold of my arm and letting me lead the way.

Standing 12 floors above Harlem, was a remarkable sight, its stalwart African American history and present was on display for all to see. The yellow light of the Apollo Theater that never seemed to fade was in the distance, and a billboard of a mohawked P- Diddy with his hands in a black power pose was nestled on the façade of the Magic Theatre. It was impressive that one hundred years hadn't changed much.

She stood close to me with her head on my shoulder and her arm tucked safely underneath mine. It was peaceful, only the howl of the wind could be heard.

"This is beautiful," she finally responded.

"It is but don't mind me if I rather look at something more breathtaking." I stared at her, wrapped my arm around her waist and pulled her close to me.

I couldn't help kissing her, couldn't help palming her ass or sucking on her neck as we stood overlooking the Harlem landscape. That was what I did. She returned the favor by sticking her hands down into my pants and massaging me while sucking on my earlobe.

Yesterday had nothing on what we were about to start. She opened my robe and started to lick my nipples with the tip of her tongue. My hands had made their way into the back of her jeans, finding the back of her pussy and starting to finger the hell out of it. Each time I entered her, she would bite my nipples, not hard, but with enough intensity that I couldn't help but moan myself.

She was smaller than I was in both height and weight, but she let me know who was in control as she pushed me down on the outdoor chaise and started to straddle me. It had been a long time since I'd had an impromptu passionate moment. What I did with the Mistress was rehearsed and with Jada, it was passionless.

My erection was prominent, standing at attention and swollen beyond belief.

"Is that for me?" she asked staring down at my little man while moistening her lips with her tongue.

"It is if you want it."

"I want it believe me, I want it," she said while making my toes curl.

I know I said that love was for the mentally impaired, but there was something between us that I couldn't explain. Mystical had the same affect on me, no matter how many times I penetrated her walls, the next time always felt like the first. This was not boring. It was heavenly.

I felt the first drop of rain on my neck; it startled me, but did not stop Angelica's forward movement. Then the clouds opened to let the waters loose. I sighed, knowing that the cold shower would probably fizzle Angelica's lust, give her another chance to back out of what we had started the last two nights, but it had the reverse affect. Straddling me, she took off the t-shirt she had borrowed, discarded her brassiere and basked in her near nakedness.

The sky lit up around us, the sound of water and thunder provided a great soundtrack to our barbaric voices.

I grabbed her wrist as she had her mind set on turning my neck completely purple, and pulled her away from me. I wanted to get a look at her body; it was the one thing I had neglected to do the night before. She seemed self-conscious, blocking her breast with her elbows.

"Don't, I want to take a good look at you." With a little probing from my hands, she allowed me to see her. "You're beautiful, your body is beautiful. Let the world see it," I said, standing and letting my robe fall to the ground.

Self-esteem is something that takes time to instill in a person. There are beautiful people that look in the mirror and see a revolting reflection. She wasn't comfortable in her own skin, the world could see that she was someone to be reckoned with, but all she could see was what mean hearted people had told her when she was a child.

"That's alright. I'm cool here. You're crazy," she said, finding security on the chaise.

I was sure the building superintendent wouldn't find anything humorous about my exhibition. There were lights on in the building across the street, could've sworn I saw a face, but I didn't care. Fucking in public had always been my dream, now they could live my fantasy along with me.

I stood by the railing with my dick sticking out, while the rain showered my body.

"Share this with me, try something new, and become uninhibited."

She shook her head no, put her knees to her chest once again. Tears began to trail down her cheeks.

"I feel so fucked up."

"I didn't mean to. I understand if you don't want to."

"I'm not talking about us. I don't know how *we* feel. I do know I did something fucked up."

She confided in me, explained to me why she needed to see me tonight. We sat underneath the pouring rain, laid across the chaise cuddled up like a loving couple. She had her head on my chest, exorcizing her demons by way of tears.

"You couldn't tell the Reverend?" I asked.

"And risk losing him. He'd never understand, he'd probably think I did something to put myself in that situation. Then I'd have to tell him about my past with Brice, I'd rather not."

"He loves you. Why wouldn't he believe you? Besides, what happened has got to be considered rape or sexual harassment at the worst?"

She sat up, cleared her throat and pulled the wet strands of hair sticking to her skin away from her eyes.

"When my relationship with Brice ended, I went to his house one night after having a few too many drinks and beat up on his wife. I got arrested for assault, Brice and his wife both took out restraining orders against me. There is no way any court in the country would believe me if I pressed charges against him. And if I was to get a date in court, that would put my affair with Brice in the open. Besides, he didn't rape me; I had a choice. Then I fucked him."

I sucked in a chest full of air, what she was saying was deep. That indiscretion she had made a few years earlier could nullify any complaints she levied against her former boyfriend. I'm sure he thought about that tidbit of information before he imposed his will on her.

"I see, but the Reverend can't hold your past against you."

"He can if he never knew I had a past."

"You mean you never told him about Brice."

She wasn't perfect as I had thought earlier, she was as flawed as I was and as unsure of herself. Sometimes when I looked at her, I saw glimpses of her inner child, so scared, so intimidated and so out of her comfort zone. And the fact that she wasn't innocent was a turn on to me. The revelation she was as dirty as Christina Aguilera, opened up many possibilities. The image that she had put on for the world was only a façade. She disguised her vulnerability with a tough as nails exterior.

Her tears weren't remorseful; they were guilt-ridden. The tears of a woman caught in a corner without the nails to claw her way out. Part of me felt she wanted to have sex with her ex, that part of her that had beat his wife's ass still resided in her. She didn't feel bad about what she did, she felt bad about the possibility of being caught. My sympathy turned off, my lust turned back on

"There were a lot of things I haven't told him about. I can't open myself to him like I can to you."

It could've been the wine speaking, I thought, as she poured herself another glass of the half-empty chardonnay, but I needed to know what she hadn't told him.

"Show me," I commanded.

When I pulled her damp body close to me, I put my fingers deep into the crack of her ass. Letting her know that there was no place I wasn't willing to go. Her nipples were hard against my skin as I lifted her from the ground and placed her on my lap. Her eyes widen, she liked my display of control.

"Do me," she said. Those two simple words meant the entire world to a man in a moment of passion.

"Do what?" I asked, wanting to confirm the cause of my elation.

"Eat my pussy again."

She said pussy, a word both dirty and beautiful at the same time and when mentioned by a woman it could cause an instant erection. When a woman said that word images of ménage a trois and girl on girl action flooded my mind. It was a whorish thing to say, but in the bedroom, discretion was a minus.

I ripped her panties off, couldn't wait any longer to roll them down the sides of her legs. She welcomed my exuberance, made her feel wanted. I grabbed her by the waist, positioned each of her legs over each shoulder, stood up and put my weightlifting class to use as I feed myself. I fed on her on my terrace, within inches of the railing and fifteen floors from certain death.

She held onto my hair for dear life, digging into my scalp with her long nails. The pain was excruciating, but for me it was a turn on. I wanted to eat the lining out of her pussy. My technique in satisfying a woman was unique, at least in my mind. I started off by paying ample attention to the lips, coating them with a hefty portion of my saliva until they parted without much probing. Then I sucked on her clitoral hood like I was trying to extract ice through a straw, titillating her nerve endings with the papillae on my tongue. This made her go wild, using the lord's name in vain.

A woman's flavor is always one of a kind. You could line up every pussy I'd ever eaten and I could name the woman it belonged to. Angelica's wetness had a sweet flavor, not candy like but a watered down sweetness. Could tell she ate and cleaned well. As I stuck my tongue inside her walls, her body went limp. She closed her eyes, was in her own zone, trying to enjoy every moment of my expertise.

I slowed down, wanting to tease her, but she wasn't having that. "Go faster," she commanded, jerking my head forcefully with her hands.

I felt my arms growing weak, so I carried her into the living room and placed her across the sofa bed. I could cover more ground that way. I put her knees into her chest and devoured her for close to an hour. Savoring the taste of her pussy, ass and anus while giving her multiple orgasms.

When her body shuddered for the last time, the look in her eye told me that more gratification was needed. "You want to do me?" I asked with my face glistening like I had eaten Kentucky fried chicken for the last hour.

I didn't want to impose my will on her. She had already been violated once and I had never been an opportunist. That was part of my inherited southern charm.

"I think I want to, but that's all I'm willing to do," she said.

She was in the frame of mind that sucking dick wasn't cheating, but there's no man on this planet who wouldn't rather find out that his woman got fucked than sucked someone's dick.

"I won't let you do it if you aren't sure."

She glanced down at my dick, rubbed her hand across her pussy and with the juices she collected, began to massage me.

"I'm sure," she said.

I had a bowl full of flavored condoms on top of the coffee table. I reached for them, but Angelica wanted to do the honors, she chose Banana flavor and opened the wrapper. She then put the condom in her mouth and tried placing it on my dick, but gagged as she got half way down my shaft.

"Been that long?" I asked smiling, while playing with the loose strands of her hair.

"I never had it this big," she admitted. "But if you can get it up, I can get it down."

I must've insulted her, because she pushed me down on the bed and started to deep throat me at a pace that I couldn't believe a person could achieve. While kneeling over me she was able to take all eleven inches from the tip of her tongue to the back of her throat in a second's time. She kept her mouth tight enough to add feeling to my dick, but not so tight, that she would scrape it with her teeth. Whenever I rubbed against the ridges on the top of her mouth, I couldn't help but bite down on my bottom lip.

It was feeling so damn good I didn't want her to stop. She was nowhere near being done; she started to jerk me off while running her tongue from the bottom of my shaft to the other side of my scrotum. She took my testicles into her mouth whole, sucking on them gently while humming. I could feel myself getting ready to explode. I grabbed the back of her neck, let out a moan and filled the condom until it could hold no more.

"Tension Release"

Angelica

After I finished him off, he turned off the lights, blew out the candles and got in bed beside me. He held me in his arms and we both lay in our nakedness as we stared outside the French doors leading to his terrace. This was how I always longed to feel. It was something remarkable about this moment. Remarkable, because it felt like it was where I belonged.

The morning came too quickly. The chirping robins perched on his terrace had awakened me. I didn't want to leave from his side. It was a workday and I wanted to play hooky. The last time I called in sick was three years ago. Today looked like a great day to catch the summer flu.

His head rested on my chest as I combed through his naps with my fingers. He had been awake for a while; I knew because I stared at his eyelashes flutter for the last ten minutes. If I could sum last night into one word, it would have to be unforgettable. This time I thoroughly enjoyed his tongue by clearing my mind of Titus and Brice. I would liken the orgasm he gave me to a release from all the problems bundled up inside my head. It freed me from all the negativity I felt for the last few years.

I didn't want to think about the repercussions of last night. It was too early for that, too early to complicate matters by thinking about my impending nuptials. All I wanted to do was learn more about this extraordinary man lying beside me. Discover why he was special enough to make me yield willingly to his advances.

"You look beautiful even in the morning," he complimented as he rose from the bed and stared at my face.

I smiled, couldn't say anything before I brushed my teeth. Didn't want to change the way he thought of me. Besides, he was only being kind, I could tell I looked like hell as I looked at my reflection in the French door windows. I needed to get a touch up on my weave and apply a fresh coat of foundation to my face.

Covering my mouth I said, "You like to talk bullshit, don't you? Do I look like I was born yesterday?"

"No, but you look starved. Stay here, I'll fix you some breakfast," he commanded once again as I gave him the look. "I meant to say, can you please stay here until I fix you breakfast."

"I'm gonna be late for work," I said.

"You ain't going to work, because you wouldn't be here if you were," he said, unwrapping himself from the sheets, revealing his naked body. Why were his tattoos starting to look so damn sexy? I thought.

He was right though and as soon as he walked out the room, I called Reba to let her know I needed a little time off. Told her the wedding was making me crazy and I couldn't take the stress. And like the great person she was, she granted me two weeks paid vacation.

Aurelius came back into the living room ten minutes later, holding a tray in his hand. He was wearing a little ass apron over his body, barely covering his chest and doing nothing to cover his dick as it bopped up and down with each of his steps.

"You like boysenberry?" he asked, sitting the tray over my thighs.

"It depends on what," I said, grabbing a hand full of his cock that at its most flaccid looked bigger than half the hard dicks I ever laid eyes on.

His eyes glowed as I massaged his thang. I couldn't believe I was being so venturesome. Since I started dating Titus, I learned to curb my tenacity, but I was feeling liberated now without his watchful eye directed at me.

"I mean on cinnamon wheat pancakes."

"That sounds tasty, but I'd rather taste it on you."

I took the syrup from the tray, moved the tray to the side, loosened the knot in his apron and poured the boysenberry on the head of his dick. The dark brown liquid dripped from his shaft and stuck to the tip as I prepared to consume all of it.

When I took him into my mouth, I heard him sigh. It wasn't easy taking him in, opening my mouth this wide was never comfortable, but he tasted so good. Sucking dick was like riding a bike and though I wasn't as thorough as in my promiscuous days, I was still proficient. Working up a good rhythm with my hands and my mouth was significant to his euphoria and I didn't want to disappoint. I learned a long time ago that using both, increased the sensation a man felt. Multi tasking always got the job done quicker.

He held onto my head, while I decided to try something new and grab onto his magnificent ass, taking him in using no hands. It wasn't exactly like trying to balance a pencil on my nose, but the act still took total concentration. I pushed his ass towards me with my hands, while I brought his dick deeper into my mouth. For ten minutes, his inaudible moans revealed enjoyment.

As my mouth started to get dry, I got from my knees, lay across the bed and inclined my head over the edge of it, with my body facing the opposite direction from where he stood. I opened my mouth, let him penetrate it and fuck it like I hoped he would fuck my pussy. I called it the half sixty-nine for I was the only one giving.

A trick I learned when I was younger from a friend of mine was the subtle suck whenever my mouth went over the head of a man dick. I thought of his dick as a straw and his cum as a thick vanilla milk shake, then suck hard, on the head of his penis, thrusting into me while his balls slapped vigorously across the top my forehead, he played with the fine hairs on my labia. He stuck his fingers into his mouth, rubbed them across my clit, dipped them deep into my nestle and tasted the nectarous juices on his fingers.

The bed started to shudder as he approached orgasm. His rhythm turned to slow, hard and delayed thrusts as he relished his looming climax. The internal passion he had suppressed the night before was finally being released. As his hot, salty cum trickled down my throat, his knees gave out sending him down for the count across the hardwood floor.

"Giving up already? I only started," I said, after swallowing, hoping he still had enough vigor to finish the job.

He looked lethargic, inebriated by a heavy dose of some good kitty. His dick had waved the white flag, lying to the side like a thirsty dog's tongue. He was sweating bullets, his body aglow as he sunbathed in the orange rays coming from the terrace.

Like a police officer rousing a derelict on a subway platform, I poked him with the tip of my feet. "Get up. I'm gonna have to rape you if you don't get that thang back up in a minute."

He held his hand up for leniency. "Damn girl, you took the life right out of me," he finally said as he caught his breath.

"Isn't that the point?" I said sarcastically. Ejaculation is life and I had sucked it from him.

"Guess it is. But damn, did you have to put it on me like that? That thang you were doing with your mouth was out of this freaking world."

"I am getting sick of the mouth. I need something a little more massive," I said standing over him ready to squat over him.

It had been so long, I was a little terrified. I couldn't remember how it felt having a man inside of me. I used my Robo cock in the last month but plastic was such a different feel than the real thing. Sexing yourself and being sexed was like apples and oranges. Being sexed is always better, especially when the man knows how to blow your back better than your hand.

"Lay on me for a minute until I recuperate."

He held the tip of my hand and pulled me down towards him. I lay across his naked body with my ears to his heart and my feet to his. I started to laugh as his rejuvenated friend prodded my stomach. And his fingertips grazed from the small of my back down to the crack of my ass.

"You must be a sodomite," I concurred.

"Only with a woman willing to go there," I said softly.

"You ain't turning me out."

"Anyone I've turned out didn't even see it coming," he bragged.

"Is that why we're on the floor instead of your bedroom? You must want to do a sneak attack on me."

"Not really, but whoever I bring into my bedroom must have an open mind."

"I have an open mind. I just sucked you off, didn't I? And didn't I nearly catch pneumonia on your terrace last night messing with you?"

"Yeah but I don't think you're ready to open your mind to what I'm into."

"Try me," I stated confidently, secretly hoping I wouldn't regret it.

When he opened the door to his bedroom, I couldn't believe my eyes. He was a freak to the tenth degree. I had never seen any shit like this before. The room was ominous, looked more like Dracula's leer than a place where two people engaged in sexual acts. The mirrors were painted black, silver restraints hung from the ceilings and wooden weapons of pain were placed meticulously across his wall. To my surprise, his bed looked rather plain; a coffin would've fit better with the décor. I looked down at my feet, noticed that at the foot of his doorway was a doormat which read "Welcome to the Dark side".

"You gonna come in?" he stepped inside and held the door open.

"I don't know if I should," I stated, looking inside his dungeon nervously.

Part of me truthfully felt like running. The hairs on my back were standing up, and nervous energy filled my stomach. There was something not right about the dark vibe of the place. Scientists say that the human body needs light; we are just like plants in that way. Without light, we'll wilt and die.

As if he was reading my mind, he said, "Let me get a little light in here." He held the door open with a dumbbell, moved across the bedroom and parted his curtains.

Against my better judgment, I entered. The sunlight didn't help all that much, the room was still gloomy, but I was at least able to see my way around.

"Do you have a sleeping disorder?" I asked. It would explain all the black.

He laughed, but I didn't find anything funny. If anything, I hoped he had a logical explanation as to why his room was so sullen.

"I figured you wouldn't like it."

"You figured correctly."

My pussy was no longer wet, my lust for him had dried up like the red sea and I was ready to leave.

"So why did you ask to see my bedroom if you don't want to understand what's beyond the door?"

I had no answer. When he said I needed an open mind to enter his room, I had no idea how wide. I did about every nasty, freaky thing there was, at least twice. However, this was the type of scene I associated with psychopaths. It was the type of setting used as a backdrop in ritualistic murders.

"Some things are best left to the imagination," I said, ready to leave the room. He grabbed my arm, pulled me close and stared intensely into my pupils. There was a child like aspect to his gaze that made me feel sorry for him.

"The imagination is superior to reality. Sometimes, it's all we have. In reality, nothing's perfect, but the imagination allows for that."

I pulled away from him. "Sorry, I've given up my imagination a long time ago. Imagining anything being perfect is an illusion."

He walked to the other end of the room, peered out the picturesque windows onto the street below. "Like the love you imagine having for the Reverend."

"You know me now," I said, sarcastically.

"No, but I do know the look of a woman settling just so she can call someone her own."

"Don't let our intimate encounters fool you. That's all they are, nothing more."

"Are you sure?" he asked.

"Yes," I responded. He came over to me, grabbed my breast in each hand, tongue kissed them both and looked into my eyes, "I'll prove you wrong."

"Here and Now."

Aurelius

We had spent the entire afternoon sexing each other like crazy, spending countless hours savoring the bitter sweetness of each other's flesh. I invaded her walls like the Grecian army, set up camp inside her private places and claimed her treasure as my own. She was a screamer, not composed as her demeanor had suggested. Her euphoric cries were intense and penetrating, like the howl of a female wolf in heat.

Being inside of her warm embrace was atoning. Her kisses had awakened desires in me that were more significant than any instinctive need of self-gratification. I sexed her from the front, to the back and side-to-side. After releasing the life force of all man inside of her, the result was unlike anything I'd ever felt. I wanted a deeper connection with her, wanted to make love to her soul. That was why I convinced her to bathe with me.

I squeezed the water from Angelica's hair, creating waves in the water that filled the bathtub. She sat between my legs thoughtfully washing my thighs. Candles were lit, Luther Vandross played on the stereo system and a mist of dooja smoke filled the bathroom. I tied her hair into pigtails and placed them over her shoulder, so I could admire her back. Her back was sleek even the pimples that spotted her skin seemed quintessential.

"What's on your mind?" I asked as her hand floated above the water. She had stared at the wall for what seemed like hours, hadn't said a word in that entire time.

"I might bore you, so I rather not say. I don't think it's something you would care about anyway."

"I wasn't made with two ears for sex appeal." I turned the music down with the remote, giving her my full attention.

"It's just that I don't feel bad about what we did. Titus has never done anything to hurt me and I don't regret it. Do you think I'm fucked up because I don't feel like I did something wrong? "

"This isn't about whether or not he hurt you directly. It's about you, about how you feel. Has he given you everything you needed from him? Has he given you his all?"

She stood, turned around, sat back down straddling my thighs and looked into my eyes. "He has a congregation to preside over. It isn't possible. I understand that."

"You can say all day you understand, your actions say you resent him for what he doesn't give to you. I know, since my last relationship ended because I didn't give all of myself."

I took my joint out of the soap dish, took a pull and blew the smoke through my nose, releasing it like I released that suppressed memory. I had never admitted to anyone why Mystical had left me; felt that if I never spoke it, it had never happened. It wasn't the smoke fogging my mind that was speaking; it was the feelings that I was beginning to develop for her that had revealed itself.

I kissed her, drew her bottom lip into my mouth and sucked on it. Her eyes were still open, not closed like they usually were when we shared a kiss, which meant there was something on her mind that she couldn't cut off.

"Is that even realistic, to have the ideal relationship? He can't spend every waking moment with me and if he did, would I even want to be with a brotha that's all up on me?"

I could feel my body member awaking underneath her. Her eyes took on a gleeful glare, the look a woman gets when they are astonished by the rigidness a man takes on just the strength of their beauty.

"It's not the moments we share together that create who we are. It's the moments we create together. Tell me one thing memorable about your current relationship and we can get out of here and never revisit this obviously strong connection that we hold."

I sat in silence awaiting her answer, but there wasn't a moment she could recall. A person that experiences great memories wouldn't have to strain in order to bring their thoughts to the surface.

"So, there aren't any," I said. She shook her head no, arched her ass back, searched for my dick with her hand and inserted my hardness into her moistness. She let out a gasp as if what I had to offer was too much for her to take in all at once. I held her waist, eased myself in slowly, giving her one inch per second.

I thought I had tamed her desires hours before, figured when I fucked her to her liking I had exhausted her libido, but I was wrong. If the tub were the ocean, we would've been in the middle of a tsunami. The waters were rough, splashing onto the tiled floor each time she bucked me. Biting into my lip without letting go, she sucked on me like she wanted to deplete my blood stream.

Working out always came in handy when I made love. I could lift two hundred and fifty pounds of dead weight, so lifting her was not a problem. I stood erect from the tepid water while she straddled my thighs, cupped my arms under her legs one at a time until her spot was on my six pack then locked onto her shoulders with each of my hands, set her on the edge of the double sink, slid into her and started to plow her relentlessly. Her knees were in her chest, her chin rested on my shoulder blade and her head was set against the mirror leaving an imprint in the misty glass.

As the curve of my manhood hit her g spot with precision, she tightened her grip around my neck saying things in my ear a sinner wouldn't even say in a confessional. But it wasn't the sex that was off the hook, it was her, and though I knew in the morning she would return to her life and I would return to mine, I hoped that somehow we could make this last a little while longer.

"Arabian Night"

Angelica

"No you didn't," Daniel said once the driver pulled away from the curb. "I'm scurred of you," he laughed, playfully hitting me on the shoulder.

Like I promised, I agreed to hangout on the town with him for a night. A friend of his was throwing an Arabian night's themed extravaganza in the Hampton's where we were bound to get into more trouble before the night was over. And since I had a home of my own out there, we packed for an entire weekend. It took him a little prodding but I didn't mind the perks Daniel was able to provide, like the chauffeured driven Rolls Royce Phantom limousine we were sitting in.

An hour earlier while I packed, I told Daniel all about the last couple of days, reiterating every single exhilarating detail and every toe-curling segment of my two evenings. He could hardly believe that I had the guts. Previously, he thought I had lost my inner hoe and went totally holy, but I proved him wrong. I felt like myself again. I needed a sex fix and Aurelius provided that for me. It was all in fun, nothing serious; I just hoped that Aurelius understood that.

Our two nights were spectacular, the sex was even better. I already had a man and there was nothing else Aurelius could give me. When I stressed my concerns, he said he agreed with me and insisted that we go the extra mile and terminate our business contract, but I sensed the hurt in his eyes when I kissed him for the last time before departing. And that was why I hadn't called him for the last two days. Yeah he took care of me when I needed him, talked to me and consoled me, but in reality, all I needed from him was a little licky, licky.

"Hell yeah I did," I bragged.

"Girl, you are no good. Now the question is; do you plan to see the mystery man again?" he asked. For the purpose of being discreet, I withheld Aurelius's name, didn't want to complicate matters. Stronger friendships ended for less. It was safer if only God, Aurelius and I knew what really went down.

"He was nothing special, he was there and it was bound to happen sooner or later. I'm allowed at least one discreet indiscretion in two years, don't you think? " I rationalized nonchalantly as I sipped Dom Perignon from a flute glass.

I reclined my chair and buried my bare feet in the plush carpeting while enjoying the high life. This would be my last taste of this life once I got married and I dressed for the occasion. I wore a Mahogany BCBG silk chiffon paisley printed dress with a plunging neckline and a pair of Giuseppe Zanotti lizard wedge sandals. Earlier in the day, I had my weave taken out and my hair permed and layered. Combined with the bright red lipstick, it gave me an exotic look.

"I can't argue with you there, home girl. But let me warn you, good dick can become overwhelmingly *addicktive*."

"People are born with an addictive personality, but I've always been good at quitting cold turkey."

"I don't know if I believe you."

"Why wouldn't you? I'm saying I'm done and that's exactly what it means."

"If I recollect, we had this same conversation the first time you met Brice. You said it was an innocent dinner the first time you two went out and look what happened."

He gave me a sly stare and that was the main reason I stopped confiding in my friends. People always use the past against you. If Daniel knew what I did to secure my promotion, he'd probably tuck that tidbit of info away to use at another opportune time.

"I didn't have anything to lose then. I have a lot to lose now. Besides, I was young and stupid."

"What do you call yourself now?"

"Old and horny as hell," I said. "Daniel, you out of all people should know not to throw stones when you live in a glass house."

Daniel cheated on his live-in lover all the time. It was common knowledge in our small circle of friends that he probably had more men than all of us combined.

"Do I have a ring on my finger?" he joked. "When President Bush legalizes same sex marriage, I'll stop cheating." We both laughed, knowing it would be a cold day in hell before that happened.

"I'm not married yet."

"You are engaged and that's close enough," he said, seriously.

"Just a week ago you were telling me to get back out there and experience life. I thought you were on my side," I told him.

"Don't get me wrong. I got your back for life. However, I think you are down playing your feelings for this mystery man."

"Why would you say that?"

"Because I haven't seen you this happy and free in some time," he responded.

No matter how much I tried to convince myself otherwise, I missed Aurelius. Part of the reason I wanted to convince myself that it was only about the dick was because I didn't want to complicate matters. In two weeks, I will belong to someone else permanently and though I could, I didn't want to change that. I wasn't going to destroy what I had built with Titus, because that was what everyone expected me to do.

As I traveled from home to home as a child, the census was always that I would end up someone's whore. For the first Thirty years of my life, I lived true to form. Now things were different, at least in Titus' eyes and I needed it to remain that way.

We were shuttled from the Hunting Inn in East Hampton to a hidden Peconic Bayfront estate. The magnificent home sat on over four acres with views of Robin Island and the North Fork and was decorated to the tee. As soon as we entered the security gates, we were in awe of what we were beholding. In the circular driveway, stood about a dozen fire-dancers, sword-dancers and sword-swallowers. As we walked through the thirty-two foot high entry foyer, belly dancers doing things with their hips that didn't seem humanly possible greeted us. They had our attention and the eyes of about twenty men that stood around watching them click their finger cymbals. We were then led down a private staircase to the beach below where Moroccan tents were set up along the sand.

The atmosphere was exotic but the ambiance was sexual in nature. Looking at everyone walking around made me feel overdressed; some women wore bikinis while some wore nothing at all. The men were even less inhibited wearing bikini underwear, g-strings and underwear with the sock like end that held their dicks.

"Where in the hell did you bring me?" I whispered to Daniel as we walked the beach.

"The other party is inside, but the real party is out here. I wanted to show you a different side of life before you put on those handcuffs." Daniel winked.

"The lord will not follow you into the devil's house," I whispered one of Titus sayings under my breath.

"What did you say?" Daniel asked.

"I said I'm hungry," I lied.

"They have to be serving food in one of these tents. Why don't you take a look?" He smiled, while admiring the bare ass of one of the waiters walking around.

I didn't think anything of it when I opened the tent closest to me, expecting to see an empty tent at the worst, but I walked in on a scene out of a porno flick. There were about five women inside and one man. He was the main course and they were starved. He looked European, had olive skin, slick black hair pulled back, a muscular build and a bulge that shattered the white man myth.

I looked behind me, but Daniel was gone. He had found his prey and was busy trying to find a way to have it for dinner. It was like a United Nations symposium in the tent. The women were all of different nationalities and each were fighting to say a few words on the mike. I stood disgusted, curious and at the same time, wondering how five women could share one man.

I never witnessed an all out orgy before; not that I was foreign to more than one sex partner at a time. While in college, I was involved in a threesome with two men. That didn't faze me though because I could wrap my mind around the temptation the body of a naked man provided. However, the body of another naked woman had always bothered me. Deep in my mind, I knew why and as I closed the tent and ran to safety, I knew one day I'd have to resolve those demons.

On the inside of the estate, the party was much different. Everyone was dressed elegantly, drinking champagne and listening to Moroccan music. The scene was a sharp contrast from what I witnessed in the tent, but I felt out of place with this particular group as well. My attire was suitable for a club, not a black and white affair. I sat alone in a chair away from most of the party and scanned the room underneath my dolce frames. Daniel was nowhere to be found. He was probably somewhere getting his freak on. Looking for him would be fruitless. I noticed a staircase leading upstairs and since I had to use the bathroom, I didn't see why I couldn't go and see where it led.

The top of the staircase was dark, but I climbed it anyway. When I finally made it to the top, I noticed sliding glass doors at the end of the landing. From the sliding glass doors, a sliver of blue light peeked in from outside. I walked to the light and was shocked to see an observation deck overlooking the North Fork.

The North Fork had to be one of the most beautiful places to look upon. Even in the dark, I could enjoy the extraordinary landscape. The full moon revealed miles and miles of the beautiful lush green grass that stood in the distance. And the scent of ripe grapes coming from the many vineyards that dotted the rolling hills, intoxicated the atmosphere. A sight was to be shared with someone special.

"Full Moon"

Aurelius

I noticed her sitting downstairs alone after I came from one of my walks along the beach. She didn't see me, she was too busy sulking. I convinced myself to approach her, wasn't sure if I should after the unprovoked cold shoulder treatment she had inflicted upon me. The unreturned calls had incited something in me I couldn't control. It was something stronger than my bruised ego.

I navigated through the horde of men that milled around the belly dancers hoping to get a glimpse of something they couldn't see at home. I parted through them like a hot knife through butter and headed towards Angelica. Before I was able to reach her, she got up and headed upstairs. At first, following Angelica wasn't in my plans, but I couldn't help it. I was drawn to her. An uninterested woman has a way of bringing out desperation in a sensible man.

I gave her room as she climbed the stairs, didn't want to startle her. The last thing I wanted was to seem overtly aggressive. There was a thin line between an admirer and a stalker. I reached the top of the stairs just as she closed the sliding glass doors. I took my time getting there. I wanted to look at her for a moment before I revealed myself.

She looked like an angel standing on the observatory deck, peeking through a telescope and glowing in the moon's embrace. Was this fate? It's not everyday that two people end up at the same party miles away from home. Especially not two people that shared what we shared not too long ago. Not in a place as beautiful and breathtaking as where we were now. Her hair was blowing in the summer breeze and my palms were wet with perspiration as I opened the sliding doors.

She jumped as I stepped onto the wood deck. Her eyes were wide with shock and as she peered through the dark to see who it was, her worried expression instantaneously turned to that of relief once she realized it was me.

"You scared the shit out of me," she said as she walked to me and gave me a one armed hug. "I thought I was gonna have to jump. What the hell are you doing here?"

"I'm here on business. I should've figured you were with friends. You work with fashion so it makes sense."

"I'm here with a friend."

"What's your friend's name?" I asked.

"Daniel... His name is Daniel and I have no idea where he is," she said looking over the deck and down towards the beach.

I couldn't help but feel the sting of jealousy, wondering if she was using the word friend as code for fuck buddy. Maybe she had moved on to someone else to quell her over until Titus return.

"Well, I better get out of here before *he* comes back," I said jokingly, but secretly hoping she'd reassure me that Daniel was truly only a friend.

She shook her head and stared at the ground avoiding eye contact. Another bone-chilling breeze blew from the lake. She rubbed her bare arms as her teeth chattered.

"Listen, I'm here all night and I have a kitchen to run. So take my jacket and give it to me before you leave." I took my jacket off and draped it over her shoulders. Then patted her on the back, moved two steps forward and looked back, smiled and kept it moving.

I opened the sliding doors and was set to leave when she grabbed me by the hand.

"Why are you so nice to me?" she asked.

"I don't know. I just can't see treating you any other way."

"But most men..."

"I've never been most men. I'm me," I said in defense.

Women in general have low expectations of men. They expect us to be uncaring, cold, physical and impenetrable at all times. And that was what I'd been for the last few years; it was a way to guard my heart from the pain I once felt. However, after spending time with Angelica, the risk of being hurt didn't matter anymore. And to think that is what I would probably feel in a few weeks when she'd marry a man she obviously does not love.

"I mean you got what you wanted. So why still bother with me?" She wanted to know.

"There's so much more to you than that. I'm insulted that you think sex is all I'm after."

"There's nothing else I could offer you. Do you remember that I'm getting married or has it slipped your mind?"

"You can push me away if you want. I can't do anything about that, but don't go bipolar on me. One day you're kissing me, then the next you're acting like you don't know me. Some things you have to explain."

"Yeah we fucked, Aurelius, but it was nothing more. It was just sex. Do I have to explain that?"

"Why give in to me when you could have waited another month? I know I'm not the first man to look at you since you got engaged," I queried.

"What do you want from me...? What do you want from me, Aurelius?" she yelled stomping her feet with tears in her eyes.

Another cool breeze blew at her hair. She rubbed her arms again and stared into my eyes like there was a secret message scrolling across my pupil's.

I told her, "I don't know what you want me to say. I don't have the magic words to make this easier."

She took a deep breath, turned her back to me, pulled my chef's jacket across her chest, held her arms across her body and walked to the railing. I learned a long time ago that when a woman acts like she wants to be alone that isn't really what they want at all. I removed my torque from my head, put it in my back pocket combed through my hair with my fingers and walked up behind her.

"This world is too big to be alone," I said, following her gaze across the lush fields.

"Being alone means living in peace. The less people there are around you, the fewer problems there are to take on."

I stood close behind her, put my arms across her body and pulled her close, "You're sounding like me. But I realize that even loners hate being alone, and sometimes they are the ones most in need of companionship."

"You think you know everything. Tell me, Aurelius, why did I cheat on Titus?"

"I read an article on Tantric practices and it said that though a man may practice celibacy and become enlightened spiritually, a woman's enlightenment comes from the electric charge of her orgasmic nature. The need to be stimulated is in your nature. He chose his path in life and you choose yours."

Normally, I hated leaving the kitchen unattended, but Angelica was loosening the belt around my waist with her teeth and I coveted the way her body felt against mine, so for the moment I didn't care if the kitchen burned down.

"Ever had sex in a strange place?"

There was that enigmatic part of her personality rearing its head. It scared me, the way she could be disinterested one minute and inquisitive the next. I didn't even know if she was aware of her own madness.

"Thought you said some things are better left to the imagination," I smiled as she released my belt and let my pants fall to my ankles.

From down below us in the tents, came orgasmic sounds of pleasure realized. And underneath the purple skies and black clouds were people enjoying the moment. We were both transfixed in that lapse of time as well.

Angelica was nymphomaniacal. She nourished herself by way of sex. I could tell from her labored breathing, that she needed me badly. She wrapped her legs around my waist, probed my mouth with her tongue ravenously, arching her back over the railing.

"I don't have any protection," I admitted.

"I don't care," she said, stabilizing herself by holding onto my neck with her arm and searching for my dick with her free hand.

I grabbed her wrist, held her in mid air. "That's something you don't want to start. Anything can happen."

"I have a better idea. When can you leave?" she asked.

"Not until I clean up."

Angelica pulled me by the collar and kissed me seductively. "If you leave now, I'd do anything you want."

"Don't say it, if you don't mean it," I said already with something in mind.

"Let's just say I'm in the mood to try new imaginative things."

"Devilish Thoughts"

Angelica

I peered into the bathroom mirror and couldn't believe what I was wearing. I resembled pure unrelenting evil in what happened to be Aurelius's notion of a sexy outfit. Before arriving at my new home, we stopped off at a specialty shop in town and picked up some things. It was he, who desired for me to wear this blasphemous getup, wanting to do a role reversal on my future place as a Reverend's wife. He picked out a devil's outfit, complete with pitchfork, sequined tail and pointy horns.

I promised to do anything he wished, so I put on the patent leather bra, panties and the fish net stockings with pride. After finally developing the guts, I turned off the master bathroom lights walked into the adjoining master bedroom and made my presence felt. The room was dark; the only source of light was the two candles that illuminated each corner of the bedroom from their wrought iron holders. Aurelius was in the middle of it all, secured to a wooden chair with cuffs and tethers. I walked pigeon toed in a sexy pair of red 6" stilettos with a patent leather ankle cuff that matched my outfit.

Aurelius was blindfolded with a huge smile on his face and naked from the waist up. Privately, I debated whether or not I wanted him to take off all his clothes, but decided that undressing him would increase the anxiety.

"Don't be nice. I get off on pain. That's if you have it in you," he challenged. I'd never done anything like this but if he wanted pain, I knew how to give it. In the drive over, he told me his history, confiding in me his sexually deviant behavior, so I had a good idea of what he wanted.

I circled the chair while tapping a leather flogger on the fatty part of my palms. I noticed how his muscles tensed up each time I whipped it through the air, creating a whistling sound.

"Welcome to hell," I said in a sadistic tone.

"I…" he tried speaking.

I hit him across the chest with the flogger, tugged his head backward and said. "Don't speak." I placed my thumb over his lips and whispered. "You can scream all you want; they won't hear you up there."

Part of me felt like I was going too far, but role-playing was growing on me. I could be whomever I wanted, say and do whatever I felt. Besides, there was no such thing as a pleasant "She Devil."

I straddled his thighs could feel his dick growing through my leather panties. I grinded forward slowly, rubbed my butt across his lap like I was trying to start a fire. He put his head back and sucked on the bottom of his lips, tried to free himself from the cuffs but was helpless in doing so.

"You aren't getting out until I'm finished. So don't even try or the repercussions will only be worse," I scolded.

He laughed, and I got mad.

I slid from his thigh got on my knees, unzipped his pants and tugged them off his body. I then walked over to the corner of the room, took one of the candles from it's wrought iron candle holder, brought it over to his naked body and poured the hot wax over his thigh. He bit the bottom of his lips, suppressing his screams while rocking back and forth in his chair.

"Laugh now and cry later," I snickered.

I finally knew what it meant to get into character. I focused my mind to no longer see Aurelius but the face of every man that had ever done me wrong. His laugh had awakened each repressed memory and he was going to be the ransom for them all.

I put the candle back in its holder, stood on top of his chair in my stilettos, applied pressure on his balls with the tips of my heels and watched as he tried to conquer his physical suffering with his mind. I didn't put all my weight on his testicles, but enough of it to make him distressed.

"Is this what you had in mind when you said you wanted to feel pain?"

He nodded his head, didn't say a thing because he was fearful of what I would do to him if he opened his mouth. I ran the strands of leather twists over his face as he opened his mouth and let each strand slide across his tongue.

"Now, let the games begin."

"My Way"

Aurelius

"What's your dream? What is it that you want most out of life?" Angelica asked running her fingers across my chest as she rested her head on my lap.

"I have many dreams. Be more specific."

"If there's one thing you couldn't die without doing, what would it be?"

Death is always unforeseen, yet mentally we all have to be prepared for it. So I thought long and hard after she asked that question. There were many things that I wanted to accomplish, but if I had to narrow it down to one, I knew what it was without a doubt.

"Open my own restaurant. If I accomplished that, I could die in peace. "

"Is that all you want? You don't want to get married one day."

"Married?" I laughed. "Nah, I don't believe in that. I believe in love, but marriage nowadays is more about status than love."

She stirred a little, sat up and removed a few wisps of her awry hair from her eyelids. "Weren't your parents married a long time?"

"And that's exactly why it ain't for me."

"At least, your parents stayed together," she said.

"My mother stayed for love and my father stayed for convenience."

"And why would they do that?" she asked in shock as if I was somewhat delusional.

There were things I knew about my parents they either didn't know about each other, or chose to ignore. My father owned a software business he dedicated his life to, and showed it more attention than his own wife. He loved it more than he loved us. I knew it because he chose to be there those five nights a week, and didn't bother to come home. I was young then and they didn't think I noticed, but I did. I knew why my mother cried everyday and fought hard to make him happy.

And when a man can't take care of his duties at home, a woman will stray. My mother was no different and after being called "Pretty Millie" by every man but her husband, she fell for the first man who gave her the attention she needed.

Dr Perry, the local gynecologist, obviously impressed her so much in his office that she let him make home visits. She never cared for him like she cared for my father. She would sneak the Doctor in the back door every night and sneak him out that back door every morning when my father was gone. Sometimes, she wouldn't wait until the morning and send him away after he did the job my father couldn't. One time I bumped into him as he tip toed down the creaky stairs and looked into his eyes, saw humiliation. From then on, I always thought a man that was content with sneaking around wasn't a man at all. Now I was doing the same.

Angelica disappeared into the bathroom to rid her skin of all evidence of our lovemaking. While she was away, I stood out on the veranda and gazed at the lush green fields down below. Her home was in the Hampton's and all the homes in the Hampton's looked the same. Humdrum shingled traditional with acres of land, a pond and a tennis court. It was made for people who hated change. Brought back memories I wanted to forget. Reminded me of where I grew up and the last time I saw my parents alive…

I saw the look on my father's face as soon as Mystical stepped onto the porch. The look of superiority was etched in his smirk, she hadn't stepped foot into the front door and he had already judged her. His condescending smile said he knew I'd bring home someone like her and he was tickled by it.

Mystical was wild and looked it. She went wherever the breeze blew her and her fashion sense embodied that attitude. The piercing on her lips and the tattoos on her body made her stand out in a crowd. Her hair was long on one side, cut short on the other. The long side was red and the short side black. She wore a white tube top, red mini skirt with sweatbands on both wrists, the color of the Jamaican flag and her pupils were dilated, just descending from her high. She had a taste for crystal meth that she could barely function without.

I hated the fact that she needed drugs. Everyday when I came from work, I feared finding her in our bedroom dead. The methamphetamines made her do unpredictable things, made her cut herself and vandalize our apartment. Once I gave her an ultimatum, asked her to choose the drugs or me, she chose the drugs. What I feared most was that she would die alone, without me by her side. So I dealt with her cravings. You could call me her enabler. I loved her enough not to see her kill herself.

My father cleared his throat, I looked at him, knew that I was his splitting image and I secretly hated it. He was an athletic man and at fifty-eight, still looked good in a tight fitting shirt. He wore a black turtleneck, black slacks and a simple gold chain around his neck. In his hand, was a glass of cognac, most likely warm like he loved it.

"Hi, dad," I said shaking his hand sternly. I hadn't seen him in a year, yet a hug was too feminine in his eyes. He didn't say a word to me just shook my hand forcefully and cleared his throat.

"And you are?" my father asked as Mystical pulled down on her mini skirt.

"I'm Mystical. Nice to meet you Mr. McKenzie," she said hugging him. She could be normal when she wanted to.

He kept his arms at his side and pulled his face away as if she was feeding him poison when she kissed him on the cheek.

He seemed more concerned with spilling his cognac than giving her a proper hug.

"That's your birth name?"

"Yes sir." She looked to me for help, all I could do was shrug and hope my mother came to rescue us all.

I could tell my father thought in his head that her parents were fools. In his mind, a parent had to start planning from the day of their child's birth for future success. Her name had indicted her D.N.A. as not being worthy of mixing with mine.

"Where's mom?" I asked my father as I stepped foot into my childhood home.

"Take off your shoes, boy," he said, exhibiting his superiority. I stepped back out and did as I was told.

I hadn't called to tell them I was coming until I was in the neighborhood; it was a spur of the moment thing. They probably thought I needed money. My father was always curt and short tempered with me when he thought I needed money. All I wanted was to show Mystical where I came from and ask the two most important people in my life a question.

I stepped back, let my father go ahead and reached for Mystical's hand. She grabbed hold tightly, as if she was nervous or scared. Reminded me of the way she held it on Halloween as we walked through a haunted house.

"Are you alright?" I asked looking back at her. "Don't mind him, he just got back from work. He's always this way," I whispered.

Her expression relaxed some and her grip did as well as we stepped into the hardwood entryway.

The smell of the house was still the same. Smelled like sandalwood, the incense my father loved to burn to cover his badly concealed marijuana habit. He only smoked when he was stressed and had to be home, couldn't cope with my mother with a clear head.

My mother came into the living room from the kitchen looking as glorious as ever, a more beguiling version of Lena Horne. Her natural beauty defined her, her grey head of hair crowned her grace. She was like a classic television show that transcended time. She would always be becoming no matter whose eyes she was seen through. She was dressed in an elegant red pair of slacks and slightly opened white cotton shirt that showed off her favorite accessory, the bodice of pearls my father bought for her on their silver anniversary.

My mother stopped in her tracks when she saw Mystical, probably wasn't who she would've picked for me, but she maintained a smile nevertheless. "Is this Mystical?" My mother asked as they converged for a hug like two lost friends. She took her hand and twirled Mystical around. Examined her, Mystical was skinny and in the south they favored a curvaceous figure. "You a frail little thang, come in the kitchen I'm fittin to feed you. Let these men do whatever they do," she said, grabbing hold of my hand and giving it a loving squeeze as she led Mystical into her laboratory.

There was a silence that covered the room as they left my father and me alone. I rarely talked to my father, didn't know his personality much, had no idea what made him smile only knew he never did so around me.

"So what are you doing with yourself? You didn't have to come out here if you needed something. I could've wired it to you."

"No dad, I'm fine. Actually, I'm doing very well. I'm head chef now."

My father leaned on the limestone mantle over the fireplace, searched his pocket for some smokes, took out a box of Newport's, tapped the package twice against his palm and extracted a cigarette. He lit it took a pull and blew the smoke in my direction.

"You ain't thinking about marrying that girl, are you? She looks like a good fuck, but she ain't wife material," he said, pointing to the kitchen with his cigarette.

If he wasn't my father, I would've punched him dead in the jaw or hit him with the closet thing to me. But he was, so I swallowed my pride, didn't say a word, put my head down like a child, his child.

My father always put me down, thought of my job as a chef as woman's work. It was nothing for him to question my sexuality. He thought I had to be gay in order to like cooking and nature like I did. When I was a child helping my mother cook or engaging in long talks with her over tea, he'd call me his "little fag." He couldn't understand why a healthy boy like me didn't play sports or get dirty like the kids on my street. That's why when I got home late that night from my first sexual encounter with that stripper, he did a search of the car, found her panties and said, "Now I know you my boy." That moment led me to believe that he viewed women as nothing more than objects.

"Boy, you gone answer me or what, you ain't planning on marrying her, are you?" he asked, dropping the ashes into his cognac glass.

"We'll talk later. I have something to say to you and mom both."

"Like I said, you can fuck all you want, but the woman you call yours should have some class," he said without lowering his voice. "I can't believe you brought this one to meet your mother. Let this be the last time you make that mistake." He stood off the mantle and took a seat in his favorite chair.

"I'm old enough to make my own decisions," I challenged him.

"You've been old enough the last nine years and that hasn't done shit for your life," he said.

He didn't even turn his neck to look at me as he spoke. Didn't care how I took it as long as I got the point. That was how all our conversations began and quickly ended.

I sat in the dining room, Mystical was helping set the table with my mother's treasured dinnerware and my father was out in the back yard hitting his peace pipe.

"Boy, why you look so mad? Smile for your mother when you see her," my mother said, running her fingers across my scalp as she kissed me on the cheek.

"Nah, I'm fine."

"You know I'm your mother, so I know when something's bothering you." She smiled at me as she put the place mats down.

There was nothing that I could get past her. I was her child and she knew me more than I knew myself.

"Does he hate me?" I asked pointing at my father as he puffed away.

She sat next to me, grabbed my hands and put them in her lap. "Your father loves you. He just doesn't know how to show it. The man knows nothing about feelings, all he's ever known is pain," she defended him like she usually did.

Thaddeus McKenzie Jr. grew up poor in Mississippi. His father of the same name could barely walk; his days in the sun picking cotton had taken a toll on his body. His mother was born blind, he adored his mother and because she couldn't do anything without his help, he gave up his childhood to take care of her. They were in their fifties when they had him. Because of the age difference, he was left to tend to his parents' disabilities while his siblings disappeared into oblivion, going on with their lives and leaving him to fend for himself. His life revolved around school and the care of his parents. He took on a part time job with a white man in his town, fixing electronics. He got so good at it, the man trusted him with his most important accounts. The summer of his high school graduation, his parents both died within months of each other, leaving him as the executor of their estate. Though they were poor, they owned a great deal of land. As the story goes, his invisible siblings started showing up out of nowhere, each wanting their share of the money.

My father disagreed, went away to college and started his own business with the money made from selling his family's property. My mother always said that jealousy and money are the two foremost things that can rip families to shreds. He had ten brothers and sisters yet I had never met one of them. They wanted no parts of my father and privately I think that gnawed at him, made him coldhearted in some way and made family irrelevant.

"Ma, I know about how fucked up his life was, but I ain't done nothing to him," I said in frustration. Her eyes got wide; she couldn't believe I had used a cuss word in her home. "Sorry ma, I didn't mean to say that."

"Remember where you at boy," she said, pulling her hands from me and standing up to finish setting the table.

Things never got ironed out between my father, and me because whenever I spoke about how he made me feel, she'd sweep it under the rug, blame his attitude on his upbringing. If I wanted to be ignored, I might as well have gone to my father and told him what was on my mind. I knew I couldn't.

My mother made roast beef, potatoes and broccoli. The food was great. No matter how many great chefs I studied with, my mother's food always proved to be the superior. We ate in silence for half an hour; the only sounds that could be heard were of the silverware hitting the plates and the smack of our lips. I wanted to wait until everything had quieted down before I said what I came home to say.

As the food on our plates dwindled down to nothing, I focused my attention on my parents. Feeling left out, Mystical departed to the bathroom, leaving my parents and me alone. There was no better time to verbalize why I came to visit them.

My mother's face was in her plate and my father was picking at his teeth and patting his stomach at the same time. Therefore, I tried my best to break the tension

"The food was excellent, ma," I complimented. She looked up at me and smiled weakly as traces of anger creased her eyelids.

"It wasn't anything special," she responded meekly, barely looking from her plate. She was no use, because when she got mad, she could be stubborn. So, as a last resort, I turned to my father.

"Dad, how's work going? What happened to the new operating system software you were thinking of bringing out on the market?"

Though I didn't know how to make him smile, I knew how to get his full attention. McKenzie Software was his baby; his first, second and third love. Speaking about it was the only time I noticed what looked like a smile cross his face.

"It's going well. We can go by there tonight if you want. There are a lot of things that you'd marvel at," he said.

"I'd like that," I said. If it would make him happy, I'd do it.

My father made no bones about me taking over his company one day. That's why we didn't see eye to eye. The career I chose for myself was something he didn't want for me. He rationalized that I was ungrateful because he had built a business for me, but I felt he would use it as another way to control me.

When Mystical sat beside me, I knew right away that she was high. That glazed-over red look in her eyes was evident. Didn't even know how she was even able to walk from the bathroom back to the table. I put my arms around her, not to be affectionate but to hold her up. To the untrained eye, she looked sleepy, but I knew the expression she wore all too well. She was just entering her altered state for her eyes were nearly closed and she was starting to nod. When we stopped off at a rest stop bathroom on my way to my parent's home, I could've sworn there was nothing in her bag because I always searched through her things when she wasn't around. However, when I looked at the bleeding needle hole on her left arm, I realized she had gotten her fix intravenously and probably had hidden the drugs.

"You alright, honey?" My mother asked. She put her hands across the table and on top of Mystical's.

"She's fine. She's been up all day. Mind if I take her to my old room," I said, hoping that I could get her to my childhood bed before my parents started to get wise.

I draped her right arm over my shoulder, held onto her waist and held her stand. "I'm alright man. Put me down," Mystical said, putting up a struggle.

"Nah, let me take you too my room. You need rest." I looked into her eyes. If she didn't get the hint through her intoxicated eyes, it would be a long night. I pulled her away from the table didn't want to break any of my mother's dinnerware.

My father stood from the table, walked over to us, draped Mystical's free arm over his shoulder and said, "You need to lay down, you look sick."

"Get the fuck off of me, put me the hell down. I want to fucking eat man."

That moment was right out of my worst nightmare. Mystical's words had only cemented what my parents already thought of her.

Mystical pulled her arm from my father's grip, causing him to fall back against the kitchen nook. "Get her the hell out my house," he said, clutching the side he fell on.

My mother was horrified; she stood across from us with her hands over her mouth looking at the developing scene.

"I said get the fuck off me." Mystical broke free from me and headed for the table. She put her bare hands in the pot of potatoes, took a bite from one and threw it against the wall. "I want some motherfucking fries, not this nasty shit."

I grabbed her by the arm, looked into her eyes, and didn't see Mystical. Someone or something else inhabited her body. When she got high, she was someone altogether different, someone mean, cold and senseless. A total contrast from the quiet, warmhearted person I knew and loved. Using drugs was her way of coping with the problems in her life; she was out of her element here. Meeting my parents made her insecure, so she sought refuge in the only thing she knew.

The sound of shattered glass rang loudly throughout the house. Mystical had tossed most of my mother's *Juliska* dinnerware to the floor. Large and small pieces of stoneware littered the tile.

"What the hell is wrong with you?" I said, grabbing her by the arms and shaking her.

"I hate you. You disgust me. Leave me alone," she said smashing a saucer against the stainless steel refrigerator. In a matter of minutes, she had redecorated the kitchen wall with butter, gravy and beef stock.

With all my strength, I lifted her from the ground and put her over my shoulder. She scratched me across the face while searching blindly for my eyeballs. She got a hold of my skin and embedded her nails into them. I bit down on my bottom lip and tried to deal with the pain. The scars on my body were evidence of other times when calamity struck.

We fought back and forth, as I tried getting her out the house. She held onto the doorframes, knocking down fragile pictures of my father's parents that hung along the wall. It wasn't exactly the way I envisioned carrying her across the threshold.

We finally made it out the house when she got away for a moment, and tried lying in the middle of the road that intersected in front of my parent's home. The lily-white neighbors were now outside their doors, standing on their manicured lawns with a box seat view of the commotion. They shook their heads; I could see the disappointment in my parent's expression as they stood on the porch. For years, they shielded me from this sort of thing, only for me to bring it into their home. I halted traffic, picked her up from the street, absorbed a punch to the face and managed to lock her into my car. I drove a '68 mustang with only one door that opened from the inside, so I placed myself in front of that door, until she tired from ripping apart the interior.

There was a lot of explaining to do, but I didn't have an idea what to say. As I ascended the stairs, the neighbors dispersed back into their homes, the fun was over.

"She's on drugs, isn't she?" My mother asked standing between my father and me.

"She normally doesn't act like that. It's just that she's been through so much. She's an addict. You don't understand addicts. They can't control their urges, "I told my mother.

"Jared, don't go telling me she can't control herself. She doesn't want to get control, that's why she does drugs. Boy, what is wrong with you?"

"Nothing's wrong with me. I'm getting sick of you two acting as if I don't have no sense."

My father crossed his arms, stood back shaking his head like he never shook it before. "That's the type of trash you bring home to me and your mother. The last time you brought that faggot, now you allow a drug addict," my father said referring to my last visit with Shane. "I thought we raised you better than that."

"You mean you raised me to be better than that or to think I'm better than everyone else," I said, pointing at Mystical. "She's a person just like you and I."

"You got to get rid of her. She's no good. Just look at her. She's used up. You want to bring a child in the world with something like that," my father reiterated.

I stepped to him. Looked him square in the eye. "Why do you care, dad? Because you think she'll be a bad parent like you. Neglect her child like you neglected me." My mother put her palms to my chest, knew it was getting heated. The testosterone was pumping at an all time high. It would take next to nothing to make the situation explode.

"If you're gonna be with her, don't bother coming here," my father said in a shaken tone. I looked at my mother, and she looked away. The tears welling in her eyes told me all I needed to know. I stood face to face with my father and for the first time I saw concern written on his clean-shaven grill. It was the first time I was in control and he knew it.

Mystical was in my car, already passed out. She would wake up with no recollection of the damage she had caused. I loved her more than I knew I could love, leaving her would pain me more than any torture known to man. And I couldn't do that.

"Okay. See you around," I said looking down, couldn't look at the pain on my parents' faces.

My mother could no longer hold her emotion, she ran into the house sobbing loudly. I heard the screen door slam closed as I walked away. My father stood on the porch with tears welling in his eyes. It was the first time I realized that he loved me. Also, the last time I'd see him alive up close.

I got in my classic Mustang, turned the ignition, heard the 168 horse power engine crank and looked over at my future bride. I came home to ask for their blessing; instead, I received their admonition. I put the car in reverse, backed out of my childhood home and drove away watching my father from the rearview mirror until he was no longer in view.

Sometimes you have to look back to see what's ahead. The relationship I was developing with Angelica would only lead to one outcome. Hurt.

"Do you"

Angelica

Since spending the night with Aurelius at my Hampton's estate, I hadn't seen or heard from him. In reality, I can't place all the blame on him for our lack of communication. While making final preparations for my wedding, I barely had time to catch a shower in the last few days. At least I knew he was alive. He still came to prepare my meals and then vanished without a trace. Maybe I was looking too deep into our relationship. Just because we were intimate didn't mean he owed me anything. It was just that the way he left bothered me.

When I came out the shower after our magnificent night, he was gone, didn't even bother to say bye. My loving wasn't even worth a cheap explanation most men give when they are done with you. The faraway look in his eyes as I stepped into the bathroom caught my attention, but I figured I'd get around to asking what was troubling him later. Guess later would never be.

After discovering his absence, I ran up the driveway in only a towel and stilettos searching for him, but he was nowhere to be found leaving behind only footprints in the dirt road. When a man has something heavy burdening his thoughts, the best thing is to be left alone, that was why I didn't bother following behind him. Maybe that was what he wanted.

The sun looked radiant as it shone its orange orbs of glory over the New York skyline. I admired its beauty from afar, couldn't sneak a glance at it too long for fear that I might go blind. A heat wave had hit the city, causing most to flock to beaches or seek refuge underneath air conditioning. I was of the hiding sort, feeling content to lie around my room in nothing at all.

In all honesty, I would've rather been out doing something, but it wasn't like there was anyone to spend time with.

Daniel had gone back home and Titus hadn't called me all week.

I would dip my finger into the melted contents of the pint of Ben and Jerry, swirled it around until it was covered in a coating of fudge and seductively sucked it off as I stared at myself in the mirror.

"So this is what married life is going to be like," I said to myself, shuddering at the thought.

My phone rang, I sighed, because after finally getting comfortable, I didn't want to move. But I did, crawling across the bed on my elbows, hoping on the other end it was someone I wanted to hear.

"Hello," I said, but received nothing but silence. "Who is this?" I reiterated, becoming increasingly irritated.

"It's me."

Those two words set my world on fire. Stirred something up on my insides the way ripple does for the homeless during the winter months. The gall and arrogance of a man to assume that those two words were all that was necessary to reveal himself, as if I had nothing better to do but wait on him to grace me with his presence. In a sadistic way, his confidence turned me on.

I waited a few seconds before mentioning the obvious. I wanted to show through my indecisiveness that he could never hold that type of power over me. The type that make's the most intelligent women seem feeble. "Is this Aurelius?" I said with uncertainty in my voice.

He responded, "So you do know who it is.?" I could tell he was smiling. I imagined those gorgeous lips twisted into a smirk.

"Not really, just taking a shot in the dark."

"That hurt."

"You just made my day," I said sarcastically.

"Just get ready, I'm going to pick you up."

"What? Who do you think you're talking to? I've got plans."
I fought just for the sake of fighting. I didn't have a damn
thing planned but a visit to the freezer for some more ice
cream.
"Just get ready. I'll be there in an hour." He hung up, leaving
me baffled and curious at the same time.

I held on tight with my arms crisscrossed against Aurelius's
chest, the wind blew in my hair while we whipped in and out
of traffic and my stomach did flips each time he hit the
redline. I felt weightless gliding down the hot, steamy paved
roads of the New York State Thruway as the scenery through
the face shield rendered me speechless.
When Aurelius showed up to my place with a motorcycle
helmet and a street-riding jacket, I nearly sent him back
home. I didn't do bikes or anything that would render me
paralyzed or deformed if I so as much as hit a pebble. But
you only live once, so I relented and went along for the ride. I
was glad I did, because life is too short to navigate slowly.
With Aurelius, I enjoyed venturing into the fast lane.
 Aurelius flashed me a smile as he made a turn that had the
motorcycle nearly touching the ground. From shear
nervousness, I tightened my thighs around his. Feeling my
heat caused him to turn around and bless me with a smile
once again.
I tapped the back of his helmet, expressed my displeasure in
his antics and playfully grabbed his package tightly for good
measure. If I got hurt, he'd get hurt; those were the rules. I
knew I was sort of a tease, but men didn't respond to
anything but the chase. That's why they are described as
bulls led to the slaughter.
We merged off the highway, followed the sign that pointed
left for Lake George and rode along the side roads lined by
silver birch trees. I got excited; riding through the
countryside on a motorcycle was more intimate as opposed to

riding in a car. I stretched out my hand, wanted to reach out and touch the lush green leaves. Then I took a deep breath, inhaling the scent of fresh grass and chopped wood that permeated the country air.

After nearly three hours on the bike, we found our destination and parked in the Cook Mountain Preserve. We proceeded to walk a steep trail for about a mile until we reached the rocky top that overlooked the entire northern part of Lake George and unpacked our lunch. I was tired, sweaty and my toes hurt like hell, but the vista in front of us was worth all the pain.

"It's beautiful up here," I said, standing on a huge uneven rock covered in moss and looking down at the sail boats moving slowly across the lake.

"I thought you would. I Saw you at that party in the Hampton's looking at the scenery and thought you'd appreciate something a little bit more astonishing," he said looking up from his knees while he set up our picnic feast.

"You drove me all this way just so I could see something I could find using the internet." I turned towards him with my hands placed on my hips.

"I'd go much further for you for much less." He smiled with a twinkle in his eyes.

I closed my eyes and wished this moment would never pass. For a second, I imagined that Titus didn't exist, hoped that when I opened my eyes Aurelius was mine and I his, but that wasn't my reality.

"And what is it that you'd do for me?" I asked seductively, taking a seat on the rock while loosening the buttons on my camisole.

"You look damn hot right now." Lust covered his face, could tell he'd love nothing more than to take me right atop the rock, thrust into me so hard that he'd split it in two.

"I'm just having fun; you do know that, don't you?" I didn't want him to feel that I was leading him on. Maybe he was confused about what we'd done. The love in his eyes struck fear in me. I wanted to make clear that this evening wasn't going to end with him inside of me.

"That's what you call what we're doing?" he responded, dipping his hand in one of the bowls to test the food.

"Not exactly, but what would you call it?"

"I think what were doing is beyond definition. You're getting married in a couple of weeks and I'm catering your wedding. Isn't that unique?" he said

"I just call it fun," I said, coming across colder than I intended. Could see that I had deflated his feelings some as he cast his eyes to the ground.

He cleared his throat and said, "So I guess when you say "I do" the fun stops?"

"It has to," I said.

"Doesn't sound like that's what you want."

"It doesn't matter what I want. Love doesn't look out for its own interests."

He chuckled to himself, didn't think I caught what he was implying. I already knew my ways were hypocritical. His cackle got me mad, made me want to kick him between the legs causing him the same physical pain he was doing to me emotionally.

I walked down the trail towards the lake, could hear branches break beneath my feet as I searched for a place of solace. As a child, whenever one of my foster parents did me harm, I'd go away, walk until the pain had numbed me. Sometimes I'd walk for hours, discover places I'd never known. Like a flash of lightning, my reality finally came to fruition. I was still a child and still running from my problems. Thinking to myself along the way that I felt trapped, like a claustrophobic animal. I wasn't a reverend's wife, hell, I didn't fit a heathen; the qualities of a good wife weren't in me.

At that moment, I knew I couldn't go along with this wedding. I'd played a role for the last two years; my portrayal of a spiritual woman could have won me an Oscar. If Aurelius wanted the truth, the truth was I didn't know if I could stop craving his touch once I became the wedded wife of Reverend Titus Rosemond.

I saw the crystal like water less than ten feet away, could barely look because the sun reflected across the lake and into my eyes. I stepped out of my shoes, put my bare feet into the lake and cleared a spot to sit. While deep in thought was when I felt his presence, felt his breath on the back of my neck, smelled his scent in the air as it overpowered the smell of the wilderness. I reached behind me, felt nothing but bare skin, and let my hand travel up until I located his stiffness.

He then pushed me into the lake without knowing if I could even swim, luckily I did. My clothes were soaked, but as I opened my eyes and wiped the water away, I could care less. Like a King entering the Euphrates River, he entered, just the way I needed him, bare.

I danced out the elevator, still on a high from my evening, still playing Bob Marley and Lauryn Hill in my mind. My head was nearly touching the ceiling the way that man had swept me off my feet. After making love, we danced to "Turn your lights down low." We were two silhouettes dancing in the orange glow that covered Lake George. He said I love you and for the first time I said it back and felt it in my heart.

As soon as I opened my door, my heart went to my throat. My lights were on and I had turned them off. When it came to keeping my lights off, I was totally anal. I heard water running, I walked in my kitchen, the faucet was off, and then I went into my bedroom, retrieved my bat and followed the sound into my bathroom. Steam blinded me as soon as I entered the door, it was coming from the bathtub and as my sight started to clear, I noticed a hand flung over the edge; saw a body lifelessly floating atop the water. I knew that tattoo, on the lower back of the person, knew those long fingernails like my own.

"Rochelle! Please baby girl don't do this to me…"

"We all fall down"

Aurelius

I revved into high gear as I headed uptown. The illuminated buildings resembled one long streak of light as I traveled at a high rate of speed. I felt safe on my bike, but feared the long winding road of infatuation that was beginning between Angelica and me. I couldn't believe those words had made their way to the tip of my tongue as we danced atop Cook Mountain.

I promised myself I'd never say those words again, because they were usually the ruin of a relationship. Many a man had experienced heartbreak almost simultaneous with mouthing that damned sentence. Hated myself for being weak in a moment of temptation, hated that her caramel tone, pouty-lips and hypnotizing eyes rendered me in an almost vegetative state in her presence.

I flashed out of my daze as I heard the screech of tires, a driver ignoring the red light, sped across the intersection of Columbus circle, nearly causing a collision, possibly resulting in my death, but I navigated my bike around the behemoth truck safely with not as much as one palpitation. That was ironic because I got palpitations whenever I thought of Angelica and she was relatively harmless.

Now I was beginning to feel guilty, after sleeping with her several times, my conscience hadn't reared its head. Now it was and I didn't know why. Was it because I was in love with another man's future wife or was it that I wouldn't stop at anything to be with her?

I paused at a stop sign, took off my helmet and put it at my side, revved my bike to its peak rpm and let the tire put tracks in the asphalt while I held it still. I pulled back on the handlebars until the front wheels were up in the air, and then I let it rip. The building lights blared past me like the speed of sound, but still failed to affect me. As I made it to the underground parking lot in my building, I could feel that twinge in my stomach. The same twinge I felt the first time I fell in love. It was fear that resided in me, turning my inside into knots.

I tucked my helmet underneath my arms as I parked my bike and walked across the gloomy lot to the elevator. When I entered the elevator, I was hit in the face by a scent that I knew all too well, the smell of Sandalwood and Vanilla, Mystical's trademark fragrance. I passed it off in my mind as being sheer coincidence but as I ascended each floor; my gut told me that she was here, here in this building. Knew it because I felt her spirit, felt it underneath my skin and in my soul.

That's why when the elevator door opened and I saw her leaning against my door, with the remnants of a Newport in her hand, I knew at that moment my heart would be divided. As much as I hated her over the years for the pain she had once inflicted upon me, I always knew that if she came back, I'd take her without a thought.

Coming Fall 2008

Blood of My Brother II
September 2008

Evil Side of Money II
September 2008

Stick N Move II
(Product of Society)
October 2008

Flipping The Game
October 2008

Hoodfellas
November 2008

The Bedroom Bandit
February 2009

Miami Noire
(the sequel to Chasin' Satisfaction)
November 2008

And More....

NEGLECTED SOULS

Motherhood and the trials of loving too hard and not enough frame this story...The realism of these characters will bring tears to your spirit as you discover the hero in the villain you never saw coming...

Neglected Souls is a gritty, honest and heart-stirring story of hope and personal triumph set in the ghettos of Boston.

In Stores!!!

Jimmy and Nina continue to feel a void in their lives because they haven't a clue about their genealogical make-up. Jimmy falls victims to a life threatening illness and only the right organ donor can save his life. Will the donor be the bridge to reconnect Jimmy and Nina to their biological family? Will Nina be the strength for her brother in his time of need? Will they ever find out what really happened to their mother?

In Stores!!!

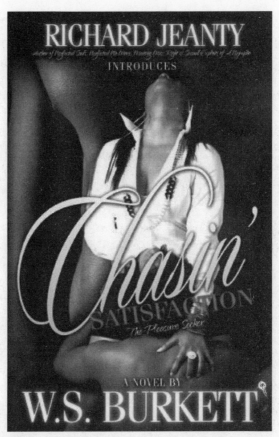

Betrayal, lust, lies, murder, deception, sex and tainted love frame this story... Julian Stevens lacks the ambition and freak ability that Miko looks for in a man, but she married him despite his flaws to spite an ex-boyfriend. When Miko least expects it, the old boyfriend shows up and ready to sweep her off her feet again. Suddenly the grass grows greener on the other side, but Miko is not an easily satisfied woman. She wants to have her cake and eat it too. While Miko's doing her own thing, Julian is determined to become everything Miko ever wanted in a man and more, but will he go to extreme lengths to prove he's worthy of Miko's love? Julian Stevens soon finds out that he's capable of being more than he could ever imagine as he embarks on a journey that will change his life forever.

In Stores!!!

The police in New York and other major cities around the country are increasingly victimizing black men. The violence has escalated to deadly force, most of the time without justification. In this controversial book, noted author Richard Jeanty, tackles the problem of police brutality and the unfair treatment of Black men at the hands of police in New York City and the rest of the country. The conflict between the Police and Black men will continue on a downward spiral until the mayors of every city hold accountable the members of their police force who use unnecessary deadly force against unarmed victims.

In Stores!!!

Just when Darren thinks his relationship with Tina is flourishing, there is yet another hurdle on the road hindering their bliss. Tina saw a therapist for months to deal with her sexual addiction, but now Darren is wondering if she was ever treated completely. Darren has not been taking care of home and Tina's frustrated and agrees to a break-up with Darren. Will Darren lose Tina for good? Will Tina ever realize that Darren is the best man for her?

In Stores!!

Ronald Murphy was a player all his life until he and his best friend, Myles, met the women of their dreams during a brief vacation in South Beach, Florida. Sexual Jeopardy is story of trust, betrayal, forgiveness, friendship and hope.

In Stores!!!

Tina develops an insatiable sexual appetite very early in life. She only loves her boyfriend, Darren, but he's too far away in college to satisfy her sexual needs.

Tina decides to get buck wild away in college

Will her sexual trysts jeopardize the lives of the men in her life?

In Stores!!!

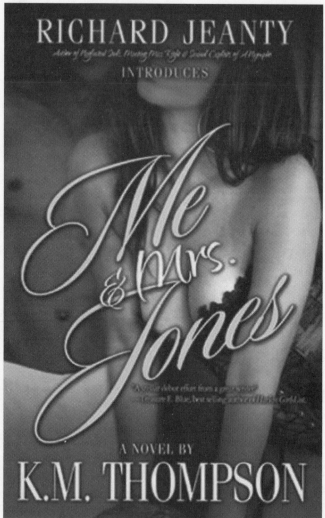

Faith Jones, a woman in her mid-thirties, has given up on ever finding love again until she met her son's best friend, Darius. Faith Jones is walking a thin line of betrayal against her son for the love of Darius. Will Faith allow her emotions to outweigh her common sense?

In Stores!!!

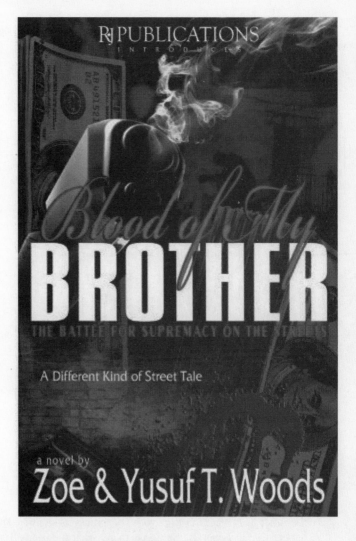

Roc was the man on the streets of Philadelphia, until his younger brother decided it was time to become his own man by wreaking havoc on Roc's crew without any regards for the blood relation they share. Drug, murder, mayhem and the pursuit of happiness can lead to deadly consequences. This story can only be told by a person who has lived it.

In Stores!!!

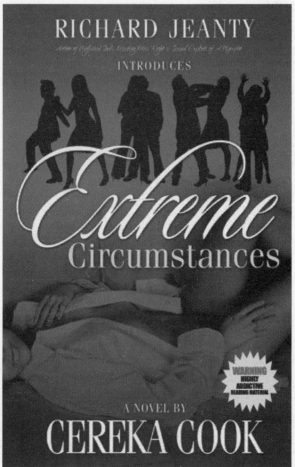

What happens when a devoted woman is betrayed? Come take a ride with Chanel as she takes her boyfriend, Donnell, to circumstances beyond belief after he betrays her trust with his endless infidelities. How long can Chanel's friend, Janai, use her looks to get what she wants from men before it catches up to her? Find out as Janai's gold-digging ways catch up with and she has to face the consequences of her extreme actions.

In Stores!!!

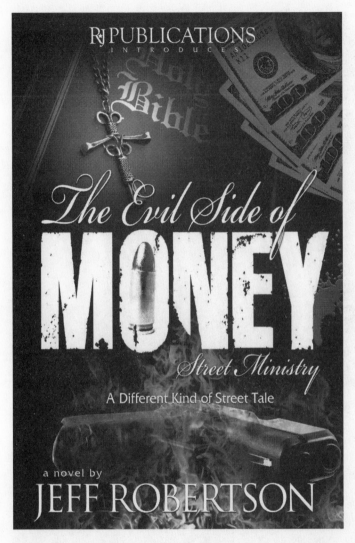

Violence, Intimidation and carnage are the order as Nathan and his brother set out to build the most powerful drug empires in Chicago. However, when God comes knocking, Nathan's conscience starts to surface. Will his haunted criminal past get the best of him?

In Stores!!

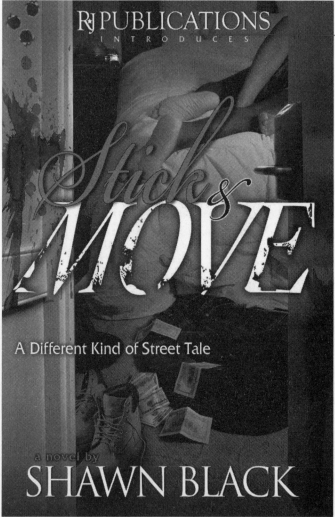

RJ PUBLICATIONS
INTRODUCES

Stick &
MOVE

A Different Kind of Street Tale

a novel by
SHAWN BLACK

Yasmina witnessed the brutal murder of her parents at a young age at the hand of a drug dealer. This event stained her mind and upbringing as a result. Will Yamina's life come full circle with her past? Find out as Yasmina's crew, The Platinum Chicks, set out to make a name for themselves on the street.

In stores!!

Ashland's mother, Bianca, fights hard to suppress the truth from her daughter because she doesn't want her to marry Jordan, the grandson of an ex-lover she loathes. Ashland soon finds out how cruel and vengeful her mother can be, but what price will Bianca pay for redemption?

In stores!!

Malcolm is a wealthy virgin who decides to conceal his wealth
From the world until he meets the right woman. His wealthy best friend,
Dexter, hides his wealth from no one. Malcolm struggles to find love in an
environment where vanity and materialism are rampant, while Dexter is
getting more than enough of his share of women. Malcolm needs develop
self-esteem and confidence to meet the right woman and Dexter's
confidence is borderline arrogance.

Will bad boys like Dexter continue to take women for a ride?

Or will nice guys like Malcolm continue to finish last?

In Stores!!!

What happens when a woman's devotion to her fiancee is tested weeks before she gets married? What if her fiancee is just hiding behind the veil of ministry to deceive her? Find out as Sean Mitchell takes you on a journey you'll never forget into the lives of Angelica, Titus and Aurelius.

Coming March 2008!!

PUBLICATIONS
BRINGING EXCITEMENT, FUN AND JOY TO READING

Use this coupon to order by mail

1. Neglected Souls, Richard Jeanty $14.95
2. Neglected No More, Richard Jeanty $14.95
3. Sexual Exploits of Nympho, Richard Jeanty $14.95
4. Meeting Ms. Right's Whip Appeal, Richard Jeanty $14.95
5. Me and Mrs. Jones, K.M Thompson ($14.95) Available
6. Chasin' Satisfaction, W.S Burkett ($14.95) Available
7. Extreme Circumstances, Cereka Cook ($14.95) Available
8. The Most Dangerous Gang In America, R. Jeanty $15.00
9. Sexual Exploits of a Nympho II, Richard Jeanty $15.00
10. Sexual Jeopardy, Richard Jeanty $14.95 Coming: 2/15/ 2008
11. Too Many Secrets, Too Many Lies, Sonya Sparks $15.00
12. Stick And Move, Shawn Black ($15.00) Coming 1/15/ 2008
13. Evil Side Of Money, Jeff Robertson $15.00
14. Cater To Her, W.S Burkett $15.00 Coming 3/30/ 2008
15. Blood of my Brother, Zoe & Ysuf Woods $15.00
16. Hoodfellas, Richard Jeanty $15.00 11/30/2008
17. The Bedroom Bandit, Richard Jeanty $15.00 February 2009
18. Blood of My Brother II $15.00 September 2008
19. Evil Side of Money II $15.00 September 2008
20. Flipping the Game $15.00 October 2008
21. Stick N Move (Product of Society) October 2008
22. Miami Noire $15.00 November 2008

Name_____
Address_____
City_____State_____Zip Code_____

Please send the novels that I have circled above.

Shipping and Handling $1.99
Total Number of Books_____
Total Amount Due_____

This offer is subject to change without notice.

Send check or money order (no cash or CODs) to:
RJ Publications
290 Dune Street
Far Rockaway, NY 11691

For more information please call 718-471-2926, or visit www.rjpublications.com

Please allow 2-3 weeks for delivery.

Use this coupon to order by mail

1. Neglected Souls, Richard Jeanty $14.95
2. Neglected No More, Richard Jeanty $14.95
3. Sexual Exploits of Nympho, Richard Jeanty $14.95
4. Meeting Ms. Right's Whip Appeal, Richard Jeanty $14.95
5. Me and Mrs. Jones, K.M Thompson ($14.95) Available
6. Chasin' Satisfaction, W.S Burkett ($14.95) Available
7. Extreme Circumstances, Cereka Cook ($14.95) Available
8. The Most Dangerous Gang In America, R. Jeanty $15.00
9. Sexual Exploits of a Nympho II, Richard Jeanty $15.00
10. Sexual Jeopardy, Richard Jeanty $14.95 Coming: 2/15/ 2008
11. Too Many Secrets, Too Many Lies, Sonya Sparks $15.00
12. Stick And Move, Shawn Black ($15.00) Coming 1/15/ 2008
13. Evil Side Of Money, Jeff Robertson $15.00
14. Cater To Her, W.S Burkett $15.00 Coming 3/30/ 2008
15. Blood of my Brother, Zoe & Ysuf Woods $15.00
16. Hoodfellas, Richard Jeanty $15.00 11/30/2008
17. The Bedroom Bandit, Richard Jeanty $15.00 February 2009
18. Blood of My Brother II $15.00 September 2008
19. Evil Side of Money II $15.00 September 2008
20. Flipping the Game $15.00 October 2008
21. Stick N Move (Product of Society) October 2008
22. Miami Noire $15.00 November 2008

Name_____
Address_____
City_____State_____Zip Code_____

Please send the novels that I have circled above.

Shipping and Handling $1.99
Total Number of Books_____
Total Amount Due_____

This offer is subject to change without notice.

Send check or money order (no cash or CODs) to:
RJ Publications
290 Dune Street
Far Rockaway, NY 11691

For more information please call 718-471-2926, or visit www.rjpublications.com

Please allow 2-3 weeks for delivery.

PUBLICATIONS
BRINGING EXCITEMENT, FUN AND JOY TO READING

Use this coupon to order by mail

1. Neglected Souls, Richard Jeanty $14.95
2. Neglected No More, Richard Jeanty $14.95
3. Sexual Exploits of Nympho, Richard Jeanty $14.95
4. Meeting Ms. Right's Whip Appeal, Richard Jeanty $14.95
5. Me and Mrs. Jones, K.M Thompson ($14.95) Available
6. Chasin' Satisfaction, W.S Burkett ($14.95) Available
7. Extreme Circumstances, Cereka Cook ($14.95) Available
8. The Most Dangerous Gang In America, R. Jeanty $15.00
9. Sexual Exploits of a Nympho II, Richard Jeanty $15.00
10. Sexual Jeopardy, Richard Jeanty $14.95 Coming: 2/15/ 2008
11. Too Many Secrets, Too Many Lies, Sonya Sparks $15.00
12. Stick And Move, Shawn Black ($15.00) Coming 1/15/ 2008
13. Evil Side Of Money, Jeff Robertson $15.00
14. Cater To Her, W.S Burkett $15.00 Coming 3/30/ 2008
15. Blood of my Brother, Zoe & Ysuf Woods $15.00
16. Hoodfellas, Richard Jeanty $15.00 11/30/2008
17. The Bedroom Bandit, Richard Jeanty $15.00 February 2009
18. Blood of My Brother II $15.00 September 2008
19. Evil Side of Money II $15.00 September 2008
20. Flipping the Game $15.00 October 2008
21. Stick N Move (Product of Society) October 2008
22. Miami Noire $15.00 November 2008

Name_____
Address_____
City_____State_____Zip Code_____

Please send the novels that I have circled above.

Shipping and Handling $1.99
Total Number of Books_____
Total Amount Due_____

This offer is subject to change without notice.

Send check or money order (no cash or CODs) to:
RJ Publications
290 Dune Street
Far Rockaway, NY 11691

For more information please call 718-471-2926, or visit www.rjpublications.com

Please allow 2-3 weeks for delivery.

PUBLICATIONS
BRINGING EXCITEMENT, FUN AND JOY TO READING

Use this coupon to order by mail

1. Neglected Souls, Richard Jeanty $14.95
2. Neglected No More, Richard Jeanty $14.95
3. Sexual Exploits of Nympho, Richard Jeanty $14.95
4. Meeting Ms. Right's Whip Appeal, Richard Jeanty $14.95
5. Me and Mrs. Jones, K.M Thompson ($14.95) Available
6. Chasin' Satisfaction, W.S Burkett ($14.95) Available
7. Extreme Circumstances, Cereka Cook ($14.95) Available
8. The Most Dangerous Gang In America, R. Jeanty $15.00
9. Sexual Exploits of a Nympho II, Richard Jeanty $15.00
10. Sexual Jeopardy, Richard Jeanty $14.95 Coming: 2/15/ 2008
11. Too Many Secrets, Too Many Lies, Sonya Sparks $15.00
12. Stick And Move, Shawn Black ($15.00) Coming 1/15/ 2008
13. Evil Side Of Money, Jeff Robertson $15.00
14. Cater To Her, W.S Burkett $15.00 Coming 3/30/ 2008
15. Blood of my Brother, Zoe & Ysuf Woods $15.00
16. Hoodfellas, Richard Jeanty $15.00 11/30/2008
17. The Bedroom Bandit, Richard Jeanty $15.00 February 2009
18. Blood of My Brother II $15.00 September 2008
19. Evil Side of Money II $15.00 September 2008
20. Flipping the Game $15.00 October 2008
21. Stick N Move (Product of Society) October 2008
22. Miami Noire $15.00 November 2008

Name_____

Address_____

City_____State_____Zip Code_____

Please send the novels that I have circled above.

Shipping and Handling $1.99

Total Number of Books_____

Total Amount Due_____

This offer is subject to change without notice.

Send check or money order (no cash or CODs) to:
RJ Publications
290 Dune Street
Far Rockaway, NY 11691

For more information please call 718-471-2926, or visit www.rjpublications.com

Please allow 2-3 weeks for delivery.

PUBLICATIONS
BRINGING EXCITEMENT, FUN AND JOY TO READING

Use this coupon to order by mail

1. Neglected Souls, Richard Jeanty $14.95
2. Neglected No More, Richard Jeanty $14.95
3. Sexual Exploits of Nympho, Richard Jeanty $14.95
4. Meeting Ms. Right's Whip Appeal, Richard Jeanty $14.95
5. Me and Mrs. Jones, K.M Thompson ($14.95) Available
6. Chasin' Satisfaction, W.S Burkett ($14.95) Available
7. Extreme Circumstances, Cereka Cook ($14.95) Available
8. The Most Dangerous Gang In America, R. Jeanty $15.00
9. Sexual Exploits of a Nympho II, Richard Jeanty $15.00
10. Sexual Jeopardy, Richard Jeanty $14.95 Coming: 2/15/ 2008
11. Too Many Secrets, Too Many Lies, Sonya Sparks $15.00
12. Stick And Move, Shawn Black ($15.00) Coming 1/15/ 2008
13. Evil Side Of Money, Jeff Robertson $15.00
14. Cater To Her, W.S Burkett $15.00 Coming 3/30/ 2008
15. Blood of my Brother, Zoe & Ysuf Woods $15.00
16. Hoodfellas, Richard Jeanty $15.00 11/30/2008
17. The Bedroom Bandit, Richard Jeanty $15.00 February 2009
18. Blood of My Brother II $15.00 September 2008
19. Evil Side of Money II $15.00 September 2008
20. Flipping the Game $15.00 October 2008
21. Stick N Move (Product of Society) October 2008
22. Miami Noire $15.00 November 2008

Name_____
Address_____
City_____State_____Zip Code_____

Please send the novels that I have circled above.

Shipping and Handling $1.99
Total Number of Books_____
Total Amount Due_____

This offer is subject to change without notice.

Send check or money order (no cash or CODs) to:
RJ Publications
290 Dune Street
Far Rockaway, NY 11691

For more information please call 718-471-2926, or visit www.rjpublications.com

Please allow 2-3 weeks for delivery.

PUBLICATIONS
BRINGING EXCITEMENT, FUN AND JOY TO READING

Use this coupon to order by mail

1. Neglected Souls, Richard Jeanty $14.95
2. Neglected No More, Richard Jeanty $14.95
3. Sexual Exploits of Nympho, Richard Jeanty $14.95
4. Meeting Ms. Right's Whip Appeal, Richard Jeanty $14.95
5. Me and Mrs. Jones, K.M Thompson ($14.95) Available
6. Chasin' Satisfaction, W.S Burkett ($14.95) Available
7. Extreme Circumstances, Cereka Cook ($14.95) Available
8. The Most Dangerous Gang In America, R. Jeanty $15.00
9. Sexual Exploits of a Nympho II, Richard Jeanty $15.00
10. Sexual Jeopardy, Richard Jeanty $14.95 Coming: 2/15/ 2008
11. Too Many Secrets, Too Many Lies, Sonya Sparks $15.00
12. Stick And Move, Shawn Black ($15.00) Coming 1/15/ 2008
13. Evil Side Of Money, Jeff Robertson $15.00
14. Cater To Her, W.S Burkett $15.00 Coming 3/30/ 2008
15. Blood of my Brother, Zoe & Ysuf Woods $15.00
16. Hoodfellas, Richard Jeanty $15.00 11/30/2008
17. The Bedroom Bandit, Richard Jeanty $15.00 February 2009
18. Blood of My Brother II $15.00 September 2008
19. Evil Side of Money II $15.00 September 2008
20. Flipping the Game $15.00 October 2008
21. Stick N Move (Product of Society) October 2008
22. Miami Noire $15.00 November 2008

Name_____
Address_____
City_____State_____Zip Code_____

Please send the novels that I have circled above.

Shipping and Handling $1.99
Total Number of Books_____
Total Amount Due_____

This offer is subject to change without notice.

Send check or money order (no cash or CODs) to:
RJ Publications
290 Dune Street
Far Rockaway, NY 11691

For more information please call 718-471-2926, or visit www.rjpublications.com

Please allow 2-3 weeks for delivery.

Use this coupon to order by mail

1. Neglected Souls, Richard Jeanty $14.95
2. Neglected No More, Richard Jeanty $14.95
3. Sexual Exploits of Nympho, Richard Jeanty $14.95
4. Meeting Ms. Right's Whip Appeal, Richard Jeanty $14.95
5. Me and Mrs. Jones, K.M Thompson ($14.95) Available
6. Chasin' Satisfaction, W.S Burkett ($14.95) Available
7. Extreme Circumstances, Cereka Cook ($14.95) Available
8. The Most Dangerous Gang In America, R. Jeanty $15.00
9. Sexual Exploits of a Nympho II, Richard Jeanty $15.00
10. Sexual Jeopardy, Richard Jeanty $14.95 Coming: 2/15/ 2008
11. Too Many Secrets, Too Many Lies, Sonya Sparks $15.00
12. Stick And Move, Shawn Black ($15.00) Coming 1/15/ 2008
13. Evil Side Of Money, Jeff Robertson $15.00
14. Cater To Her, W.S Burkett $15.00 Coming 3/30/ 2008
15. Blood of my Brother, Zoe & Ysuf Woods $15.00
16. Hoodfellas, Richard Jeanty $15.00 11/30/2008
17. The Bedroom Bandit, Richard Jeanty $15.00 February 2009
18. Blood of My Brother II $15.00 September 2008
19. Evil Side of Money II $15.00 September 2008
20. Flipping the Game $15.00 October 2008
21. Stick N Move (Product of Society) October 2008
22. Miami Noire $15.00 November 2008

Name_____
Address_____
City_____State_____Zip Code_____

Please send the novels that I have circled above.

Shipping and Handling $1.99
Total Number of Books_____
Total Amount Due_____

This offer is subject to change without notice.

Send check or money order (no cash or CODs) to:
RJ Publications
290 Dune Street
Far Rockaway, NY 11691

For more information please call 718-471-2926, or visit www.rjpublications.com

Please allow 2-3 weeks for delivery.

Use this coupon to order by mail

1.   Neglected Souls, Richard Jeanty $14.95
2.   Neglected No More, Richard Jeanty $14.95
3.   Sexual Exploits of Nympho, Richard Jeanty $14.95
4.   Meeting Ms. Right's Whip Appeal, Richard Jeanty $14.95
5.   Me and Mrs. Jones, K.M Thompson ($14.95) Available
6.   Chasin' Satisfaction, W.S Burkett ($14.95) Available
7.   Extreme Circumstances, Cereka Cook ($14.95) Available
8.   The Most Dangerous Gang In America, R. Jeanty $15.00
9.   Sexual Exploits of a Nympho II, Richard Jeanty $15.00
10.   Sexual Jeopardy, Richard Jeanty $14.95 Coming: 2/15/ 2008
11.   Too Many Secrets, Too Many Lies, Sonya Sparks $15.00
12.   Stick And Move, Shawn Black ($15.00) Coming 1/15/ 2008
13.   Evil Side Of Money, Jeff Robertson $15.00
14.   Cater To Her, W.S Burkett $15.00 Coming 3/30/ 2008
15.   Blood of my Brother, Zoe & Ysuf Woods $15.00
16.   Hoodfellas, Richard Jeanty $15.00 11/30/2008
17.   The Bedroom Bandit, Richard Jeanty $15.00 February 2009
18.   Blood of My Brother II $15.00 September 2008
19.   Evil Side of Money II $15.00 September 2008
20.   Flipping the Game $15.00 October 2008
21.   Stick N Move (Product of Society) October 2008
22.   Miami Noire $15.00 November 2008

Name_____
Address_____
City_____State_____Zip Code_____

Please send the novels that I have circled above.

Shipping and Handling $1.99
Total Number of Books_____
Total Amount Due_____

This offer is subject to change without notice.

Send check or money order (no cash or CODs) to:
RJ Publications
290 Dune Street
Far Rockaway, NY 11691

For more information please call 718-471-2926, or visit www.rjpublications.com

Please allow 2-3 weeks for delivery.

PUBLICATIONS
BRINGING EXCITEMENT, FUN AND JOY TO READING

Use this coupon to order by mail

1. Neglected Souls, Richard Jeanty $14.95
2. Neglected No More, Richard Jeanty $14.95
3. Sexual Exploits of Nympho, Richard Jeanty $14.95
4. Meeting Ms. Right's Whip Appeal, Richard Jeanty $14.95
5. Me and Mrs. Jones, K.M Thompson ($14.95) Available
6. Chasin' Satisfaction, W.S Burkett ($14.95) Available
7. Extreme Circumstances, Cereka Cook ($14.95) Available
8. The Most Dangerous Gang In America, R. Jeanty $15.00
9. Sexual Exploits of a Nympho II, Richard Jeanty $15.00
10. Sexual Jeopardy, Richard Jeanty $14.95 Coming: 2/15/ 2008
11. Too Many Secrets, Too Many Lies, Sonya Sparks $15.00
12. Stick And Move, Shawn Black ($15.00) Coming 1/15/ 2008
13. Evil Side Of Money, Jeff Robertson $15.00
14. Cater To Her, W.S Burkett $15.00 Coming 3/30/ 2008
15. Blood of my Brother, Zoe & Ysuf Woods $15.00
16. Hoodfellas, Richard Jeanty $15.00 11/30/2008
17. The Bedroom Bandit, Richard Jeanty $15.00 February 2009
18. Blood of My Brother II $15.00 September 2008
19. Evil Side of Money II $15.00 September 2008
20. Flipping the Game $15.00 October 2008
21. Stick N Move (Product of Society) October 2008
22. Miami Noire $15.00 November 2008

Name_____
Address_____
City_____State_____Zip Code_____

Please send the novels that I have circled above.

Shipping and Handling $1.99
Total Number of Books_____
Total Amount Due_____

This offer is subject to change without notice.

Send check or money order (no cash or CODs) to:
RJ Publications
290 Dune Street
Far Rockaway, NY 11691

For more information please call 718-471-2926, or visit www.rjpublications.com

Please allow 2-3 weeks for delivery.